W9-COV-236

THE GAME.

Car, restaurant, car, restaurant, car. Hyde could almost hear the words, hear their repetition inside the car. Lip-reading. Difficult, not impossible. Time to get back.

Light rain. He shrugged his shoulders and looked up. A long-range microphone protruded from the upstairs window of the unlit shop like a gun barrel. Hyde drew in his breath, felt his frame tremble with alertness. At that distance, the microphone would be picking up Aubrey and Godwin's voices, their words. He studied the microphone, then he began running.

Godwin appeared relieved to see him.

"What is it?" Aubrey asked as Hyde sat down, his back to the camera and microphone.

"There's a lip-reader using infra-red, and there's a long-range directional mike, both of them trained on you," Hyde replied. "Don't react, just listen. If you've been talking about our friend back at the house, then they may have been able to learn the name of the game. Understand?" He had gabbled in a hoarse whisper. "I see you have."

Godwin had gone pale, his mouth opening slowly like that of a fish. Aubrey lowered his head in admission.

"Then you could have given the whole bloody game away!" Hyde blurted out.

"Yes," Aubrey said, not looking up.

Jade
Tiger

Craig Thomas

BANTAM BOOKS
TORONTO · NEW YORK · LONDON · SYDNEY

JADE TIGER

A Bantam Book / published by arrangement with The Viking Press

PRINTING HISTORY

Viking edition published August 1982

Grateful acknowledgment is made to the following for permission to
reprint copyrighted material:

Doubleday & Company, Inc.: Excerpt from *Under Western Eyes*
by Joseph Conrad. Copyright 1911 by Doubleday & Company, Inc.
Penguin Books Ltd., London: Four lines from *Hard Is the Journey*
by Li Po, from *Li Po & Tu Fu*, translated by Arthur Cooper. Copyright
© 1973 by Arthur Cooper. Selections from the poetry of *Meng
Chiao* from *Poems of the Late L'ang*, translated by A.C. Graham.
Copyright © 1965 by A.C. Graham

*Bantam Export edition / March 1983
Bantam edition / August 1983*

ISBN 0-553-23517-6

Published simultaneously in the United States and Canada

PRINTED IN THE UNITED STATES OF AMERICA

O   0 9 8 7 6 5 4 3 2 1

for
GEOFF *and* **PETE**

ACKNOWLEDGMENTS

I wish to acknowledge at the beginning of this book, and most importantly, the companions of my travels, especially my wife, Jill, for being secretary, assistant, prompter, ally and editor.

I would especially like to thank Ms. Dorothy Goss, of Melbourne, for her generous and valuable assistance in tracing maps, reference works and the like, while also acting as hostess and guide.

Lastly, I wish to pay tribute belatedly to the late Anthea Joseph, whose untimely death occurred last year. She was responsible for accepting my first novel, *Rat Trap*, for publication, and it was her encouragement and enthusiasm that launched me upon my present course. She is gone, and I miss her, as do countless others.

BIBLIOGRAPHICAL NOTE

The People's Republic of China has in recent decades adopted a specific system of alphabetic script known as *pinyin*. This is gradually replacing systems such as that invented by Wade which is still widely used in the West. The author of a novel which uses Chinese proper and place names is therefore confronted with a minor problem, i.e., which system to adopt. There are two ways of highlighting the differences between the *pinyin* and Wade systems. The city of Peking, as Wade renders it, becomes Beijing in *pinyin*. Obviously, any Western novel set in Peking would lose by employing the new system. This is true also of places like Canton and perhaps especially Shanghai.

Therefore, the reader familiar with Chinese as rendered alphabetically must forgive me for employing a rather random selection of both systems. I have chosen convenience of recognition and familiarity above considerations of accuracy or exclusivity. Thus we have Peking, Shanghai, and Canton, while we have Deng rather than Teng in rendering the name of the most powerful man in post-Mao China. I only hope that he, and the reader, approve my eclecticism.

In researching this novel's background, I was indebted to the Nagel Guides to Spain, China, and the Federal Republic of Germany, and the Michelin Guides to Spain and Germany. Also, that valuable (and shorter!) volume, Keijzer & Kaplan's *China Guidebook*. In Australia, Roma Dulhunty's two books on Lake Eyre and Michael Page's *South Australia* kept me company.

Other principal sources of reference employed during the writing of the novel include *The Chinese War Machine*, edited by Ray Bonds; *British Intelligence in the Second World War* by F. H. Hinsley; Terence Prittie's *The Velvet Chancellors;* Purnell's *History of the Second World War*, vol. 2, and *The Encyclopaedia of World War II*, edited by Thomas Parrish.

Hard is the Journey,
Hard is the Journey,
So many turnings,
And now where am I?

–Li Po (AD 701 – 62)

The senior foreign operations officer from the Ministry of Public Tranquility reached his slim, long-fingered hand into the pool of light cast by the anglepoise lamp at the edge of his desk. The fingers stroked the back and flanks of a jade ornament carved in the shape of a tiger. Its green was too light, artificial and almost plastic to the American's eyes. It did not look valuable, though he supposed it was. The tiger had been remounted on a cheap, varnished wooden plinth which bore a small brass plaque with an inscription in Chinese which commended the socialist revolutionary zeal of the occupant of that desk and that office. The inscription faced outwards into the darkened room, presumably to impress visitors. To the American, also, the tiger appeared tubby, ill-formed, Buddha-like. Smug, too.

The occupant of the office then spoke, in an American-accented English without slurs or hesitation; and with great politeness.

"Yes, with your permission, of course, we shall call this operation *Jade Tiger*. Do you agree?"

The American nodded. "Sure. Good name. I agree."

"Excellent."

The overweight, fat-sleeked tiger continued to smile smugly from its little plinth in the white lamplight.

Preludes

He had been swimming now for a long time—for a little under three hours, he corrected himself sharply, feeling the edges of his consciousness curl and become fuzzy even as he attempted clarity of thought. Ahead of him, no longer retreating with every stroke but rendered a haze of light that had neither form nor movement. Kowloon and Victoria blazed. There was a patch of darkness between those two bunches of light hanging from the night sky, which was Victoria Harbour. The Star Ferries—there was one of them now, a bell clanging almost lost in the weariness-sounds in his ears—moved across that ten-minute gap between the lights. Then, at once, he was no longer certain of what he had registered, what he had thought . . .

The ferry, yes, that was it. Fingers of lights reached up into the darkness; the hotels on Kowloon. Then the roar of an airliner, lights pricking beneath its belly, coming in to land at Kai Tak.

Colonel Wei knew that if he was not picked up by one of the police patrols soon he would stop swimming, tread water wearily for a while, then slip beneath the dark, placid, oil-tasting water. And it would all have been for nothing. He splashed forward feebly, arms wrenching in their sockets. He had trained to swim much farther than he had come; from the Chinese mainland, a deserted though patrolled spot on the coast where swimmers launched themselves off from the People's Republic, making for the slums and the junk ghettoes of Aberdeen harbour. Yet he was wearied already, after less than ten miles, to the point of surrender. His body was warm rather than cold, warm and numb, and he could not make himself afraid and wary of that. The adrenaline had flowed too quickly, too crudely in his veins, dissipating itself. Now, nothing remained, nothing spurred him on.

1

Where were the nightly harbour patrols? He knew their routine well, their assiduous sweeps of the bays and harbours and roads around the islands. He should have encountered a patrol boat, been pinned gratefully in its searchlight beam, long before this, while he was still swimming across Deep Bay, or Urmston Road. A map flickered like an old piece of celluloid in his mind, and was gone. The names cost him an effort of thought. Hundreds of other swimmers would have been picked up by now, why not him? They would be sent back, he would not. Did they not realize that, out here in the dark water, he was beginning to drown? He, Colonel Wei Fu-Chun of the Ministry of Public Tranquility, Foreign Department, was drowning, and all the uniqueness that was him and the more valuable uniqueness of what he knew and could tell was drowning with him. Rage filled him for a moment, a back-of-the-throat rage like the last vomit of an emptied stomach, a thin bile of anger.

His body stopped. He worked his legs, so far away from him and so numbly warm, but he felt the weight of his torso pressing down into the water. His mouth closed as it went below the water, then he thrust up, arms waving and back arched, his breath roaring as if he had been submerged for minutes. He bobbed more successfully on the water, his head swinging slowly, like that of a tired and wounded bull, searching for the prick or wash of light across the harbour. He should have made straight for the shore, he should not have tried this over-elaboration, he should have . . .

He blew the water from his mouth, but he had already swallowed some and it made him cough and retch. No lights, no darkness, the rush and press of the water, the frantic, copulatory arch of the body, as he thrust back to the surface. Leaden arms, legs no longer there at all, slim body so heavy. Lights again, the hazy sunrise of lights and the gap of darkness between them now growing, seeming closer. His past life invaded him as a vague, hopeless, infinite longing to which images—pale and shadowy and unimportant—clung like burrs. His mission, his importance, his game-plan, all were rendered meaningless by the imminence of his death, a death he perceived with a dimmed kind of certainty. He felt abandoned by his past, by his self.

He shook his head with great effort. The water and his panic roared in his ears. The noise would prevent his hearing the puttering of the launch when it came. Light was flowing over him like pale lava. The noise of his blood, calling now. Something in him was trying to attract his attention.

Water as solid as earth in his nose and throat. He was being buried alive. He could not breathe. Darkness.

Then a thrust of futility, and a sound chuckled through the water, its laughter surrounded him. Puttering. Then only the arms, his body being moved, the dragging sensation, the pressure on his back, his legs being worked, something clamping over his mouth while something else held his nostrils tight. Again and again, spasms injected into his lungs. He kept his eyes closed, retched water in a dribble from the slack corner of his mouth, dragged in air without assistance, retched again, coughed in a spasm.

A white face was staring down at him, out of focus. An indifferent face, a face already expressive of decision, and dismissal. One more to be sent back.

"No—" he said, and began coughing again. He grabbed the man's arm, detaining him. "No! My—my name is Wei, I am a senior official of the Ministry—Ministry of Public Tranquility. I wish—wish to talk to someone from the British int-intelligence service. Do you understand? Colonel Wei Fu-Chun—"

The face went on looking down at him. He could do no more to make his situation clear. It was a crucial moment, perhaps the most crucial. Everything—*everything,* he reminded himself—depended upon that moment. Yet he could not repeat his words. The face slipped out of focus, lost form, went. Wei slept.

"My languages aren't what they might be, Peter, but I definitely heard German—as you'd expect—and I *know* I heard Russian, too."

Peter Shelley stood at the drawing-room windows, watching the garden slip into shadow. The tree that was the focal point of the part of the garden on which his attention was fixed was a blaze of crab-apples. Some of the earliest to fall lay like bright beads on the grass. A large Victorian house in a village to the north of Birmingham, and after dinner, with the sound of a last, distant lawnmower from a neighbouring property, Michael Davies had made his announcement, almost without preamble. It was as if he were continuing the telephone call that had invited Shelley from London in the brief interval while his wife, Marian, stacked the dinner service in the dishwasher. Shelley stared down at the brandy balloon in his hand, and swilled the pale liquor slowly.

"But—Zimmermann? Russian?" he said, without turning from

the window, as if consciously posed against its last golden light like an actor positioned upstage of Davies, at ease in an armchair.

"Yes."

"Tell me again. You fell ill in Wu Han—business trip."

"Yes. Food poisoning or something." Davies chuckled. "Overdoing the food and drink, no doubt. In hospital for a couple of days, business colleagues solicitous and out to steal the contracts I wanted to negotiate with the Chinese at the same time." He chuckled again. "The second day I was in, Zimmermann is rushed in. He's got food poisoning or something, as well. You'd have seen it all in the papers."

"Yes, I did. Very embarrassing for the People's Republic. Deng makes a brief appearance in Wu Han to commiserate. The German Chancellor's top adviser, his strong right hand, struck down by sweet and sour pork. Too bad."

Michael Davies laughed loudly. "Didn't do the Krauts any harm, mind. Their trade mission scooped up orders left, right and centre—sort of apology, I suppose. By the time Zimmermann was transferred to Shanghai Hospital, there must have been a dozen deals on the cards—ball-bearings to TV sets. My illness didn't produce such spectacular results."

Shelley turned from the window. Davies's florid features, good-humoured, shrewd, amused, were caught by the setting sun, which made him squint-eyed and golden. A successful Midlands' businessman, owning his light engineering company, and an occasional—in times past—courier for SIS. Uncaught and unsuspected, unlike poor old Greville Wynne and others like him. Someone Shelley had operated, instructed, liked. Trusted.

"Michael," Shelley said, almost proffering his glass, "thank you for dinner, which was excellent—Marian's cooking continues towards perfection—and thank you for the pleasure of your home." Shelley's eyes wandered over the drawing-room. "But this tale of yours, the purpose of my visit?" Davies nodded, his face expectant. "What is it you're really trying to tell me?"

"I want you to do something about it—can you tell Aubrey?"

"Is there anything to tell?"

"Look, Peter, you're Aubrey's closest confidant. What's he now, by the way—deputy director?" Shelley nodded. "In that case, he ought to know. He ought to be interested."

"In what, precisely, Michael?"

"I heard Zimmermann talking in Russian, bawling out, crying, weeping, screaming, stuttering. You couldn't avoid it. I was in the room across the corridor. He was like a bad five-act tragedy in there, and you know as well as me what that means.''

"Do I?''

"Dammit, Peter, don't be so cagey! He was drugged, and not to make him sleep. There were little, official-looking Chinamen in and out of his room like a railway station. Staying for hours. *Not* locals—the kow-towed-to brigade was there in force. Then they whisked him off to Shanghai. A week later he was back in Bonn, at Chancellor Vogel's right or left hand. The second most powerful man in the West German political firmament, the architect of *Ostpolitik,* was in a provincial Chinese hospital, yelling for his mother in Russian and attracting a lot of *professional* attention! Don't you think it all rather strange, Peter?''

Shelley sat on the chaise in front of the french windows, smoothing the creases in his trousers with his free hand. Again, he studied the brandy in his glass, his face exhibiting the concentration of a drunk at his car wheel attempting to count his alcohol intake. Finally, he looked up.

"Probably nothing in it—merely curious.'' He raised his hand. "Very well. Aubrey's on holiday, but I'll ring him about it, since you're worried—''

"I'm not. I just think Aubrey should be. Zimmermann was being interrogated in that hospital room—it was like one of my old courier's nightmares half the time—and he was being interrogated in Russian.''

The house was perched above Hong Kong Central, looking down from Peak Road over Victoria Harbour and Causeway Bay to the Manhattan-like skyline of Kowloon across the blue water. Colonel Wei, however, was not given the privilege of the view. His room overlooked a dusty, bright courtyard, and the hills rose directly behind the house, cramping the perspective from the locked window. There was ineffectual-looking wire netting across the window. The room was hot, the dusty fan turning slowly, as if continually losing power. Colonel Wei lay on the narrow bed, dressed in borrowed shirt and slacks, a belt pulling the waistband into his flat stomach. Unfortunately, too, he had to turn up the trouser legs a matter of three inches. He considered that the clothes represented a planned humiliation.

For most of the morning, after the doctor had left him, Colonel Wei gave himself up to the task of filling the metal ashtray, blazoned with a brand of local beer, with cigarette stubs, and clouding the room with blue smoke which the fan moved like an element as viscous as treacle. Godwin, when he came in, unlocking the door noisily, wafted a disparaging hand at the smoke. He re-locked the door, and drew a chair to the side of the bed. Colonel Wei pushed his body into a more upright position against the bedhead.

Godwin was young, ruddy complexioned, his forehead showing a white, sunhatted line between his fair hair and the folds of his brow. He perspired freely in the humid atmosphere of Hong Kong. His pale suit was creased and rumpled. His pale blue eyes appeared ill at ease, almost furtive. He seemed to exude the kind of nervousness he might have displayed before his own superiors.

"You—" he began, then cleared his throat. "You claim to be Colonel Wei Fu-Chun of the Foreign Department of the Ministry of Public Tranquility, the intelligence service of the People's Republic."

Wei shrugged. "I am he—I do not claim it." He touched the small, waterproof packet suspended from his neck by a thin gold chain. They had inspected it, then evidently replaced it while he slept.

"We know about that," Godwin said dismissively.

"You have had the photographic negatives developed and enlarged?"

Godwin nodded. "Yes. If you're not Wei, you obviously seem just as important as he is. Unless the pictures are faked."

"They are not."

"Why does an intelligence colonel take the peasants' route into Hong Kong? You almost drowned."

"It seemed safer."

"You could have provided yourself with false papers, with travel warrants, with anything you needed to arrive anywhere in the West officially. If you are who you say you are."

"I realise that. I am sorry, I can only ask you to believe that I was watched, that I was under suspicion, that I could not do the things you have suggested without being unmasked."

"Why was that? Had you fallen into disgrace?"

"I was falling, shall we say?" Wei lit another cigarette from the butt of the one he had finished. He drew in the smoke like an opiate, exhaling reluctantly and after a lengthy pause. The blue smoke enfolded the fan that moved sluggishly through its soup. "I was in the Ministry of Public Tranquility in Shanghai. Does that give you a clue?"

"How long had you been there?"

"I am from Shanghai—I grew up there."

"You learned your English in America."

Wei shook his head. "No, my teachers did, not I. As I was saying, I entered and progressed in the MPT in Shanghai. I am now forty years of age. During the Cultural Revolution—"

"Ah," Godwin said, his eyes widening, growing bright with perception and self-congratulation, "you're tainted by the Gang of Four, then?"

Wei nodded. "Yes. The present leadership is suffering a renewed bout of Party purification. Now it is associates of associates of associates who are suspect, who will be disgraced. Myself among them." Wei shrugged. "It was becoming difficult, almost too late. I arranged a provincial journey, to Guangzhou— Canton, as you call it—to retrieve an individual arrested for bourgeois revisionism and crimes of counter-revolutionary publication. Instead of going there, I came here, swimming just like, as you say, a peasant."

"I see." Godwin's voice became official-sounding. "What, precisely, do you want, Colonel Wei?"

"A great deal of money. And I wish to go to the United States of America—to the arms of the Great Enemy." Wei smiled humourlessly. Even for an Oriental, he seemed to lack expressive facial muscles. He might have been lightly drugged, so bland and unchanging had been his expression throughout the interview.

"I see. America. Money. What have you to offer?"

"A great deal. But not to you. I will talk only to a senior officer of the CIA, *and* to your deputy-director."

"There isn't a deputy-director here. You're misinformed. My senior is the station head, Mr. McIntosh. He's in Macau at the moment."

"I mean the deputy-director in London. Mr. Aubrey. I will talk to him, perhaps only to him."

"What?" Godwin's mouth had fallen open. "Impossible, I'm afraid—"

It was as if Wei had moved in to finish off a boxing match. Another body blow winded Godwin. "You must signal London. Tell them I have information—a great deal of information—concerning a plot by the Soviet revisionists to discredit the whole government of West Germany. A man named Zimmermann is the keystone of this plot. Please tell Mr. Aubrey in London that I will talk of this only to him. And please inform the senior CIA officer in Hong Kong of my arrival." Now Wei smiled broadly, but his eyes were directed at his hands, at the smoke that curled from between his fingers. "The name is Zimmermann, remember."

* * *

"So, Shelley has rung Aubrey?"

"At last, yes. There was no way to hurry matters. The man Davies could not be prompted. A free agent."

"I accept that. Shelley also has received signals from Hong Kong concerning Wei. That was confirmed this morning."

"Good. A pleasing and effective conjunction, then?"

"It is to be hoped so. Aubrey's curiosity is famed. Sometimes, it clouds his judgment."

"I agree. Is Wei good enough, do you think?"

"Aubrey is clever—so is Wei. He has been trained in Aubrey's methods of interrogation. He understands Aubrey. Yes, Wei will perform his task."

"There'll be quite a convergence on Hong Kong, then. Everyone will be running for the train."

"Indeed. The Germans, of course, will miss their train."

"Let's hope so."

"Do you really believe in the fortuitous, Peter?"

Kenneth Aubrey removed his straw hat and wiped his damp forehead. The noon sun glared above the garden in an almost colourless sky. Shelley's tall, angular figure remained beneath the shade of the low-boughed apple tree. In his dark suit, he had brought the atmosphere of conspiracy to the small, walled garden of Aubrey's Oxfordshire cottage, which seemed foreboding to Aubrey. As for himself, he felt diminished by the garden shears in his hand, his rolled-up sleeves, his momentary breathlessness.

"I—don't know what to think, sir."

"I took your call here yesterday. Now, today, you arrive out of the blue to tell me that a very important Chinese intelligence defector has arrived in Hong Kong and regaled the station there with similar dark mutterings about the German Chancellor's principal political adviser. Do you really *believe* in it, Peter?"

While he spoke, Aubrey advanced on Shelley, shears extended as if to do him some physical injury. Aubrey entered the shade of the apple tree. Shelley wiped aside a lock of fair hair that had fallen over his brow.

"It's—curious, sir."

"Perhaps. A Soviet scheme to discredit the German government, a German-speaking Russian in a provincial Chinese hospital. Curious is putting it rather mildly." Aubrey replaced his straw hat, jamming it on his head as if a sudden wind might spring up. He studied the shears as if considering their purpose, then he let them fall, point first, into the grass. "Mm."

"Wei can be brought here, sir," Shelley suggested.

Aubrey shook his head. He turned his back to Shelley and contemplated the whitewashed walls of the cottage, then its thatch. His study might have been valedictory. He sighed.

"I can't see that working. Godwin and McIntosh would have to come, too, denuding Hong Kong station. Time would elapse, Wei would be on guard. The CIA might well have him *under wraps*, as they would put it, by that time. The man wants to go to America?" Shelley nodded. "No. I shall have to go there."

"Hong Kong, sir?"

"You don't think the trip worthwhile?"

"We're not even sure Wei is who he says he is."

"Agreed." Aubrey rubbed his mouth. "I haven't offered you a beer, Peter." He made no move towards the cottage. Birds quarrelled above their heads, amid leaves. "Perhaps I would not take such a precipitate step except for the fact that the Berlin Treaty is to be formally ratified between the two Germanys and the Soviet Union in a fortnight's time. *There* is the real fortuitousness of these two pieces of information. There, perhaps, is their significance and their danger. I think I had better talk to this Colonel Wei." Aubrey nodded vigorously. "Yes, I had better."

"You think this has something to do with the treaty, sir?"

"Zimmermann has *everything* to do with that treaty. Berlin to become an open city, virtually all travel restrictions between the DDR and the Federal Republic suspended for a trial period of a year. A referendum on reunification early next year. And the great symbolic act: the pulling down of the Berlin Wall. It is all Zimmermann's achievement, you know. He and Chancellor Vogel. They've gambled everything, including the imminent federal elections, on that treaty. It is a vastly important piece of legislation. *Ostpolitik* rules, OK?" Aubrey smiled. "Talk of plots and schemes and the Russian language from a hospital room makes me a little jumpy."

"You need me there, sir."

"I'll take Hyde."

"The swagman?" Shelley sounded disappointed rather than contemptuous.

"I'm old, Peter. I need legs. I need a Jason to carry me across the river, bundle of bones that I am. Hyde is a runner. Besides, I need you here." He patted Shelley's arm. "Come into the house. I have some rather gassy lager in the refrigerator." He looked round the garden again, and sighed. "I must arrange for the lawns to be cut, at the least," he said, steering Shelley towards the cottage with his hand on the younger man's arm.

"You'll want the files pulled?"

"Of course. Did I tell you that I know Zimmermann—*knew* him rather? During the war. Beginning of the war, really, just before Dunkirk." He looked up at Shelley. He was smiling broadly. His pale blue eyes sparkled with a kind of boyish mischief. "Wolfgang Zimmermann was once my prisoner in France."

12 May 1940

It was evident even to himself that he appeared more of an ornithologist than a man of action; thornproof tweed jacket and plus-fours, heavy walking shoes, a knurled stick, a deer-stalker. A costume that was an affectation in the Hague or Brussels or even yesterday in Arras, was here a piece of self-mockery, of self-deprecation that Kenneth Aubrey resented, lying at the crest of a hillock overlooking the Meuse and Sedan and Guderian's XIX Panzer Corps moving up to the river. The binoculars which brought him closer to the Germans also completed the inappropriateness of his appearance. The problem was, there was no prescribed uniform for spies, and there had been no time for a convincing gesture in the direction of French or Belgian peasant dress. There had only been enough time to contact his two local men, be led through narrow lanes and past tiny villages filling up with uniformed French, arrive at this hillock sheltered by heavy-boughed trees, and begin watching.

The French had abandoned Sedan on the other side of the river during the day, and the Germans had flooded into it and up to the eastern bank of the Meuse like a slow, inexorable tide of grey mud. Only an hour before, at seven, while the smoke was clearing from the demolition of the bridges and debris still bobbed and idled in the river, the assault infantry and the tanks had reached the far bank of the Meuse. With evening darkening the scene, Aubrey's certainty increased. Guderian would order his infantry, probably with artillery and aircraft cover, to cross the river the following morning. The battle for France was about to begin—was already lost?

Aubrey put away the thought. The Germans had been assumed incapable of negotiating the Ardennes, then assumed capable of being held for nine or ten days. That had been two days ago. Now they were across the French frontier, into Sedan, at the river. Tomorrow, they would cross. Now, Aubrey knew, French senior commanders would be assuming, possessed as they were by the spirits of the last war, that it would take the Germans five or six days to force a crossing. Aubrey, suddenly and utterly Francophobe, like the army commanders and intelligence seniors who had dispatched him from his SIS mobile unit with GHQ of the British Expeditionary Force, believed that Guderian's corps would cross the Meuse the following day.

Aubrey disliked the Francophobia, just as he disliked the defeatism that so easily and readily pervaded SIS during 1940. After the capture of two SIS senior officers in November 1939, morale in the intelligence service in the Low Countries had been dealt a blow from which it had never recovered. Raw and inexperienced young men, some of them with the correct languages, some of them with completed practical training, had been drafted in to replace blown agents and networks. Aubrey had been one of these barely-down-from-university young men. By May 1940, there was, for all effective practical purposes, no British intelligence service operating in Europe. Even here, above the river and the town of Sedan, Aubrey could conceive of himself in no other terms than that of the boy with his finger in the dyke.

"M'sieur?" Henri murmured behind him to attract his attention. Aubrey swept his glasses once more along the darkening river bank. Shattered bridges, a broad, moving stretch of water, the smoke of deliberate or inadvertent fires lowering above the town. And field grey and artillery and tanks everywhere, a heavy margin drawn along the right bank. Aubrey rolled onto his back and sat up.

"Oui, Henri?"

"Food, M'sieur." Henri offered him a hunk of bread he had cut from a long loaf with a clasp knife. There appeared to be no butter, but there was a strong-smelling cheese and some young red wine. Henri had obviously decided not to wait for the return of his brother, Philippe, before supper. Aubrey chewed on the bread, feeling it stick to his palate.

"Good," he said. He had recruited the two brothers, who farmed near Verdun. Their intelligence responsibility had been the Franco-Belgian border from Verdun north along the Meuse to Charleville. They were enthusiastic, anti-German since their father had been killed in the last war and their farm destroyed around their childish heads during the battle of Verdun in 1916, and they were conscientious in the performance of their surveillance duties. They represented, in embryo, the kind of network that Aubrey believed, with the arrogance of inexperience, he could develop and maintain, given time. Guderian, as much as anyone, had robbed him of that time.

"Merci," Henri murmured. Philippe, the younger brother, was more communicative than the darkly complexioned Henri. "What do you intend, M'sieur?" Henri continued, as if to contradict Aubrey's reflection on his taciturnity. "Tomorrow, the Boche"—here, an obligatory spit—"will be across the river, uh?"

Aubrey nodded reluctantly. "I think so, Henri."

Henri pointed westward, where the clouds were dyed a violent pink against dark blue. He spat again. "The French cavalry—ordered to hold Sedan! The retreat has begun."

"What we need to know is . . . as much about their plan of campaign as possible."

Wine dribbled from the corner of Henri's mouth. It made him look retarded. And his brother Philippe was in the nearest village, using an ordinary telephone to communicate with Aubrey's unit and pass on his report and conclusions. None of it seemed sufficiently serious, or sufficiently professional, to place in the path of Guderian's army like a buried mine. Henri wiped the wine from his chin.

"They'll be sending over patrols tonight," Aubrey said. Henri nodded, and indicated his throat with a cutting motion. "No. But if they were like us, *spies*, they might know a great deal, don't you think? We might learn a great deal."

"True, M'sieur." Henri appeared disappointed. "But only from an officer, uh? We need an officer."

"Perhaps we can find one."

Aubrey rolled onto his stomach again, and raised his binoculars to take advantage of the remaining daylight. He scanned the near bank of the Meuse, the concrete pill-boxes and the trenches of the French appearing stout, and yet shadowy and insubstantial in the gloom, behind the belt of barbed wire. Behind Aubrey, on the Marfée Heights overlooking Sedan and the river, the French had massed artillery. If the Germans sent out intelligence gathering patrols across the river, then it would be the heights that would interest them. Later in the night, perhaps, the small inflatable rafts might be putting out from the far bank.

He heard a click behind him, and rolled onto his back again. Henri was checking the big pistol he held in his hands, squinting down the barrel, pretending to fire. Aubrey found the gesture, and the concentration in the play-acting, strangely poignant. The gun belonged to the last war, a bulky, long-barrelled Mauser. It was effective, and outdated. The tanks and artillery and P38s and new Mausers and machine pistols and Kar 98 rifles of a modern war lay on the other side of the Meuse. And he was a short man with thinning hair, dressed like a country squire. Ridiculous.

Yes, he would have a German, catch himself a Wehrmacht officer, when Philippe returned and before the night was through.

13 May 1940

Noises now, quiet mouse-pattering noises, the disturbances of old leaf-mould, new grass, the night air itself. Aubrey glanced at the luminous dial of his watch. Three-fifteen. Henri and Philippe were away to his left, towards where the copse straggled out on the Marfée Heights. The noises indicated a small party, perhaps three. The path through the copse lay like a parting in dark hair in the moonlight. It seemed impossibly arrogant that the German patrol would use the path, as if out for a stroll, for exercise. Perhaps they were that confident...

The noises ceased. The path slipped away from Aubrey, into the trees that marched down the slope towards the river. Distantly, the night was filled with the muted orchestration of German movements. Heavy artillery, the rumble of tanks, the occasional noise of aeroplanes overhead. A war gathering in the background, making itself real. Aubrey felt damp, stretched on the grass and leaf-mould; damp, ineffectual, reluctant, excited.

Noises again, and the bobbing of a helmet climbing the path, moonlight glancing on it above a bulky shadow. Then the glimpse of a slim rifle, caught in the pale light. Then a second German soldier toiling up the slope. No disguises, no real caution. The slope was already part of a greater Germany. The third man was an officer. Aubrey watched him pause and remove his cap, wiping his forehead. So confident...

The first soldier passed Aubrey's hiding-place, moving cautiously but steadily down the path towards Henri and Philippe. Aubrey experienced a sudden and fierce delight at the prospect of the man's death. The second soldier turned to look back at his officer, and was motioned forward. The officer replaced his cap, and hastened up the path. The second soldier moved on, his back now to Aubrey.

A long pause, each footstep the officer took punctuated by an intense silence where the noises from across the river seemed to have reduced to a static-like hum. The ether of war. Then sudden noise, muffled, struggling, hand-over-mouth noises that Aubrey could envisage vividly. Knife—the clasp knife that Henri had used to cut off chunks of the loaf—across throat, into side, up through ribs...

The German officer stiffened. There was an instant recognition that seemed without puzzlement or guesswork. This man *knew* the noise of assassination in the dark, and Aubrey was suddenly afraid of him. Aubrey pushed himself to his knees. The officer had drawn his pistol, and cocked it—cocked his head too, listening ahead of him. Aubrey moved the gun—it was clumsy, heavy now—out in front of his body in a two-handed grip, realising he had never killed, never even wounded, must not do so now...

"Halt!" he snapped in German. The German officer spun towards the sound of his voice. A crashing of something into a bush, then silence from further up the path.

The German's gun came up. Aubrey was still on his knees, as if praying, his Webley aimed at the middle of the German's form, his hands white around the gun butt. The German saw the gun, didn't see the gun, *must* see the gun in this light...

The German officer lowered his pistol to his side. Aubrey was afraid to get up or to lower his own gun. He felt weak and helpless, anxious for the two Frenchmen and their arrival.

The German officer laughed softly, incongruously, then shrugged his shoulders. Then he spoke.

"You're not even a soldier," he remarked, disappointment evident in his tone. He was no more than six or seven yards away, but his face was in shadow. He sounded young, looked tall and slim. Aubrey hated being still on his knees, damp from the ground soaking through the plus-fours. "What are you? French? Not French?"

"Englander," Aubrey felt obliged to explain.

"Where is your uniform?" Footsteps coming down the path. The German flinched, almost precipitated himself into activity, then shrugged again. He had Guderian's army at his back. It was bad luck, but only temporary. "Wait—you're an agent—a spy, then." The German laughed softly. Henri and Philippe appeared on the path. Aubrey could see their white teeth, grinning. They'd killed...

"Perhaps so. Like yourself, then."

Aubrey felt excitement—a febrile, arcane, secret excitement he had rarely before felt—rise in his stomach like a tickling, mild indigestion. He had captured his first German of the war.

Henri tugged the pistol from the German officer's hand, and

Philippe frisked him for other weapons. The German seemed indifferent, even bored. Aubrey stood up.

"Name, rank and serial number," Aubrey snapped.

Yes, the German was taller, perhaps a few years younger; slim and handsome in uniform, unafraid.

"Hauptmann Zimmermann," he said, nodding, "at your service."

PART ONE

Towards the Unknown Region

As cold waters to a thirsty soul,
So is good news from a far country.

Proverbs 25:25

ONE

Orient Express

The rush of houses slipped beneath the belly of the aircraft—Hyde glimpsed washing thrust from windows on bamboo poles—and there was the sense of being amid the tall fingers of the hotel blocks, before the seeming lurch settled the 747 above the runway stretching out into the blue water. It was unnerving, as if the pilot had somehow shrugged the huge aircraft into alignment with the finger of concrete in the bay. Then the wheels skidded and bit, and the 747 was moving like a fast powerboat level with the water, and Kai-Tak's airport buildings were scurrying towards the windows.

Hyde shrugged himself upright in his seat as the aircraft slowed and taxied. The businessman who had kept him company all the way from London to Hong Kong looked rumpled, tired, but smelt of the applied wakefulness of after-shave. Hyde's knowledge of the clothing import business had become compendious during the flight, to his increasing boredom. His own biography as a freelance journalist had been used to fend off further assaults of information and anecdote. Aubrey, naturally, had travelled first class.

Hyde squeezed out from the window seat into the aisle before the rush to anticipate the disappearance of the seatbelt light, collected his bag from the locker over his head, and pushed down the aisle towards the nose of the aircraft. One stewardess watched him, but Aubrey had arranged matters satisfactorily, and his progress was not impeded nor was he instructed to return to his seat. He pushed aside the curtain into first class as the aircraft finally slowed to a halt. Aubrey's eyes instantly met his, and the old man smiled. He looked tired, and eager; an almost-hunger about his features, even in the pale eyes. In a room somewhere in the teeming city, a man waited to be interrogated. It was as if

19

Aubrey could taste the man's presence, scent it in the dry air of the fuselage.

Immigration officials entered in crisp khaki shirts and shorts and sprayed the aircraft, which had stopped at Bombay, from oversized aerosol cans. Five minutes later, Aubrey and Hyde stepped into the passenger gangway, Hyde carrying his own bag and Aubrey's, the old man's being emblazoned with the British Airways legend. It was virtually unused. Hyde wondered whether some of Aubrey's evident excitement was connected with the mere fact of travelling—a grandad journey, but not quite to relatives in Aussie.

The tunnel of the gangway was hot, insinuating a stifling, humid day outside. Then they stepped into the air-conditioning of the main airport building and its reasserted, artificial cool.

McIntosh and Godwin were waiting for them at passport control. Hyde observed a florid young man who emanated a subtle, and possibly crucial weakness, and an older, lined, sunburnt man who stooped, appeared clever, and was close to retirement. Aubrey shook hands with them, introduced Hyde, and was then ushered by the two men towards the terminal building doors. Godwin glanced at Hyde, following behind.

Hyde understood the way in which the two men from Hong Kong station had ignored him. They recognised him; recognised his type, his function, to be perfectly accurate. Aubrey's minder, his runner. The thug. Hyde grinned at McIntosh's stooping back in its creased linen jacket. Disrespect was something he offered freely, and received back by a process of compound interest. The uncomfortable, sidelong way in which the Third Secretaries and Trade Attachés of the intelligence service regarded him was in itself a marking-off, a distinction. He was one of the night-soil men, and there would always be a job with SIS.

He leant against the car, squinting in the hard sun. McIntosh was already in the car, inspecting his briefcase for something Aubrey had demanded. Aubrey, perspiring freely, visibly wilting in the temperature, which Hyde guessed was perhaps just nudging eighty degrees, and unable to cope with the high humidity, was fussing with his straw hat, then his club tie, then the creased jacket he wore.

"McIntosh," he said suddenly, and the station head plucked himself from the hot interior of the small, battered Ford and looked at Hyde, startled; a sense of insult spread across his lined face immediately it emerged.

"Yes, Hyde?"

"Who's the little man watching us from the observation gallery?"

McIntosh's mocking smile revealed new and different folds and erosion gullies in his face. "Local colour, Hyde—just local colour. One of the KGB irregulars. Taken photographs, as usual, has he?"

"Not yet. Get in the car, Mr. Aubrey."

"He goes everywhere with us," McIntosh protested. "You can't expect to come here without arousing professional interest, Mr. Aubrey."

"Agreed," Aubrey said as he obediently got into the car.

"You could save on expenses by sharing the same transport," Hyde remarked.

McIntosh shrugged dismissively at Hyde's back as the Australian climbed into the Ford. Godwin grinned.

As Godwin turned the car out of the airport and onto the road leading through Kowloon to the cross-harbour tunnel to Hong Kong central, McIntosh turned in the passenger seat and handed Aubrey a sheaf of papers.

"There are the full transcripts, Mr. Aubrey."

Aubrey glanced at them. Hyde slumped back in his seat, watching another 747 coming in to land. He had glanced to ensure that the car that had turned out behind them was still following, and then he relaxed. His talents and intervention were not, at that moment, required. A cooling breeze blew on his face from the open window of the car. On the opposite side of the road, the hotels crowded like white trees down towards the blue water.

"Your impressions, McIntosh," Aubrey requested, looking up from the papers. "What are they?"

"Of Wei?"

"I've talked to him most, sir," Godwin remarked.

"Very well," Aubrey replied in a heat-exasperated tone, "what is your impression of Wei?"

"Very clever, sir."

"What are his reasons for defecting to us?"

"Money and fear, I think."

Ma Tau Wai Road was crowded with cars, rickshaws, bicycles. It poured humanity and vehicles along itself like a gully accepting new flood water. Hyde sensed the unimportance of one Chinese defector amid the seething, appalling collision of humanity that was Kowloon. He realised that Hong Kong was in the process of seducing him to its vision of itself.

"Fear? Does that fear of reprisal, of arrest and disgrace, ring true to you?"

"Yes, sir. As far as we can check back. He's a Shanghai MPT man. We know there have been shake-ups there, a weeding out process. Deng's very thorough, sir, and he controls China now."

"After smashing the Gang of Four..." Hyde recited in a mocking imitation accent that belonged to the music-hall.

"Precisely," Godwin replied primly, his China-watcher's credentials mocked by the Australian thug. "Deng's very thorough, and his people are prepared to sift and sift and sift, find anyone and *everyone* who might be suspect. He does not intend to find himself or his Great Leap Forward imperilled—*ever*. Chairman Hua has gone—Colonel Wei is just a minor case of purification."

"Accepted, provisionally," Aubrey remarked in a smoothing-over tone. "He's given you sufficient background for you to believe he may have had superficial connections with the Gang of Four and the Shanghai People's Commune period?"

"Yes, sir, he has."

"This money business—going to America. You find that equally convincing?"

"It...seems to fit the man—"

"Like a glove," McIntosh interrupted. "He's a greedy bugger. Clever, smart as paint, man-of-a-thousand-masks type. Oriental to the bone. No bloody Communist or Maoist or Dengist—just the usual selfist. An operator."

"I see."

The crowds pouring into the railway terminus on Hong Chong Road appeared to Hyde like a mass of the faithful pouring into some modernist temple. The search for faith was unceasing, desperate, hurried.

"The local CIA are very interested, sir."

"I imagined they would be, Godwin. I've had signals from Langley expressing great concern. In fact, I expect no less a personage than the Deputy Director here to supervise."

"Buckholz? He's coming?"

"He's as intrigued by the matter of Colonel Wei's proposed revelations as myself. I take it you have been unable to elicit anything further?"

McIntosh shook his head reluctantly. Hyde glimpsed the glittering, wild blue of Victoria Harbour from which Colonel Wei had been fished, then the tail-lights of cars glowed and bobbed ahead of them as they entered the cross-harbour tunnel.

"Tight-lipped bugger," McIntosh muttered. "Just Zimmermann,

and a Soviet plot—dark hints, with that bland, cheesy, self-satisfied grin on his face and a fag in his mouth morning, noon, and night.''

Aubrey suppressed a smile.

"Does it add up to something important, sir?" Godwin asked in a voice that failed to conceal his excitement.

"I don't know, Godwin—I really don't.''

"But the Berlin Treaty, sir?"

"Yes, Godwin. Two weeks away from ratification. And you have a Chinaman you fished out of the harbour above us who suggests it is all a Russian plot. I take your point. But I wonder how a Chinaman knows, and why he should want to tell us, don't you?"

The car emerged into blinding sunlight at the end of the tunnel. Dark green hills climbed above Hong Kong into a haze of humidity that clung like mist. To Aubrey, the hills above the white concrete town resisted him. It was as if they concealed and sheltered Wei and what he knew. At the other end of the world from Zimmermann and his Chancellor and the Berlin Treaty, he had entered a world of secrets; a darkened room which contained a formidable, forewarned opponent.

"Kenneth."

"My dear Charles, welcome!"

Aubrey shook hands with Charles Buckholz, Deputy Director of the CIA. The ice rattled in his tall glass of lime juice as he got up and crossed the room to the American. The last sunlight before the quick tropical night splashed against one wall of the fan-cooled, open-windowed room like a decorator's anger. Buckholz looked about him as if he expected Wei to join them, or to be concealed behind a piece of furniture. Then he looked at Aubrey intently, weighing him, his glance distinguishing the elderly Englishman as a relic of empire.

"I never realized how well you'd fit in surroundings like these," he commented. Aubrey glanced down self-deprecatingly at his cream linen suit and recently whitened shoes.

"Ah," was all he said in reply.

"You've talked to Wei?"

Aubrey motioned Godwin from the room, then indicated the drinks arranged on a sideboard. Buckholz inspected them without expectation, then found a bourbon and poured himself a large measure, adding a handful of ice to the tumbler. He raised his glass to Aubrey.

"Yes, I've talked to Wei."

"What do you make of him, Kenneth?"

"He will be, as they say, a hard nut to crack. Something particularly hard and shrivelled and dry." Aubrey remembered pickled horse chestnuts on knotted string. Conkers. A school quadrangle. The next day had been Armistice Day.

Buckholz looked puzzled. "I thought he was eager to talk to you?"

"Oh, I have little doubt of that. I haven't allowed him to discuss the material he says he has brought—not yet. What I meant was—to establish the truth of what he says will be difficult. His genuineness."

"Oh, yeah." Buckholz walked to the open french windows to the first-floor balcony. He was outlined in orange sunlight, hard to look at without squinting. Aubrey sipped the chilled lime juice. What hadn't he asked Buckholz? The man seemed in such a hurry.

"Did you have a good flight?" Yes, that was it. Pleasantries.

"What . . . ?"

"Flight. A good flight?"

"Sure." Buckholz turned to him. "You have doubts about this guy Wei?"

"I would have doubts about anyone who claimed to know that the German Chancellor's closest adviser is a Russian agent-in-place."

"He said that?"

"As near as dammit. Wolfgang Zimmermann was interrogated—so the claim runs—in Wu Han, then Shanghai, and officers of the intelligence service elicited that he was a long-term KGB agent."

"Like Guillaume, who brought down Willy Brandt."

"Precisely. Lightning striking twice."

Buckholz moved away from the window towards Aubrey's chair. He appeared purposeful, quick, youthful. Aubrey glanced towards the sofa, where the small briefcase with which Buckholz had entered the room now lay. Buckholz swallowed at his tumbler of bourbon.

"We have to know the truth about this, Kenneth."

"I realize that, Charles. I realize that."

"Jesus, if it's true, then the whole of *Ostpolitik* is no more than playing into the Russians' hands—it could even be a

Russian game that the German Chancellor is playing. Jesus." He swallowed the last of his bourbon, refilled his glass, clinked in the handful of ice, then turned once more to Aubrey. Orange light, darker now like a dying fire, lay like a birthmark on one cheek and fringed his cropped grey hair. "I never liked that guy, Kenneth, and I never liked his games of footsie with the Kremlin. But this . . ." He shook his head, drank again. Then he moved like some caged and dangerous animal towards Aubrey's chair. The Englishman sipped like a nervous bird at his lime juice. "You realise we've already withdrawn more than a hundred thousand troops from the Federal Republic, in agreement with this Berlin Treaty nonsense?" Aubrey nodded.

"We have done the same, in proportion. In two or three years there will be no more than token NATO forces in West Germany. It will be the probable case that West Germany will leave NATO. Will have to if any referendum on reunification proves— *successful*?" Aubrey smiled apologetically. "These are world events, Charles. Not quite my responsibility. It is happening, it will happen."

"And it could all be the motivation of a Russian agent? Listen, Kenneth, if Wei is telling the truth, that changes everything."

"I suppose it does. Certainly, if it were proven against Zimmermann, there would be no Berlin Treaty."

"We have to find out."

"I agree."

It was Buckholz's turn to appear apologetic.

"It's going to be difficult, Kenneth." He sat down in a chair opposite Aubrey. "Since this guy Wei went over the wall, all our people in Shanghai are under the closest surveillance."

"Your Chinese nationals?"

"No. But my channels to them are stopped up. I can't get anyone near them."

"It would be the same with my people. I realise that."

"But we need to check this out. Wei has to be checked out. Zimmermann has to be checked out."

"Quite. What do you propose?"

"Send in a man—a Chinese. One of my people."

"And?"

"I have people he can talk to in Shanghai. He goes to this Wu Han place if necessary. He's got to learn if Zimmermann was in those hospitals, who visited him, when and how often—the whole ball of wax."

"One man?"

"It has to be done. Everything you get from Wei—*we* ge
from Wei—has to be checked out. Every detail he feeds us. You
agree?"

Aubrey was thoughtful for only a moment. He disliked the
haste being thrust upon him. It was more than simply Buckholz':
characteristic thirst for action, the American's effective impatience. Yet the deadline was unavoidable. Aubrey felt himsel
pushed reluctantly into what he could only regard as an arena, an
amphitheatre. Wei's story might be true. If it were not, then
Aubrey could not comprehend the man's motive; if it were true
then its implications were appalling. If Zimmermann was a KGI
agent . . .

Aubrey did not complete the speculation, but said: "It goe
back as far as 1938, you know."

"What?"

"Zimmermann's relationship with Moscow. Not quite as long
as Philby, but longer than most of your doubles." He smiled

"In my briefcase—" Buckholz began, indicating it with his
tumbler. "I debriefed Zimmermann, a long time ago." Buckholz'
eyes were gleaming with recollection and speculation. "At the
end of the war. I was with G-2 then, army intelligence. He was
captured near Frankfurt. He was an Abwehr *Oberst,* but they al
had to fire guns in the front line by that time." He leaned
towards Aubrey. "Read the file, Kenneth. Zimmermann was no
Nazi, not to me. He surprised me then. With what Wei has on
offer, I wonder just what he was. I read the files on the
airplane."

Aubrey nodded, almost dismissively. "This man of yours
Can he do any good?"

"He has to. My people are hamstrung by surveillance. We'l
get nothing out of China on Wei without a new face. A Chinese
face."

"Where is this man?"

Buckholz looked at his watch. "No more than two, three
hours away. He's on the next flight from the States. Just in case
you agreed we needed him."

"Quick," Aubrey murmured.

"He's one man, Kenneth. If we send him in and then come up
with another idea, so what? We have nothing to lose, except by
doing nothing."

"I suppose not." Aubrey paused, then added: "Strange, isn'
it? I once had Zimmermann as my prisoner."

"You're kidding."

"No. Early on in the war, before Dunkirk. In France. I interrogated him, too."

"And?"

"Not a Nazi, as you say. No, not a Nazi. But that means nothing, of itself."

"No? You read my file. Five years—*those* five years—are a long time. He may have changed—hardened."

"I wonder. You say you can do nothing in Shanghai with your establishment there?"

Buckholz shook his head vigorously. "No way. They're all pinned down in the foxhole. We need a wild card—my tame Chinaman."

"Hospitals, you think?"

"Who was there, how often, the records, even the MPT. There are one or two low-graders in the ministry he can tap." Buckholz shrugged. "It's not just an offer of help, Kenneth. Everything looks like it could be coming down to the wire. We have to crack this one, and we've got two weeks. Just two weeks."

Soft morning rain from a grey sky. Except for the temperature and the mugginess of the atmosphere, it might have been early winter in the Marienplatz in Munich. The rostrum had been set up on the steps of the Neues Rathaus, the town hall, and Wolfgang Zimmermann stood below it, looking up at the figure of Chancellor Dietrich Vogel as the West German leader addressed a large crowd in the main square of the Bavarian capital. Vogel was on his opponent's territory, in the heartland of right-wing, conservative Germany, and he was displaying the wares of the Berlin Treaty with all his customary style and simplicity and effectiveness. He held the microphone close to his mouth so that his tone and style remained conversational, and he was wearing his familiar check cap, borrowing an image of ordinariness for his purpose of self-portrayal as a man of the people. Elegant of mind, easy of manner, quietly passionate, Vogel demanded admiration, even affection, and Zimmermann rendered it.

It was a good crowd, and a receptive one. Whatever his opponents' suspicion of Moscow or East Berlin, and whatever right-wing fears he was able to mobilise, Vogel possessed the dream. It had been handed down from Adenauer and Erhard and Brandt, and it had lost none of its potency during the transmission. The German dream: the reunification of Germany. In the shadow of the Neues Rathaus and beneath the twin towers of the

Frauenkirche away behind Zimmermann, Vogel paraded the
dream-becoming-reality once more, and its magic was potent
enough to win elections.

"Look," Vogel said, without histrionics or rhetoric, "I know
you don't trust the Russians—I find it hard myself sometimes—"
Laughter, a few cheers, very little adverse comment from the
crowd. "But if we don't trust, we get nowhere. And the people
we really have to trust are in East Berlin, the people on the other
side of that obscenity of a wall and a border fence. And they're
Germans like you and me." Cheering now, a swell of sound. To
Zimmermann, it appeared that the crowd had raised its collective
voice precisely because Vogel had not raised his. Vogel waved
for silence, and continued. "I know that's easy to say, and I
could be accused of making cheap political capital out of it. But
it's also true. They're Germans, just like us. They live in
German cities like Dresden and Leipzig and Halle and Magdeburg
and Berlin—" Vogel was interrupted by another cheer. He
waved again for silence. "They don't live in Russia or Poland,
that's all I'm saying. And we have time to see whether it will
work— whether East and West alike will let we Germans make it
work. The referendum on reunification will not take place until
next year, and then *you*—all of you—will have the chance to
vote on it. We won't do anything without you. There are nearly
sixty million of us, and less than twenty million of them. How
can they impose on us? If *you* want a reunited Germany, then it's
in *your* hands."

More cheering. Zimmermann studied the nearest faces. Yes,
he concluded. Vogel and the Social Democrats would win the
election, and the Berlin Treaty would be signed. The Wall would
come down.

Zimmermann suppressed a smile, knowing it would be smug,
knowing there might be a film camera on him at that moment as
he looked up towards Vogel. It would work, though, he repeated
to himself. They would win. NATO would leave German soil. It
would be, again and after so long, just Germany; not East and
West. Germany. Nothing could go wrong now, nothing could
stop them.

"Don't be afraid," Vogel was saying, still in his conversational style. "As a great American President once said, we have
nothing to fear but fear itself. Don't be afraid."

The french windows were still open, despite the moths and
insects that flew into the room periodically, attracted by the soft

light of the table lamps. In the darkness outside, Hong Kong glowed with light. Its noise ascended the hill to the house as a hum; urgent, vibrant, enervating. It was a noise that seemed to tauten the atmosphere of the room, to bring the walls closer to the soft lights. It emphasized shadows and rubbed against nerves. It was, Aubrey considered, the noise of a dentist's drill, heard from the waiting-room.

McIntosh and Godwin, present out of courtesy rather than necessity, hovered at the edge of the lamplight, as did Hyde, who leaned on the frame of the open windows, arms folded on his chest, an observer who might have been carved or inanimate in some other way. Aubrey and Buckholz sat on chairs drawn closer to the room's large sofa. On that piece of furniture sat an Oriental; small, slim, brown, he appeared diminished and made child-like by the size of the sofa. He looked very young and, to Aubrey at least, vulnerable. David Liu. Correctly, Liu Kuan-Fu. His American persona possessed the name David.

He should be wearing spectacles, and have neatly cut hair and be dressed in a narrow-lapelled suit and be white, Anglo-Saxon and Protestant, Aubrey reflected. In that skin, he would appear more clearly what he was, a recent college recruit to the CIA. There had been many such young men, during the sixties and seventies, who had melded into a single image of the young CIA officer in Aubrey's mind, so that he could not help but see this Liu's Oriental guise as no more than a veneer. It only partly disguised his inexperience, his youth, merely delayed the reluctance Aubrey felt at having to trust the verification of Colonel Wei to him. Hurry, hurry, he reminded himself. They were moving at Buckholz's pace, with his energy. Yet there seemed no virtue in deliberation, nothing to be gained from procrastination. It was best to let Buckholz continue to handle the penetration operation, while he concentrated upon the enigmatic Colonel Wei.

A small heap of papers and documents lay on the coffee-table before the sofa. Liu's new identity—identities, rather. Liu had brought them with him from CIA headquarters, Langley. They were safe and current. Liu had been thoroughly briefed by Buckholz, and the penetration operation had been planned and organized before either of them had left America. There was no reason—except an old man's reluctance—to delay Liu's departure any longer.

"From the border to Kwangchow, then you take the train to Shanghai," Buckholz was saying. "An army officer, returning from home leave in the south, to 20 Corps headquarters outside Shanghai.'' Buckholz turned to Aubrey. ''He's Political Department, so he should be safe from any army personnel he meets.'' Aubrey nodded. The repetition of Liu's route and cover were for the benefit of those in the room.

''We require medical certainties—if you can obtain them,'' Aubrey said, addressing Liu. Liu's attention turned to the old man with a kind of robotic deference. Ancestor worship. ''Who came to see Zimmermann, yes, what they talked about—but why Zimmermann was there, what treatment he received, that kind of thing. If we know his illness and his treatment, that may tell us whether or not he was interrogated.'' Aubrey turned to Buckholz. ''This man Davies's story indicates the administration of highly specialized drugs. One hint of that, one shred of proof, might be all we need.''

''Agreed.''

''What access to the hospital does your cell in Shanghai have?'' Aubrey asked.

''Some. Probably enough. Shanghai station has built up a good range of contacts—industrial, political, domestic, even medical. They should be able to put Liu in touch with someone from the hospital. He has the freedom to frame his actions to the kind of person he reaches, and how much they can tell him.''

''You understand the gravity of your undertaking?'' Aubrey persisted, addressing Liu.

Hyde, from his vantage at the open windows, a moth touching his neck at that moment and startling him to wakefulness, saw the movement of the old man as one of doubt, disquietude. Aubrey looked pale in the light, drawn. For his own part, Hyde sensed the inevitability of Liu's mission. He had weighed the Chinese-American for himself, and suspected reserves Aubrey evidently doubted.

''I do, sir,'' Liu replied with archaic courtesy. ''I realise, also, that I am expendable as clearly as I understand the importance of my mission.'' He smiled swiftly and briefly. ''I consider your task with Colonel Wei just as difficult as my own.''

Buckholz laughed. ''Get off the boy's back, Kenneth. He'll do a good job for you.'' He turned back to Liu. Hyde studied the slim brown hands crossed almost primly on Liu's lap. They did not move, did not appear tense. ''OK, David, you know what we want, and how soon we want it. Mr. Aubrey's added what he wanted to your Stateside briefing. You ready?''

Liu nodded, as if dismissing them from an audience he had held. "I am, sir."

Buckholz looked at Aubrey, who nodded, then up at McIntosh, who came forward into the light. "OK, let's get this show on the road."

Liu stood up abruptly, mechanically.

"Patrick, you accompany Mr. Buckholz," Aubrey instructed. Then he reached out his hand, and shook Liu's slim fingers. "Good luck, young man," he said. "Very good luck."

Wei was sitting up on the bed, almost in the same position he had adopted during Aubrey's first encounter with him that afternoon. The ashtray was again full of stubs, and Wei was smoking. He seemed to treat American tobacco—he had insisted on that—as a source of infinite satisfaction. Aubrey wondered whether the man was allaying, even sidetracking, an opium habit, and then dismissed the idea. There was too much control there for a smoker of the stuff.

Aubrey closed the door of the room behind him. A bright moth fluttered at the heavy mesh across the window, desperate to escape into the room. Wei seemed to possess no such urgency to leave it.

"Ah," he said. "Mr. Aubrey. I heard a car leaving. I take it the young American-Chinese I glimpsed earlier is beginning his journey?"

The perspicacity Wei displayed surprised Aubrey. "I beg your pardon?" he bluffed.

"Come, Mr. Aubrey. You must check on me. Obviously, I am not to be trusted. I would imagine some new face would be required. Your people and those of the Americans would be under the heaviest surveillance since my disappearance."

"I see."

Wei lit another cigarette from the stub of the one he had been smoking. The nicotine of his habit was revealed even on his brown fingers. He stared upwards, watching his exhaled smoke roll like dragon's breath along the low ceiling. A long-legged insect that had climbed through the mesh hovered around the bulb overhead.

"Well, Mr. Aubrey?" he asked, still regarding the ceiling with an intent, satisfied gaze. His manner angered Aubrey, as it was meant to do. "Are the arrangements proceeding for my reaching the United States of America?"

"At present, you're going nowhere," Aubrey snapped impatiently.

Wei shrugged. His face remained impassive. "How did you come into possession of the information concerning Herr Zimmermann? Were you present at any of the interrogations you claim took place, either in Wu Han or later in Shanghai?"

"Ah," Wei observed. Surprisingly, he stubbed out the unfinished cigarette, and did not light another. Aubrey stood by the bedside, and saw Zimmermann's face against the creased and soiled pillows, and wondered about the drug-truths the German was purported to have uttered. There was Davies's evidence, dammit, otherwise he could have freely chosen to disbelieve this Chinaman. "No, I was not present."

"Then it is all hearsay. It is a great pity, Colonel Wei Fu-Chun, that you could not have smuggled out some verification of your story, along with your photographs which may or may not prove you are who you say you are."

"It was much too difficult," Wei replied in a slightly apologetic tone.

"Then all of this could be nonsense, Wei!" Aubrey snapped, steeling himself to accelerate the interrogation and establish a new relationship between them. He moved closer to Wei, drawing a chair to the side of the bed. His movements were studiedly brusque and confident. "Every piece of information you have supplied, or have hinted at, could be nothing more than fabrication on your part."

"Perhaps."

"Your motive is obvious."

"Yes?"

"Certainly. What are you worth to us, in the present climate of growing cooperation between China and the West? We would be far more interested in a KGB officer from one of their foreign departments, perhaps even in a Cuban. So, you invent a grandiose lie concerning a senior German political figure, to make yourself more interesting. It is the shy and lonely child's effort to make himself interesting to others." Aubrey spread his hands like a benediction. "In what other light, pray, am I to regard this story of yours?"

"As the truth?"

"Ah, what is truth? What are facts? I accept, for the moment, that you are who you say you are, but I can accept nothing else. We know that Wolfgang Zimmermann fell ill in Wu Han, and was transferred to Shanghai. Within a week, he was back in Bonn, none the worse for his experiences. Yet in that time, you tell me, he confessed to being a long-term Russian agent? Why haven't your superiors used and exposed this vital piece of information? Why does it need your escape to bring it to light?''

Wei shrugged himself more upright on the bed. It was clear that he felt disadvantaged by his prone position. Aubrey leaned forward on the chair, his face expressing disbelief, yet without contempt or indifference. He appeared, half-shadowed from the overhead light, like a priest taking confession, weighing the moral nature of an unexpected and peculiar act of sin. The posture and appearance were intended.

''I do not know why, or whether they eventually intend to release the information,'' Wei said. He looked at his opened pack of cigarettes, but did not reach for them. Aubrey cursed the impassivity of Oriental facial muscles. Wei's hooded, expressionless eyes were similarly of no help. He felt he could never know the man as he must. ''I am using the information, Mr. Aubrey, for my own benefit, as no doubt my government will do—in time.''

''Who interrogated Zimmermann in Wu Han?''

''General Chiang.''

''And in Shanghai?''

''Chiang again—and others. A special team.''

''One of your so-called Harmony of Thought units?''

''Exactly.''

''Drugs, hypnosis.'' Wei nodded. ''Your motives for leaving China—what were they?''

''We have already discussed them.''

''It won't bore me. Explain once more.''

''I was, very briefly, connected with the Shanghai People's Commune, in the days when the Gang of Four ruled Shanghai. I—there was evidence against me, being compiled by my enemies, which indicated arrests I had made, certain methods of re-education I had used on peasants. I—had hidden the evidence as well as I could. I had—removed the witnesses. But families of—of peasants and intellectuals who had undergone re-education continued to press for investigation, for knowledge of the whereabouts of those they regarded as missing. When Deng—'' Wei's face crumpled into something virulent for a moment, then smoothed itself to a bland mirror once more. ''When Deng finally replaced Hua as Chairman, and the trial of the Four was complete, Deng's people turned on others. I would have become one of those others.'' He looked into Aubrey's face when he ended his recital. ''For personal reasons, Mr. Aubrey, it was not safe for me in Shanghai, or anywhere in China.''

"I see. You worked in the Anti-Revolutionist Department of the ministry?" Wei nodded. "Which section?"

"Rice Bowl."

Aubrey shook his head. "Vietnam, Kampuchea, Thailand. Not a great deal of use to us, Colonel Wei. As I suggested earlier, you *need* this story about Zimmermann for us to regard you as a prize worth having. You have a rank greater than your abilities or your entrustment. I am inclined to disbelieve the whole matter." Aubrey stood up dismissively, moving his chair away from the bed. His face was harder in the direct light from the ceiling. Wei studied his expression. "We'll talk tomorrow. Perhaps your story will have improved. Dig for the bedrock of facts that alone will convince me, that's my advice to you. Good night."

David Liu lay pressed flat against the pebbles and shingle above the tide on the narrow beach. The rowlocks of the dinghy that had brought him to the water's edge still sounded in his ears, though he knew by now that the faint squeak was out of earshot. Its betraying memory remained with him, vivid and jumpy like a live wire beneath his hand. Deep Bay stretched away from the shore behind him, and he was lying on a narrow beach that was part of the Kwantung province of the People's Republic of China. A different world.

The lights of Hong Kong and the New Territories glowed softly behind him, dimly mirroring from a low, heavy, thunderous cloud cover. The lights of the town of Paoan were dimmer, more diffused and less assertive ahead of him, beyond the narrow, shelving beach.

He lay until his breathing had returned to normal, and the clothes he had adopted on the launch no longer itched and seemed unfamiliar. He lay still until his ears no longer heard the tiny, rat-like squeaks of the rowlocks, and heard instead only silence. He lay still until the impression of clinging to a ledge at the edge of an unknown and dangerous world left him. The darkness ahead of him had been as palpably ominous as threats in an unknown language.

He stood up and dusted down the shapeless grey Mao-suit he wore, his hands running over remembered denim, recollecting mohair and wool. He took the baggy, small-peaked cap from his pocket and donned it. He patted his pockets for his papers, and then began walking up the beach onto the rocks. The stretch of coast where he had been landed was deserted, the fishing port of

Paoan the only real settlement, except for temporary homes and a few farming communes. The coast was patrolled, but to prevent potential escapers rather than to deter illegal immigrants. Liu was, however, mindful of light and noises as he clambered over the low rocks.

When he reached the grass beyond the rocks, he looked out to sea. Deep Bay lay in darkness, pricked by the navigation lights of freighters and fishing vessels. There was no sign of the launch, nor had he expected to see it. Hong Kong, another alien world, lay alight with the deceptive familiarity of San Francisco. He turned away from it quickly.

The rolled, coiled barbed wire that had been laid along the verge of the rocks had been damaged on numerous occasions and never renewed. Escapers, holiday-makers, Party officials objecting to the effort required to reach the beach. His hand closed over the wirecutters in his pocket as he moved swiftly, half-crouching. It was no more than a minute or so before he found the wire lying like the shed skin of a snake rather than the serpent itself, and he began stepping gingerly through it, lifting his feet high in an exaggerated, comic walk. He was aware of his ungainly appearance. It did not seem fitting as his first act of penetration into the People's Republic. He paused at the edge of the wire, regained his breath, then bent to study the strip of bare earth, recently dug and flattened. A compromise between convenience and security. Someone had decided to place anti-personnel mines opposite the largest gaps and rents in the barbed wire. Yes, there was the warning notice. He picked it out in the thin shaft of light from his small torch, then flicked off the light. He moved slowly along the edge of the wire until he reached scrubby grass again.

The glow of Paoan was less than a mile north of him. He knew the road lay mere hundreds of yards inland of the wire. He began to move towards it. He would be on a night train to Kwangchow, and by morning on his way to Shanghai.

It happened suddenly.

There were lights, and yells, and the noise of whistles. No dogs, for which he was momentarily grateful. But figures moved like shadows around him, until one rushed into him, knocking him sideways. He staggered, blinded by the searchlight mounted on a truck which swept over him, hovered, then returned, then began pursuing the fleeing, half-naked figures who scattered in the hollows and folds of the land to avoid it. It was like some frenzied poolside party, everyone drunk, whistles instead of laughter. The truck's engine roared into life, and the searchlight bobbed towards him, as if to swallow him.

It was a trap. He felt the irony of its having embraced him accidentally. They had known about these potential escapers. Someone had betrayed this party of ten, twenty, thirty swimmers before they reached the beach and the bay, and they had waited for them with lights, a truck, guns . . .

Shots, now. Liu looked about him, panicking, yet unable to move. More shots, cries and screams; panic and injury.

It was a joke, a cruel joke. Boo, and we jump out on you, wearing demon-masks. Too bad.

He threw himself prone on the grass, felt someone blunder onto him and stumble over his body. The whistles reached a climax of enjoyment, there were a few more shots, and then there were the voices giving orders, the pushing around, the slaps across the face, the turning over of the bodies . . .

He was turned over with a rifle butt in his ribs. The man with the torch, who was dressed in the uniform of a Border Defence unit, seemed surprised to discover he was still fully clothed. Liu was kicked and ordered to his feet. He raised his hands above his head and began trotting towards the small, frightened herd of bare-chested men who huddled in the glare of the searchlight. It had taken him less than fifteen minutes in the People's Republic to become its prisoner.

Patrick Hyde jumped from the deck of the launch onto the jetty inside the typhoon shelter flung out like a cradling arm into the bay from the glittering Kowloon waterfront. Buckholz himself threw the mooring rope to him. It landed heavily across Hyde's shoulder, and he looped it over a bollard. The launch bumped against the jetty and its row of car tyres. The engine cut out, and the sounds of Kowloon swilled into the momentary silence. Buckholz came heavily up the wooden steps from the water, Godwin moving more lightly and swiftly behind him, ahead of the two CIA locals who had crewed the launch.

Lightning blared across the water, seemingly dimming the lights of Kowloon and the tall bright stalks of the new hotels. The wind rushed against Hyde's face like a rough, damp flannel. He helped Buckholz onto the jetty.

A second flash of lightning was accompanied by the thunder from the first. A flat, eerie, dead light lay across sky and water and town for a moment, then it was black again. Hyde, turning away from Buckholz, saw the white face at the corner of a low warehouse at the end of the jetty. It was as if a grubby spotlight had been turned upon the man, so much so that Hyde was easily able to recognise the KGB man that Godwin had called Vassily, the man who had been on the observation gallery at Kai-Tak that morning.

Hyde's hand clamped over Buckholz's arm as the rain began, a sudden emptying of the clouds accompanied by the second roll of thunder.

"I've just seen one of the KGB locals," Hyde announced in a conversational tone.

"What? Where?"

"Over there, by the warehouse. You want me to take a look?"

Buckholz was silent for a moment.

"Anything wrong?" Godwin asked. His cream-coloured suit was being stained black across the shoulders by the rain. A car engine started, and they heard the noise diminish in the distance.

"Leave it," Buckholz murmured, then he snapped out: "Damn! Did anyone see him when we left?" He turned to Godwin and his own men. "Anyone see a guy tailing us when we came down here?"

No one had. Hyde shook his head.

"That's you and Mr. Aubrey they've seen in Hong Kong," Hyde remarked. "I think they'll become very interested in what's going on here, sport, don't you?"

"Damn."

TWO

Border Country

"Too much hurry, Mr. Aubrey," Hyde warned. He was standing at the foot of the stairs, and Aubrey, ascending, turned to look back at him. A gritty, irritating tiredness assailed Aubrey's eyes and skin, and he felt a vast reluctance to continue up the flight of stairs to Wei's room.

"You think so?" he snapped.

Hyde sipped at his beer. "I think so."

"You assume the right to tell me, too."

"Look, Mr. Aubrey, I haven't got a tan suit on and a blue shirt, and I haven't got steely blue eyes." Hyde grinned. "If you want the strong silent automaton type, get in touch with the CIA or the KGB." He sipped again. Then he pointed his glass up the stairs at Aubrey. "The KGB know you and the deputy-director of the CIA are both in Hong Kong at the same time. They may know you've mounted a penetration operation against the People's Republic. I don't think that's top-drawer security, do you?"

"No, I don't. Damnation," Aubrey added softly. "You're right, of course." Aubrey shrugged. "There's nothing that can be done now. Except to keep all the doors closed in future."

"You going up to see old slit-eyes?"

"I am."

"Good luck, mate."

Aubrey reached the head of the stairs, cross the landing, and moved along the corridor to Wei's room at the back of the house. A young man, whose name Aubrey could not recollect, was seated tiredly on a hard chair outside the door of the room. Aubrey berated himself for his precipitate disbelief. It is because you did not believe in the importance of these matters, he told himself. He had given the debriefing of Wei the codename *Wild Goose*, and now the name mocked him. He had deliberately employed that name, the feeling of futility increasing within him almost from the moment in his garden when he had decided to fly to Hong Kong. It was a futility that had reached its apotheosis during the first interview with Wei.

Wei, he had concluded and still believed, was a frightened man clutching at the straw of notoriety. He was a materialist buying his ticket to America with an inflated currency. He did wonder, as he nodded to the young man who opened the door to Wei's room for him, whether his judgment of Wei sprang in any sense from an old man's tiredness and bouts of inadequacy; frailty of perceptiveness. Then he quashed the idea. The story about Zimmermann was a fabrication, and he would prove that it was.

Wei was reading a newspaper. The grilled square of the window was a black hole above and to one side of his head. Two moths and some unidentifiable insects lay on the sill between the mesh and the glass, exhausted into death. The fan turned slowly, asthmatically. When Wei looked up from his reading, Aubrey saw a flicker of calculation as bright as greed in his eyes, and the assumption of defiance about his lips and jaw.

"I have decided," he said, "that I have nothing further to say to you. I will talk only to the Americans now. Please arrange for my transfer to American custody." He folded the newspaper casually and laid it on the rucked, creased counterpane.

Aubrey drew the single chair in the room close to the bed. He was puzzled by Wei's attitude until he resolved it to his satisfaction as a further species of bluff. The man had absolutely no cards in his hand.

"I don't think we can do that, Colonel Wei."

"Why not?" Wei, like most English-speaking Chinese, lisped and hissed slightly as he grappled with an alien alphabet, barbaric phonetics. His accent was faintly American. "I am quite certain that Mr. Buckholz would welcome my company."

"The problem is, the CIA do not operate harbour patrols. If you wished to be rescued by them, you should have chosen another method of entry. Besides, a European interest, shall we say, would have intrigued my service more than the Americans. Which is why you came to us."

"But I am no use to you. You do not believe me . . ."

"I think your story is a complete and utter fabrication." Davies, *Davies*, he told himself. The one reason why you cannot abandon this man or this investigation. Davies, who is trusted by

Latymer, heard Zimmermann talking Russian, saw the interrogators . . .

Damn.

"You seem to doubt your own words," Wei observed sharply.

"Not at all."

"Ah."

They listened to the fan, to the hum of the city below the house, to the retreating thunder. The air was already losing its freshness outside as the humidity climbed once more. An airliner swung over them, roaring towards Kai-Tak.

"Tell me everything," Aubrey said finally. "Everything you know about Zimmermann."

"I could not see the files, of course."

"I understand." Wei seemed puzzled, guarded rather than disarmed by the paternal tone Aubrey employed. Infinite patience, infinite wisdom; compassion for shortcomings, for failure. "You tell me again what you heard, what you guess."

"Very well. May I walk about the room?"

"Of course." Aubrey stood, and moved his chair against the wall. He would be able to watch Wei's face, his body. Then he gestured for the Chinese to stand. Wei nodded briskly.

"Much of my information comes in the form of rumour, and gossip," he explained, beginning to pace the room immediately.

"I understand."

"Chiang received a report from the hospital in Wu Han, and left Shanghai immediately—that began the rumours. The German had been taken ill, possibly food poisoning."

"That was the official explanation," Aubrey remarked. "It is what Zimmermann and Bonn believe to this day."

"It may have been true—I have never heard a different story. Whether a mild delirium or a maladministration of drugs caused the first concern, I am not sure, but the gossip was that Zimmermann had begun speaking in Russian, rambling. There was no one in Wu Han who spoke it, except for one of our low-grade officials. He was summoned, and then he summoned General Chiang."

"And Chiang summoned others?"

"No. Chiang had doctors recommend that Zimmermann be transferred to Shanghai. That is when the German underwent Harmony of Thought techniques, in Shanghai."

"How was this concealed from German consular officials, and from members of the trade mission from Germany?" Aubrey's voice was unfailingly gentle. His eyes, when not studying Wei, cast about on the threadbare carpet and the linoleum that appeared at its borders, as if he searched for runes of comfort or conviction.

"Drugs are advanced. You do not use them?"

"There are occasions—I am not an expert, Colonel."

"I see. Zimmermann was permitted visitors, but he was always sedated. Our doctors reassured enquirers."

"What was learned?"

Wei shrugged. "Here," he explained, "I enter the realms of half-gossip, third or fourth hand."

"Proceed, nevertheless."

"Zimmermann had been an agent of the Soviet revisionists since before the war—since his time in Spain."

"Zimmerman *was* in Spain, with the Condor Legion."

"It was there—Republicans captured him, he was persuaded of the truth of Marxist-Leninism, persuaded by infidels, as it were," Wei smiled, "and from that time he never deviated in his loyalty to his masters in Moscow."

"A road to Damascus, then?"

"I do not understand."

"It doesn't matter. Zimmermann went all through the war fighting on the wrong side, a side which must have been repellent to him?"

"Presumably so."

"And after the war?"

"Presumably, he remained a sleeping dog." Wei shrugged. "It is all in Chiang's file, I expect."

"But what did you hear?"

"That he was not an active agent."

"Never?"

"I cannot say. I did not hear so." Wei paused in front of Aubrey. His hands were in the pockets of his too-large trousers. "I can tell you very little more, Mr. Aubrey."

"You know nothing about contacts, about his Moscow control?"

Wei shook his head. "They exist. The usual, but very discreet, periodic contacts. Mr. Aubrey, I have given you sufficient indications of good faith. I can do no more to convince you. Of course I wish to impress you. That is why I give you this story. I knew, when I heard it, that it could be my passport to America. Now my fate rests with you. You must establish the truth."

Davies, Davies, Aubrey's mind chanted to him in an insistent, maddening whisper. He was there, he confirms part of this. The damned Chinaman may be telling the truth. Aubrey entertained a vision of a long ugly concrete wall tumbling to the ground, raising dust. On the other side of it, people were cheering in Russian. He shook his head.

Zimmermann, so high, so influential. The shape and contours and fate of the West might be in his hands. The Berlin Treaty . . .

He could not afford to dismiss Wei or discount the story. He had to establish the truth of the man's story. He *had* to elicit the truth about Wolfgang Zimmermann.

David Liu was pushed in the back, and the wooden, barbed-wired gate of the small compound was shut and locked behind him. There was laughter from the guards, the sniggering of anticipation. He hardly attended to it, grateful still for the lack of a body-search. The carelessness of superiority, of imposing humiliation. Clothed among the half-naked, yet he created little individual attention. The guards classed them all as captives, as failed escapers. As butts, dolts, animals. His wire-cutters and papers were still in his pockets.

He was soaked through from the downpour soon after they were captured. The night air was warm, but his teeth chattered from tension, from the effort to absorb his changed circumstances and alter them once more. The men around him, most of them young, crop-headed, thin, cowed, brushed against him or huddled aimlessly. Their teeth chattered, they rubbed their arms. Fear also made them cold.

The compound was part of the nearest commune. From the gouts of old manure scattered on the bare earth, it evidently served as an animal pen, and perhaps also as a punishment enclosure, as at present. A small wooden dais had been erected on one side of it, presumably for some official to mount and berate the occupants. One of the guards, a platoon commander, was indeed on the dais, but there was no crowd of peasants from the silent, dark commune beyond the searchlight to witness the scene. They would not be lectured, then, on their treacherous revisionism, their heinous desertion of the People's Republic. Two guards dragged something like a flat snake into the glare of the light. Liu recognized it, and slipped behind the bodies of a group of the others. A hose. They would be humiliatingly drenched with water, the compound would be turned into a quagmire, for the amusement of their captors. They had abandoned all humanity with their clothes.

The hose spurted, trickled, then sprayed at them. Men scattered, to raucous laughter. One slipped, then another. The hose washed them across the rapid new mud of the compound floor. More laughter, high and almost hysterical, from the border defence unit who now surrounded the barbed-wire compound. The jet of water jabbed at Liu's shoulder, washed his flanks, punched at his chest and back, flinging him off his feet, skidding him across the compound. His hands instinctively protected his pockets containing his cutters and his papers, as dearly as he might have clutched his groin against injury. He lay still. The water licked over him, then pursued others. He climbed slowly to his feet, knowing that to remain lying still would attract further attention.

The border guards and their platoon commander jeered and yelled, shaking their fists. Cultural Revolution images flicked in his mind as vividly as on a screen; rioting mobs of students, flags, the tearing down of posters, statues, buildings, people; the chanting, the fist-shaking, the book-burning—the ritualized, formalized hysteria unnerved Liu.

The water jetted over him again. The noise, the humiliation, the mud covered him. The prisoners, too, were screaming. He felt himself splashed, washed at, eroded by the sea of noise and movement. It was as if the nightmarish scene focused upon him, had been created specifically for his anguish.

He cowered on the floor, hands over his head, clutching his ears, oblivious to the water and the mud, uncaring with regard to his papers and his cutters. Like elements of his identity, the noise was sluicing them away. Louder, louder . . .

Then, like a climax achieved, the light had disappeared and the noise had stopped. He was in darkness as close and complete as that of a cupboard, hunched into his own senses. The guards were gone, the searchlight was gone. Silence rang in his ears. Small, snuffling-animal noises nearby. The sucking of sodden mud like some reminder of a trench war. Men groaning, stirring, accepting humiliation. Personality soused and sluiced away. Unpersons. A dramatic foretaste of the remainder of their lives.

The mud was repellent as he crawled across it, hand extended in front of him, eyes still blind from the glare of the searchlight. He touched men's bodies, and his hand shrank from the contact. Then he grazed his fingers against barbed wire. He lay exhausted and paralysed of will. Dimly he could hear the border unit still enjoying the huge, hysterical joke in the distance. Behind him, the prisoners were gathering into a huddle in a far corner of the compound, whispering softly in tones bereft of comfort.

Eventually, as the noises of the soldiers diminished further, he was able to reach into his pocket and check his papers. They were contained in a plastic envelope, and were still dry. Then he took out the wire-cutters and examined the stretched, ugly pattern of the wire.

The first snapping click of the wire sounded horridly, betrayingly loud. He listened. Only the defeated, impotent whispers behind him. He cut again, then again, and peeled back the barbed wire gingerly. Then he eased himself with a dancer's sinuosity through the gap he had created. He paused, and listened once more. A raucous laugh little louder than a whisper. The platoon might well be billeted in the commune, just as the local police, civil servants, and suppliers would all be contained within the perimeter of the commune. A town in miniature.

Liu moved rapidly away from the compound. There were lights, one or two weak and scattered streetlamps, or lamps hanging from the eaves of low buildings. The smell of brackish water was stronger than the scent of the sea. Paddy fields. He had glimpsed them from the truck. He estimated they were perhaps a mile or so inland of the road, perhaps two or three miles from Paoan and the railway station.

A soft rain began to fall. His footsteps sucked and pouted his presence. He began to shiver with relief, and with anticipation. He needed dry, clean clothes. He was moving through a hostile country, a hostile town. Teachers, doctors, soldiers, peasants—anyone might open a shutter, open a door, and light would fall on him.

He had no idea of the arrangement of the commune, nor its extent. The clothes of a doctor or a teacher would be best, but the buildings between which he now walked, heading in the general direction from which they had entered the commune, were long, low, shedlike. Peasant workers' dormitories. Too many people too close together for him to take the chance. And there might be others already at the hole in the wire behind him, eager to escape, making noises of relief and speed that would attract attention.

He entered a wide space which might have constituted the equivalent of a town square. He pressed against the wooden wall of one larger building, and removed his torch from his pocket. He flicked its light over the nameboard. The dispensary, and the doctors' names. Luck. It made him shiver. Luck had entered the arena and demanded acknowledgement. Liu was fatalistic about luck. It shortened the time-scale, it had its own momentum and logic. It ran out. He crept along the wall of the dispensary, then down the alley between it and the next building, looking for an open window. The soft rain insinuated depression, a sense of failure.

An open window. It made him swallow. More luck. Time was running out.

He reached up over the sill and gently touched the frame, dabbing his fingers over it. Caked with drying mud, they were insensitive. He inhaled, and then pushed at the window. It slid up almost without noise. He hoisted himself to the sill, and pushed his body halfway into the dark room. A slight smell of disinfectant and medicines. The shadowy outline of a long room with a low ceiling. Beds, empty, against the far wall. He ducked his head back out, and levered his legs over the sill. He sat for a moment, and then dropped into the room. His hand touched something that moved, something cool and metallic which shivered, then wobbled. He grabbed for it, making it squeak, felt it fall, cupped his other hand, clutching the object to his chest. Then he crouched beneath the window, his breath roaring in his ears and chest.

He examined the object in the faint light coming from the lamp at the corner of the next building. A kidney bowl, chipped white noisy enamel. He returned it to the table on which it had been resting, and stood up. He moved to the centre of the room, straining eyesight to perceive impediments. There was what appeared to be a door at the end of the room. He moved, well clear of the beds, towards it.

Slowly, he opened it. His blood ticked away the seconds in his ears. His chest thumped with anticipation, his thoughts were alive, as in the light of a flickering fire, with images of recapture. A corridor. He closed the door behind him.

A narrow, wooden-walled corridor, without plaster or paint, smelling of disinfectant. Doors without names or numbers led off the corridor. Light coming from beneath one of the doors. He listened, but there was only silence beyond the chorus of his own tension. He tiptoed past the door which leaked light, on down the corridor. Bedrooms, he supposed and prayed.

He listened at each one. The sound of snoring encouraged him, and he tried the door handle. It eased silently open. A scent of soap, and possibly of perfume. Mothballs, too. A small high window, an outside light filtering through the thin curtains. A narrow bed beneath the window. Drawers, a wardrobe, a dressing-table reflecting the square of the window's dim light.

He moved towards the wardrobe, the sleeper accompanying his tiptoed steps with noisy inhalations and exhalations. A subconscious protest or grumble at his intrusion. The form of the sleeper was small, but fit was a luxury. Dryness of clothes the only imperative. The wardrobe door opened with a jerk, and he stilled it with his other hand. Then he reached into the mothballed darkness, touching clothes swiftly, carefully. A smock? He bent and sought shoes. Sandals, very small, not a man's...

Silence in the room. Then a stirring noise from the bed. He waited, sitting on his haunches, feeling a tremor begin in his thighs and calves. Sitting up? He did not dare to turn and look. Mouth-clearing noises, the slapping of tongue against dry gums, roof of mouth? The noises maddened him with their sinister anonymity.

Snoring. Like an engine stuttering to life. Regular snoring. He controlled his breathing, quashing the jumping of his heart. He got shakily to his feet and left the room, closing the door with exaggerated slowness. A woman, snoring.

He listened at the adjacent door. Silence. No light. He opened the door, passed into the room, shut the door. He took one careless step before his eyes picked out the contours of the room, and he jarred his shin against the frame of the bed. The same small high window, the same furniture, but the bed near the door.

"Uuuh? What?" The word if not the noise was formed in wakefulness. A light sleeper had come quickly and totally awake. A doctor, used to interruptions to his sleep. "What is it?" Then, as Liu's training analyzed the information that the man spoke in northern Min dialect as opposed to his own expatriate Yue dialect, a piece of clear, professional irrelevance, the orbit of the man's thoughts changed. "Who is it? Who is there? Speak."

An upright torso, a hand extended towards what must be a light cord above the bed. Liu was frozen for a moment, realising that the man was bigger, paunchier than himself, then he moved, and struck his stiff forearm across the man's nose. An escaped bubble of pain gurgled in the man's throat, and his head banged back against the thin partition wall. Liu groaned softly at the noise, even as he dragged the pillow from beneath the man's body, pressed the man flat on the bed, and thrust the pillow over his nose and mouth. Claw-hands scrabbled across Liu's forearms, drawing blood in diminishing protest. Then stillness, one arm hanging down by the side of the bed, the other folded in death across the man's chest. Liu released the pillow, and his hands were shaking with a palsy.

Over-reaction, over-reaction...

He had been wrong, even under the weight of his cumulative tension and the steady growth of desperation. It had been wrong, stupid to kill. It created enemies, a pursuit, it was like finger-prints or a note. *Professional*.

He hurried to the wardrobe, dragged out a Mao-suit, measured it against himself, then stripped off his own clothes in the now hot darkness. Airless room. He thrust his legs into the rough cloth trousers, pulled on the too-big jacket. Belt, belt . . .

In one of the drawers, he found a narrow belt. He tightened it around his waist, then buttoned the jacket. He removed his papers and torch and pocketed them. Then he bundled the sodden jacket and trousers under his arm, and opened the door of the room. No one in the corridor. He hurried down it, entered the long room with the beds, crossed to the window, swung his legs over the sill, and dropped to the ground. Later, when he could pause, he would strip off the lining of his jacket and remove the twenty high-denomination notes and the second set of papers. Not here, though. Outside the commune.

The streets of the commune were deserted. Speed now was a comfort, the plaster holding luck together, the child's hand pulling luck out longer like chewing gum. After the narrow alleys and the wooden huts and barns and store-houses was the smell of the paddies. It had stopped raining. A thin, weak, watery moon indicated the paths along the banks above the level of the water. The lights of Paoan were dim to the north. He glanced at his cheap watch.

One-thirty. In half an hour he could be at the station in Paoan. He hurried on, the dead man behind weighing on him, heavy not on his conscience but on his sense of safety.

Aubrey, in a half-sleep, the bedroom fan stirring the humid air that moved over his face and arms, dreamed vividly. The temperature would not allow him to achieve real sleep, and he was sufficiently conscious, as the past claimed him, to resist belief in the vivacity and the detail of words and appearances and events that had happened more than forty years before. The thin cotton pyjamas restricted and enveloped him, and for almost all the moments of the dream he was aware of the single sheet lying heavily on his limbs with the weight of numerous blankets.

When Zimmermann had been disarmed and body-searched by Henri and Philippe, they hurried the German officer through the woods on the Marfée Heights, along winding, climbing tracks, past French outposts and patrols, through the French artillery lines away from the Meuse. Aubrey was regarded with a certain admiring futility by the French soldiers who inspected their papers. The *sale Boche* was the occasion of numerous remarks and much contemptuous spitting. Zimmermann, Aubrey now recollected clearly though he would not have claimed to have attended to it that night, was amused by the reactions of the French. Aubrey, in his dream, where many of the images achieved a point of view not his own, as if he were watching a film of the events, saw Zimmermann as the archetypal Prusso-Nazi, his manner and movements a swagger. He distrusted those images especially, as he mistrusted the sounds he heard of disturbed animals and birds in the trees, the night-scents that could have no place in the foetid air of the Hong Kong bedroom where he dreamed. The noises of bats, of nocturnal monkeys and even a domestic dog impinged upon his semi-awareness, but they were distinct and distinguished from those Ardennes noises. The heavier, more corrupt scents of tropical flowers were also distinguishable from the smell of grass crushed beneath their hurrying feet.

After more than an hour of interrupted travel, they arrived at a farmhouse near Flize which was owned by a distant cousin of Henri and Philippe. Aubrey had failed to enlist the man, but the occasional and unspecified use of one of his barns had been grudgingly contributed to the intelligence service. While Philippe went up to the farmhouse to announce their arrival and to obtain food, Henri and Aubrey directed Zimmermann into the barn. Henri lit an oil lamp, then returned it to its bracket near the door. One old horse stirred in its stall at the light and noises. Two Friesian cows grumbled and stamped. Aubrey, lying on his bed and standing again at the door of the barn, was assailed by the warm smell of dung and hay. The scene was lit by a localized shadowy, Rembrandt light. Henri pushed Zimmermann down onto a bale of hay, as if deliberately to erase the elegant posture of the German.

Again, Aubrey the old man saw his younger self from an impossible, filmed point of view, as if he looked into the Nativity painting of the barn's scene. He felt, very vividly, at a loss, traced with a finger-like recollection the remark that had passed through his mind, *First catch your German . . .*

"What do you want of me?" Zimmermann had enquired conversationally and as if reading Aubrey's indecision on his face. "Do you mind if I smoke?" His hand patted the breast of his tunic.

"Of course. Be careful where you throw your matches."

Zimmermann smiled. "Naturally."

Aubrey seated himself opposite Zimmermann, his hands on his knees, while Henri remained at the door, the big gun tucked obviously into his waistband.

"Now, we have time to talk," Aubrey announced.

"Certainly. What is it to be?" Aubrey had spoken in German, but now Zimmermann demonstrated his fluent, almost accentless English. "Literature, painting, music, current events?"

Aubrey's eyes narrowed. "I think current events, don't you?" He glanced at Henri. A suitably menacing presence, soon to be reinforced by the return of his brother. Yet the German officer seemed relaxed, at ease, confident; as if the guns were in his possession, they his prisoners. There was no sense of isolation, of being cut off from help. Training had emphasised that as an important factor to exploit. The person undergoing interrogation always feels cut off, isolated.

Aubrey realised, quite suddenly and with an insight he suspected but which the dreaming old man on the bed approved forty years later, that this German officer, despite his motorized infantry regiment *waffenfarben* and his standard Wehrmacht uniform, was something other than a common-or-garden soldier. A kindred spirit; someone like one of his instructors in SIS, even his recruiting officer at Oxford. Intelligence. *Abwehr*.

A dog barked in the tropical night; Philippe caused the barn door to protest on its hinges as he opened it. The two noises were concurrent, and distinctly heard by the dreaming Aubrey. The satisfaction of the moment of recognition replayed itself in his mind, was held in focus even though he had attended to Zimmermann's reply almost in the moment of recognition.

"Ah," the German had said, exhaling smoke, watching Philippe and the food he brought with a bright, intent gaze, "precisely what kind of current event? Perhaps you really mean fortune-telling? A little crystal gazing?"

The old man heard Zimmermann's words and regarded the feat of memory as impossible. Imagination, rather. Yet he wanted to prompt the young self. *Crystal Night*. The pun would have been a thrust, would have helped Aubrey forty and more years later, would perhaps have exposed the Nazi, or the Russian agent. But the youthful Aubrey did not play elegant mental games like his older self.

"I think so. Yes, Philippe, give our guest something to eat."

Philippe slapped a rich, lumpy stew onto a plate and thrust it at Zimmermann, who courteously thanked the Frenchman. Then Philippe served Aubrey before carrying the pot and the last two plates to his brother. Zimmermann ate eagerly, complimenting the meal again and again.

"Excellent, excellent . . ."

"What is the campaign strategy?" Aubrey snapped, textbook-like. "How long is the front to be? What is the timetable?" Henri, reacting to tone of voice like an alert hound, drew the Mauser from his belt and laid it in front of his plate, across his knees.

Zimmermann stirred the air in front of him with his fork. "Ah," he said. "I see." He did not, however, so much as glance in Henri's direction. "Your men here would, of course, kill me. I do not think you would. We are of an age, but you are very young in this work, I think. It is my judgment that I am safe from harm with you." Aubrey struggled to keep his expression neutral.

"You will answer my questions, Herr Hauptmann."

"Oh, I don't say you would not have me beaten up a little. But you will not kill me, I am certain."

"You're Abwehr—correct?"

Zimmermann's features snapped shut on an expression of surprise.

"Nineteenth Panzers," he replied with studied evenness. "I'm sorry to disappoint you. Perhaps I would be dressed more like you if I were a spy." He laughed softly. Aubrey flushed, unable to prevent expression of his embarrassment.

At the laughter, Henri growled. His fork rattled against his empty plate like a warning. "Fucking Nazi pig!" he snapped.

Zimmermann coloured. "Nein!" he snapped back, then pressed his lips tightly together to prevent the escape of more words. He smiled then, his face relaxing into an habitual, engaging self-confidence. "Infantry," he explained to Aubrey.

The dream had followed chronology, had moved at an even pace, edited in some professional and slick way, highlighting instants of drama and interest. Yet Aubrey was warned as the moment approached, as if he knew he had reached the climacter-ic of some involved plot. *Fucking Nazi Pig,* that was it, snapped out in French, snarled almost, and the hurried, definite, con-temptuous cry of denial from Zimmermann. The scene instantly retreated, the film in Aubrey's dream snapped, and he came hotly, sweatingly awake in the bedroom in the house on Peak Road, overlooking the city of Hong Kong.

He had *not* imagined that, he told himself, and smiled as he sat up and switched on the bedside lamp. Three-thirty in the morning. Half an hour or so before the quick dawn spread like mercury across the harbour. The purpose of the dream had been revealed. His half-sleeping, half-waking mind had worked towards that point with the detail, chronology and care of a writer. Zimmermann had vehemently, deliberately denied he was a Nazi, in May 1940.

What had he been? What did he believe?

Aubrey threw back the sheet and got out of bed. He felt hot, but now his temperature was the effluent of excitement. He removed his spectacles from their case and the file Buckholz had given him from its folder. He sat himself in the room's one armchair, adjusted an angle-poise lamp on the dressing-table, and switched on its white light. Sighing with a kind of happiness, he began to read.

Zimmermann had been captured, with the survivors of his unit, in a pocket of German resistance to Patton's US Third Army east of Frankfurt. He had by then become in fact as well as in pretence an infantry officer. The date of his capture was given as 5 April, a month before Hitler's suicide and the German capitulation. Charles Buckholz was then a very young intelligence major in command of a G-2 unit attached to the U.S. Third Army. Zimmermann had fallen into his hands by virtue of his rank of colonel in the *Militaramt* of the RHSA, which had absorbed the Abwehr in 1944.

The inner folder of the file was stained—old rings from coffee mugs, smeared cigarette ash, even a thumbprint. Aubrey recognised on its label, as well as on most of the tied-in pages, a bolder, more confident version of Buckholz's handwriting. It was the transcript of Zimmermann's debriefing, which had been conducted by Buckholz himself and a lieutenant called Waleski, who seemed, from the outset, to have acted as the darker side of the interrogation team. Much of his colourful language had been preserved in the record, which had obviously been typed on an old, heavy American portable by an inexpert typist. There were numerous mistakes and corrections, the spacing and blocking were erratic. For the most part, it was a simple question-and-answer transcript, with occasional conclusions or inferences which had been dictated later by Buckholz, more occasionally by Waleski.

Aubrey hurried through the transcript. There were no evocations from the text. If he envisaged Zimmermann at all, it was in the terms of his own dreaming recollection of 1940. This was his second reading, and he arranged and selected the material on which he focused in terms of his dream. Most of the subject matter of the interrogation—local conditions, Werewolf units, SS and Gestapo individuals' whereabouts, local atrocities, mined roads and buildings, attitude of the local German population, the fate of local Jews—was irrelevant in content, except where it revealed Zimmermann himself, his inner lights and shadows. These Aubrey plucked from the text.

Zimmermann was tired, defeated, cynical. Resentful of defeat, too. Question: *You fucking Nazis are all the same, uh?* Aubrey drew in his breath sharply. Waleski was the questioner. Henri's epithet applied to Zimmermann five years later. Answer: *I said, if you wish. As you wish.* Question: *Major, the guy admits it. This one admits it.* Answer: *I am a German, isn't that enough for you? German equals Nazi.* Question: *You admit to being a member of the Nazi party?* Answer: *I was never a member—but, you see, there is at once disbelief on both your faces, when I deny this.* Question: *You're going to tell us you're a Red, right?* Answer: *I am not a Communist.*

Aubrey smiled, and flicked a number of pages over swiftly. Question: *What did you think when the bomb plot against Hitler failed?* Aubrey realised the changed circumstances of the conversation. After a meal, perhaps, and drinks? Buckholz and Zimmermann alone. Aubrey realised that the conversation must have been recorded rather than taken down in shorthand. Answer: *Oh, that. It was bound to have failed.* Question: *You did not support the plot? I find that strange.* Answer: *Strange? Romantic fools.* Aubrey had ignored this conversation the previous day when he had read the file. Later, he recalled, the conversation became almost metaphysical. Yesterday, these general speculations, the evidence of Zimmermann's *weltschmerz*, even his nihilism, appeared of little significance. Now, they loomed larger. They went beyond defeat, beyond failure. Question: *You would have advocated doing nothing?* Answer: *It failed, didn't it? Like all the other attempts to get rid of that lunatic.* Question: *You thought the Führer mad?* Answer: *I thought Germany mad to follow him.* Question: *Explain that. You fought in Hitler's army.* Aubrey nodded unconsciously at Buckholz's adoption of the persona of an opponent in debate. Answer: *I did not wish to go to the camps, or be shot, like the Jews and the*

Communists and the gypsies and all the others. Question: *You felt this way ten years ago?* Answer: *Yes. But a war is worth fighting when you're going to win. My father was in the army, so I went into it.* Question: *After university?* Answer: *Yes.* Question: *You felt no attraction to Nazism in university?* Answer: *No, nor to the Communists, either.* Question: *The Communist party was illegal by that time. Why do you keep insisting you were not a Communist, are not a Communist? Is it important?*

Aubrey laid the file across his lap. Buckholz had pencilled into the transcript a reference to the fact that Zimmermann had merely shrugged and given no answer. Buckholz led him back to plots against Hitler and anti-Nazism in the Wehrmacht. Aubrey admired the foresight of Buckholz, beginning his career in post-war intelligence, gathering these insights like a commodity that would leap in value once hostilities ended.

Aubrey rubbed his eyes. *Is it important?* he read on the dark, red-flaring screen behind his closed, pressed eyelids. Was it? He recollected other instances—many, now that he considered it. Zimmermann had expended a great deal of effort convincing Buckholz, and through him the Americans, that he was not, had never been at any time, a Communist. More time than he had spent persuading them he was not a Nazi.

Strange. Emphasis after emphasis, almost at every possible opportunity. Strange. Simply one of Gehlen's protégés with an eye to the main chance, hoping to be enlisted in intelligence work by the Americans? Aubrey shook his head in answer to his own question. Unlikely. A cover-up, a chance to place on record his political purity? Possibly.

1940 and 1945. Poles apart. The same intelligent, subtle, experienced intelligence officer. Letting be known only what he wished to be known about himself. *I am not a Communist.*

"Are you?" Aubrey's voice surprised him. "Wolfgang Zimmermann," he added dramatically, "what, precisely, are you?"

Kwangchow station, on Huanshi Road. The city's old name of Canton, the one most familiar to the American segment of himself, kept running through Liu's head. What was it in *Hanyu pinyin,* the official system of transcription of Chinese characters? Guangzhou? Yes. He had found that one of the most difficult hurdles to clear, the transposition of names and spellings and pronunciations that he had regarded as traditional and correct, had grown up with, into some other and alien system. It had made him feel less Chinese, less than Chinese. Just as the Cantonese dialect which, though his own and familiar in San Francisco among friends and their parents, was now a further alienation. He felt like a tourist, a foreigner, his version of Cantonese stumbling, slurred, changed by his being the grandson of immigrants to America. His Mandarin, too, which his cover as a Political Department officer required him to speak—the language of Peking, of officialdom, of the police—felt furry and unused and stale on his tongue.

He felt unprepared, and he could not dismiss that feeling as mere reaction to having killed the doctor or medical ancillary or whatever he had been in the darkened bedroom. Admittedly, he had not buried the shock of it with a weighted stone at the same time as he had rid himself of his sodden, mudstained clothes in one of the paddy fields. Under the moonlight, he had hurried along the raised earth banks between the paddies, the landscape of rice-fields laid out under the strengthened, pale moonlight like frozen, formalized ripples on the surface of a vast lake or sea.

Paoan had been almost empty, yet his arrival at the station had caused little interest. He had shown his railway warrant at the ticket office, and the man's eyes had widened in respect and an anticipatory nervousness, but Liu had left him with a nod. He had reached Kwangchow on a slow, nearly empty train in a pearly, soon-lifted cloudy light. The train moved out of the unrelievedly cultivated countryside, dotted with the wooden and stone and concrete buildings of communes, into the south of the town, through factories and warehouses and chimneys belching smoke into the increasingly blue sky; the fingers of concrete blocks of flats seemed to remark the smoke and fumes of industry, advertising progress and the Four Modernizations. Liu observed the People's Republic like a tourist. A small inner part of him regretted the absence of any sense of homecoming. He had to admit to himself that his racial identity survived only as part of an American minority. He was not Chinese *here*, in this place, among these people.

Kwangchow was going to work as he crossed the town by bus to the main railway station to Shanghai. The city was almost carless, and yet deafeningly noisy with the horns of trucks and the bells of bicycles. The thousands of cyclists on Chiefang Road, the main north-south thoroughfare, created in Liu a sense of the backwardness of the new China, and its huge and scarcely tapped energy. Thousands, perhaps hundreds of thousands, of limbs pushing at the pedals of bicycles. Unsmiling faces bent over handlebars, shoulders bowed. A curiously unreal and yet perceptive moment. China was raw human energy. That was its brute fact. Numbers.

The station received the waves of a human tide. Liu ate a breakfast of rice gruel and salted fish from a breakfast stall on the station concourse. As soon as he began eating it with the spoon supplied—he had almost expected chopsticks—and the first raw, strong, appetising mouthful was swallowed, his stomach rebelled, expressing the tensions of the night in a ravenous hunger. He offered the stallkeeper one of his own grubby ten yuan notes for a second bowl of gruel. It satisfied his hunger, and staved off the hollow sense that was more metaphysical; his gradually, inexorably increasing sense of loneliness.

Liu sat finishing his rice gruel on a rough wooden bench against one wall of the station concourse. The roof arched over the concrete expanse like the ribs of a whale. The grimy glass roof let in a diffused, smoky sunlight. The station was headily scented with the unfamiliar smoke of steam engines. Liu watched a man in railway police uniform approach the line of breakfasters of which he was a member and, beginning at the far end of the row of benches, initiate an inspection of papers. Next to Liu a man in the uniform of an artillery captain, his newly reintroduced badge of rank stitched brightly onto the four pockets that formerly would have distinguished his status as an officer, belched loudly, and grumbled. Liu, glancing at the older man's eyes, saw that he had been drinking. A smell of rice gruel, salt fish and what might have been wheat wine hung about him.

"Bloody papers," the captain muttered, patting his breast and side pockets. "Here somewhere." The captain spoke in Mandarin dialect, but probably because he was from the north rather than because of education or official status. He grinned. "Mou tai," he explained, dropping his army passbook and travel warrant at his feet, scrabbling them up. Liu smiled. Wheat wine, almost pure alcohol. His grandfather had once given it to him as a child, out of devilment he had always suspected. It had made him violently ill. "Here he comes."

The railway policeman stood in front of the captain. The army officer leaned back, staring into the other's face. There was a subtle sense of hierarchy and challenge about the two uniformed men. The railway policeman would be Public Security Bureau while the officer was merely army. Yet he was evidently senior in rank. A draw was declared by a cursory inspection of the papers and a slight nod on their return. Then the policeman was holding his hand out for Liu's papers.

Liu was acutely conscious of the army officer—the shuffling feet, the quiet burping, the exhalations of salt fish and wheat wine on his breath—as he withdrew his papers from his breast pocket. He was aware, too, of the too-baggy suit he wore, even of his physical smallness inside the belly of the whale-ribbed station. The railway policeman took the papers, and turned the yellow Political Department of the PLA card over in his hand. The army captain coughed. Liu felt him lean slightly towards him, his interest caught and held.

"Thank you," the policeman said, returning the ID card and the travel warrant. He nodded with a less perfunctory politeness than he had employed with the army officer. Liu hurried the papers back into his pocket.

"Political Department, eh?" the captain said slowly. "Shanghai district?"

"Yes. Twenty Corps."

Liu attempted to analyse the officer's reactions to the discovery he had made. There was caution, of course, as well as surprise. Yet there was almost amusement; perhaps, too, a self-contained sense of superiority. This captain existed as an army officer, before he was aware of himself as a finger of the Party.

"I'm Feng Yantai," the captain said, offering his hand. "I'm with Sixty Corps, at Nantung."

"Liu Kuan-Fu."

"PLA Political College in Peking?"

"Yes."

"War College," the captain explained of his own military education. It was evident he regarded himself as socially superior.

"Congratulations."

"A long time ago." Feng shrugged. "You've never seen action, I suppose?"

"No."

The contempt was evident, just for an instant. Liu felt himself moving into a dangerous jungle area, mined and full of snipers and other forms of sudden ambush. Feng, drunk or sober, was more than competent, probably clever and shrewd. How to get rid of him?

"Not to worry," Feng said good-humouredly. "You people have your work, we have ours." He belched again, then rubbed his lips. "Mou tai leaves you dry as dust," he observed, then:

"I've been in most of the hotspots. Mm, along the Amur now, there's fun there with the Russians." He laughed. It was evidently an intimidatory biography. Liu had considered Feng might be cowed—at least made respectful—by his political status within the People's Liberation Army. Evidently, this was not so. Feng was strangely Western, a military man belonging to his own elite, some obscure and stereotyped universal brotherhood of arms. He was self-confident, boastful, contemptuous—and therefore more dangerous. "Yes, Tibet for a spell—too cold—and Vietnam a couple of years ago." He tucked his thumbs into his belt. "Yes. Shanghai's a dull posting."

"Of course," Liu murmured, and Feng looked at him sharply, his mind turning over the stone of the words, looking for a biting insect beneath.

"We'll have a talk, on the journey. Get drunk, eh?" He laughed again. Liu inwardly shuddered. It was worse than he had imagined. Feng had become attached like a burr. How could he shake him off? Liu smiled weakly. "Don't look so frightened!" It was obvious Feng had not the least nervousness of him. He was to become Feng's butt for the eleven-hundred-mile journey to Shanghai. "Come on, we'll board the train now, get them to serve us drink."

"But—"

"Forget the regulations. Throw your weight about. We'll be allowed on the train early, they won't refuse your papers when you order a drink. Come on!"

Liu stood up unwillingly.

"Very well," he said.

"Where's your luggage?"

Liu pointed to a cardboard suitcase near his feet.

"Is that all?"

"Yes." Buckholz had had the suitcase, with a change of clothing inside it, deposited by one of his people in Kwangchow in a left-luggage locker at the station. It now appeared, under Feng's scrutiny, a very feeble additional disguise. Feng picked up his own suitcases.

Liu trailed Feng towards the platform and the Shanghai train. He might have to spend thirty hours in the man's company. The thought unnerved him. Feng was clever. Liu could not believe that his cover could bear thirty hours of close, drunken scrutiny.

"Godwin?"

"Yes, Mr. Aubrey?"

"Get a signal off to London right away, would you?"

"Sir."

"Shelley. Ask him to dig out the files of my 1940 interrogations of Wolfgang Zimmermann—if he can find them. Tell him he may have to go down to the warehouse at Catford. And tell him it's urgent. He'd better send me the complete post-war biog on Zimmermann, too. *All* the background."

"Yes, sir."

"I want it as quickly as possible."

"Sir."

"Good tucker," Hyde observed, and Aubrey became more convinced that the Australian had booked their table on one of the floating restaurants in Aberdeen Harbour in part for the anticipated amusement of watching Aubrey eat Cantonese food with chopsticks. However, those morsels of crayfish that he had managed to convey to his mouth persuaded him to be lenient towards his subordinate.

"Indeed," Aubrey murmured, reaching towards the bowl containing the crayfish more in hope than expectation.

"Sir," Godwin murmured. "Perhaps if you held the sticks in this fashion?" He held out his own hand. "Bottom stick tucked tight into the joint there...that's it, sir." Aubrey glanced into Godwin's face. His eyes daunted the florid young man, who added: "This one pivots, sir, like this..."

"Thank you, Godwin," Aubrey replied huffily, and waggled the chopsticks, gradually adopting a more correct rhythm and a snapping-puppet movement unlike his former feeble attempts to imitate knitting needles. He rescued a piece of crayfish, wobbled it in the sticks, placed it in his mouth. "Thank you, Godwin— like this, mm?" Sudden bonhomie, the sticks snapping like jaws at the younger man. Godwin smiled with relief.

"Yes, sir."

"An excellent idea of yours, Hyde. Splendid food."

"Chicken next," Hyde observed. Aubrey, after two more morsels of crayfish, looked at his surroundings. Splashes of light on the dark water of the harbour on the southern coast of Hong Kong island. Other floating restaurants, rich with coloured lights and paper lanterns; beyond these splashes of colour and affluence the dimmer, strung-out, faltering smudges of light from the hundreds of sampans and junks that housed the floating population of the harbour. Colourful, crowded, noisy poverty by day had become a dim, staining light which uncomfortably reminded, insisted its presence. After a moment, Aubrey studied the moving firefly lights of water taxis, then closer, the lamplit faces of his fellow diners on the deck of the sampan that was a restaurant. Near-sightedness induced well-being.

The crayfish was cleared away, fresh plates supplied, and then the chicken was served. As soon as Aubrey and Godwin began to serve themselves from the bowls, Hyde stood up, finishing the beer in his glass.

"Just going for a pee," he explained, and moved away from the table. "Shan't be long."

Hyde ducked his head and descended the stairs. He passed quickly along the corridor beneath the deck, the odours from the kitchen assailing him like a vivid, complex emotional experience. Then he climbed another stairway leading to the stern part of the deck, where other diners crowded around small tables and other waiters glided between them as if on castors. He paused for a moment in the shadow of the awning over the deck, red lamplight spilling over him from a lantern, and then he walked along the companionway to the jetty. The island's hills loomed over the town of Aberdeen, dotted with house lights. The harbour's shops and restaurants and cafés were a gilded strip of gleaming lights ahead of him. He hurried into the shadow of a small warehouse at the end of the jetty.

Hyde removed from the pocket of his windcheater a small, slim pair of binoculars, almost a child's version of field glasses. With his back to the wall of the warehouse, lounging as if he had little business and much time, he began to scan the harbour front. In the narrow field of vision of the glasses, the scene was enhanced with an eerie, orange-red light. Cars that were only shadow took on shape, semblance of colour, passengers. Hyde knew that any watchers would be in cars rather than on foot. He felt no sense of danger, merely curiosity and a restlessness prompted by inactivity.

Café windows—Oriental faces, the occasional white. Men and women, leaning towards one another over café tables, or more intent upon their food than each other. White males, Oriental women. Ubiquitous yellow-brown skin more scorched, darker in the enhanced, false light of the glasses. Shadows moving beyond the lanterns and lamps overhead or on the tables. Hyde pried upon fifty tables, a hundred and fifty people. No one attracted more than a cursory, dismissing inspection.

Then the cars. Most of them empty. Then bored taxi-drivers, loiterers, pimps—dark, shadowy girls' faces in doorways, profiled against lighted, gleaming windows, explained the pimps—a face wreathed in cigarette smoke, another shadowed by a girl's raven hair. Car after car, along the harbour front, until he saw, at the point where clarity was beginning to seep away and the eerie light was itself as substantial as the faces and forms, the two men, one of them with a sniper-scope employed as a telescope. A jump of the heart at the instrument that should have been mounted on a rifle, and then he began moving.

He crossed the street, avoided the blandishments from a dark doorway and the child-like face that emerged into the streetlight for a moment, and began strolling in the direction of the car. Rock music jarred against him like a blow from an opened café door, car horns engaged in some unseen quarrel. He paused fifty yards from the car, leaning back against an unlit shop window, and trained the miniature field glasses again. Two men, one with a thick neck, both with clipped haircuts, their profiles turned to him, eyes looking slightly back behind them towards the floating restaurant. Hyde swung the glasses, and Aubrey jumped at him from behind the dark straight hair of a Chinese woman. He was using, firelit in the glasses, his chopsticks with dexterity. Godwin, side-on to Hyde, seemed to be looking for his return. On the table, the chicken that had been served had diminished in the bowls in the centre of the table.

When he swung his glasses back to the car, the man with the thick neck was using a camera with a telephoto lens and presumably with infra-red film. The sniperscope remained trained. Hyde saw the squinted-up cheek of the man using it, and the movement of the man's lips, as if he was talking.

Little danger, then. Too far off. He swung the glasses again. No immediate danger. But they were interested. The arrival of Buckholz and Aubrey in Hong Kong in the same period of twenty-four hours had acted like a distress maroon, riveting their attention. It was time to consider moving Wei. Aubrey's face was now in the glasses again, animatedly talking, brushing his chopsticks to one side in a gesture of disagreement. His face was thoughtful, and peremptory with authority. Godwin was making a point forcibly. Glasses back to the car. Sniperscope man's lips moving. Back to the restaurant. Aubrey arguing, making a point with the drum-like emphasis of his chopsticks on the tablecloth. Car again, the man's lips moving in the same methodical, hesitant, robotic way, without any increase in tempo. A recitation rather than a conversation.

Car, restaurant, car, restaurant, car. He could almost hear the words, hear their repetition inside the car. Lip-reading. Difficult, not impossible. Time to get back.

Light rain. He shrugged his shoulders and looked up. The long-range microphone protruded from the upstairs window of the unlit shop like a gun barrel. Hyde drew in his breath, felt his frame tremble with alertness. He trained the glasses on Aubrey. Still talking, still laying down the law. At that distance, the microphone would be picking up a morass of sounds, yet it could be filtered and enhanced later. They might be able to isolate Aubrey and Godwin's voices, their words, the task made easier by the fact of their speaking English in a background mush of Chinese. He studied the microphone protruding from the half-open window above him, then he began running.

Godwin appeared relieved to see him, but Aubrey noticed the wetness of his shoulders and hair and the heightened colour of his complexion.

"What is it?" he asked as Hyde sat down, his back to the camera and the microphone.

"There's a lip-reader using infra-red, and there's a long-range directional mike, both of them trained on you," Hyde replied. "Don't react, just listen. If you've been talking about our friend back at the house, then they may have been able to learn the name of the game. Understand?" He had gabbled in a hoarse whisper. "I see you have. Shit."

Godwin had gone pale, his mouth opening slowly like that of a fish. Aubrey lowered his head in admission.

"I see," he said. A piece of chicken remained clamped in the chopsticks, which quivered slightly.

"Then you could have given the whole bloody game away!" Hyde blurted out in the same hoarse whisper and broader Australian accent.

"Yes," Aubrey said, not looking up.

THREE

Shanghai

The station lamps at the end of the platform were haloed and diffused by the soft, rain-misty night as the Shanghai train stopped at Nanchang in Kiangsi province, almost halfway to its destination. The platform along which Captain Feng walked was gleaming darkly with the rain. David Liu watched him go, ostensibly to buy something to read, and felt his stomach quickly empty and become hollow with an enteritis of foreboding. His cover had not been good enough, he had not been able to sustain it during thirteen or fourteen hours of conversation with the army officer, cramped into a small compartment with four others, Feng's unchanging glance upon him, his voice eroding the pretence of himself as an officer in the army's Political Department. It was a cover designed to discourage scrutiny, not to bear it.

Feng—he must find out what Feng was up to, where he was going. He opened the door of the carriage and stepped down onto the platform, glancing up immediately at the damp night sky, knowing that Feng would see and remark on the wetness of his hair and clothes when he returned to the compartment. He scampered for the shelter of the station roof. Feng, fifty yards away, had passed the still-open bookstall and seemed to be heading for the station exit.

Nanchang station possessed a small, partial concourse like that of a railway terminus, but most of its traffic was heading for Shanghai, Wu Han or the north and its proportions were those of a provincial railway station. The platforms seemed short to Liu, almost empty, exposed. Feng had only to turn to see him. There was nowhere Feng could logically be heading, unless he had decided to leave the train—an impossible, silly hope that Liu immediately quenched. He was certain Feng was suspicious. There had been too many hesitations, too many evasions in his

answers, too little offered in his conversation. Over all these
hours, he knew he had made mistakes sufficient to alert Feng,
who was no longer drunk.

*Do you know . . . ? What do you think of . . . ? Aren't they a
strange lot at headquarters?* Liu had no army experience to rely
upon, and his briefing had not been deep enough. *Ever been on
the border? Tibet? Vietnam? Kampuchea? Thought you might
have been a political adviser there? No?*

The questions reiterated themselves in a harsher, more incisive
voice than Feng had used.

Feng paused, and looked about him. He had reached the small
concourse which abutted the platforms for local trains. He stood
with his hands on his hips for a moment. Liu halted and pressed
back against the political daubs that occupied the spaces where
he might have expected commercial hoardings. A stylised, digni-
fied, almost Westernly-handsome Chinese, out-of-focus next to
his cheek as he leaned against the poster, gripped the staff of a
People's Republic flag and exhorted him to devote himself to the
Four Modernizations and directed him forward to the second
millennium. He felt his heart pumping with wasted adrenaline.
Feng, apparently satisfied, crossed the concourse swiftly towards
the office of the railway police. Liu cursed the arrogance, the
presumed immortality of his Californian self. Because Feng was
boorish, in uniform, slurred in his speech, he had kept slipping
into contempt for the man. Feng was in command of the
situation, and had been from the beginning.

A railway policeman in green jacket, dark-blue trousers and
peaked cap was standing at the doorway of the office. Feng
approached him, and at once began a hurried and evidently
emphatic explanation. He was explaining Liu, it was obvious.
Liu could not bring himself to move closer. Feng and the
policeman were perhaps sixty yards from him. It was as if he
could hear them, or lip-read their conversation. He remained
beside the handsome, exhorting Chinaman in his Mao-suit,
horridly fascinated, a rabbit with prevision or a sensitive imagination regarding the snake. He expected Feng and the policeman
to move back towards him at every moment.

The policeman's attention was caught. His head kept flicking
towards the Shanghai train, declaring the subject of the conversation. Feng pointed towards the door of the office, and the
policeman shook his head and stiffened his carriage. It was
evident that he possessed sufficient authority to deal with the
matter. Then the policeman made as if to move towards the train,

but Feng restrained him and then proceeded to dissuade him from action. Liu was puzzled. The lips of the Chinaman on the hoarding now appeared to be shouting a warning. Feng kept his hand on the policeman's arm and talked quickly and urgently for some minutes. Liu began to be aware of the gruntings and breathing of the steam locomotive just behind him. The train would depart in a few minutes' time. Feng laughed, and the sound carried. He made a sweeping, dismissive gesture with his arm, and his hand closed into a tight fist. The policeman nodded, nodded again, replied. Feng commented. They had reached agreement. Then Feng glanced towards the locomotive.

A whistle sounded, startling Liu. Feng stepped away from the policeman, who made vigorous assertions to him. Then Feng hurried back towards the train. Liu felt weak, almost pushed himself away from the hoarding. The handsome face on the poster gleamed with pleasure and triumph. Liu turned and ran back along the platform, climbing into the third carriage so that Feng would not see him.

He hurried down the carriages towards his own compartment. There was a yell of steam following a second whistle, and when the train lurched into motion he felt as disorientated as if the earth had moved; as if some tectonic plate in his personal continent had groaned and moved.

Shanghai. Feng had arranged matters. He would be arrested for questioning when they reached Shanghai. He hurried on, trapped on the train, pushing through passengers who seemed intentionally to restrain and impede him.

Chancellor Dietrich Vogel looked out of the window of his suite in the Hotel am Schlossgarten, down at Stuttgart's main railway station, then altered the direction of his unseeing attention towards the Schlossgarten, its concrete paths whitened against the darkening grass that submitted itself to the sunset. Shadows lay across the grass, and rush-hour traffic crowded into the station square, along the Schillerstrasse. The tower of the railway station flung itself towards the darkening gardens. Behind him, Wolfgang Zimmermann's voice insisted on the emphases of that evening's election speech in the Rathaus.

"Yes, yes, Wolf," he murmured, sipping at his whisky and sensing only the separation of glass between himself and the people of Stuttgart below him. Zimmermann did not need to remind or rehearse him. He knew he could not falter or be in error now. The mood in the Federal Republic, in Germany, was the mood he felt himself. He was at one with the German people.

He smiled inwardly. Too grandiose, he thought. Too like others who have claimed to speak for the German people. But true nevertheless, he reminded himself. He was going to sweep back to power in this election, and he was going to do it precisely because of his *Ostpolitik*.

"Don't be impatient, don't be too confident," Zimmermann said in what might have been a hurt tone. Vogel turned away from the window and its darkening scene, and confronted his chief political adviser and oldest friend.

"Sorry, Wolf," he said. "Listen, you must have sensed it, mm? Even in Bavaria, where he might have expected a rough ride. We have a *winner* here, Wolf. The people want what we offer—they want the Berlin Treaty."

"Perhaps."

"You're so cautious, Wolf!" Vogel crossed the room and sat down in the spilled light of soft lamps in a chair next to Zimmermann. Zimmermann's handsome features expressed doubt; expressed, too, the nervousness of a man on the verge of some momentous act or triumph. His look struck Vogel. "You believe in it more than any of us, don't you?" he said softly. "You've worked harder than any of us. Sometimes, I almost feel as if you hypnotised me into this *Ostpolitik* thing." Zimmermann's face narrowed with what might have been conceived as spite, dislike. "It wasn't my political priority at one time, you know. After poor old Willy Brandt's failure, it looked like a dead duck." He patted Zimmermann's arm. "You lit the torch again, Wolf. I'm grateful to you."

Zimmerman shrugged. "It's your work," he replied diffidently. "Your work."

"My salesmanship, your work. Or your salesmanship, perhaps?" Vogel's eyes glittered with amusement. He lit a cigarette, inhaling deeply. "God, you even taught me to trust the Russians! Because you trust them."

Zimmermann nodded, his face grave, yet closed. "Yes," he said. "I trust them."

Already the morning freshness had gone from the air and the brazen sky seemed to press down on the white house on Peak Road. Aubrey looked down over the Happy Valley racecourse, then towards the tiny, whiter-than-white toy buildings of Government House and the smudges of green of the zoological gardens already softening into a haze. His mood was angrily, recalcitrantly guilty. Hyde had, of course, been right. He had been remiss, even lax, in discussing Wei with Godwin the previous evening. The young man's questions had been energetic and flattering, and Aubrey had displayed his knowledge and his assumptions out of little more than a complacent sense of self-congratulation.

He had mentioned Wei by name, many times. He had referred to Zimmermann also on numerous occasions. He had expressed his doubts, beliefs, theories, insights. He had been—*insecure*. The word rankled in his thoughts like a nagging, worsening headache. Just as his temporary surrender of the process of decision to Hyde, the field agent, distressed him.

Walk on the terrace, Hyde had said. *With Wei. Keep the conversation bland*. The look in Hyde's eyes as he gave those instructions had mortified Aubrey, rubbed against his pride. Simple instructions for an old man.

Thus, with Godwin acting as minder, seated on the low wall of the terrace, his face discomforted by the bulge of the shoulder holster beneath his linen jacket, Aubrey walked in a conscious, instructed parade with Colonel Wei.

"The open air is to your liking?" Aubrey murmured, glancing at his watch. *Make it ten minutes, no more, no less,* Hyde had instructed.

Wei appeared nonplussed. "It is thoughtful of you," he replied.

"Your early career," Aubrey said. "You were loyal, of course. You grew up in the Party?"

"This is necessary? I would have imagined these matters would have come later."

Don't let him get onto the subject of Zimmermann.

"I am conducting this debriefing," Aubrey replied huffily.

"Where is your running dog?" Wei asked, nodding in the direction of the florid-faced Godwin. "This is not this one's real game."

"Running dog? Oh, I see. On an errand."

"Ah. Yes," Wei continued, returning to the subject of Aubrey's question, "I was, of course, loyal to the Party. In the People's Republic . . ." He spread his hands. "It was impossible not to grow up in the Party. Crèche, school, military service, all of them form a fine net." He linked his fingers, twisting them tightly together. "One does not escape, there is no thought of escape."

"Under Mao?"

"It is still the same. The objects of revulsion have changed, as have the objects of belief. But we are all totally as we were, the creatures of the *People's Daily.*" Wei smiled enigmatically. "There is a cliché cupboard, rack after rack of trite and most-used Party phrases, at the offices of our great newspaper. It is as full as it ever was. Some of the phrases have changed, that is all."

Aubrey studied the man carefully, stopping in mid-stride. Modulations, a singing voice, hypnotic like that of an actor. The sentiments were sophisticated and clever, established disillusion very effectively. But something about the tone of voice struck Aubrey. Was he being played upon? Wei's eyes watched him as if for a reaction.

"I see. Disillusion is your keynote. Not avarice?" The sounds of the city ascended to them, enfolding them like a cloud of insects drawn by their body heat. Aubrey waved one long-legged hovering insect away from his face dismissively.

"Avarice, yes," Wei admitted. Then his lips shaped themselves in a bitterness which Aubrey could not but accept as a genuine emotion. "The Great Leap Forward and the Four Modernizations are not thought. They are artificial, pre-packaged items." Wei turned the Western colloquialism easily. "Do you understand? A man of intelligence can accept only so much, and only for a certain period of time."

"I understand." There was an evident appeal to Aubrey's own intelligence, a subtle flattery there. He glanced at his watch. The ten minutes had passed. "Shall we go in now?" he asked, ushering Wei towards the house.

"As you wish." Wei turned with him. Looking at the man's narrow back and neatly clipped hair as he moved ahead of him, Aubrey felt himself baffled by Wei. Hyde's instruction to keep their conversation away from sensitive areas had only increased the sense of mystery surrounding Colonel Wei.

Aubrey glanced back once, across the hot flagstones of the terrace, before he passed through the doorway. Hyde's task was perhaps easier than his own. He did not doubt that Hyde would have learned what he desired to know, somewhere on the slopes and the road below the house.

Hyde studied the house, the two figures on the terrace, then swept the glasses over the bush-strewn, rocky slope that dropped gently away from the house towards Peak Road. There was a car on the road, parked as if to sightsee the city spread out below and the shimmering white towers of Kowloon across the pale bay. It was empty, and was the same car that had been parked on the harbour front at Aberdeen the previous evening. Hyde grinned when he spotted it, opening his lips and inhaling the superiority of the unseen watcher like oxygen. His skin prickled with awareness, his mind raced, his frame was compact, reliable, employable around his senses. The gun pressed against his back in a hollow that might have been designed to absorb its shape and dimensions. The glasses swept back once more, examining each bush, each outcrop of rock, each fold of the slope.

The house that was Hong Kong Station for the SIS perched on a flattened area of the hillside which stretched greenly up to the peak of Mt. Kellett and fell away to his left towards Magazine Gap. The best vantage points for any observer were on a level with the house, before the slope dropped away to the road. The cover was thick in places where bushes had grown back across the gouges of excavation made when the house was built. Rocks, too.

A glint of momentary light? Bottle top, broken shard of glass, gunsight? Hyde focused the glasses, and waited. Perhaps fifty yards below him and to his left. He shifted a leg that was becoming cramped, and a small fall of dust and pebbles slid away from his suede shoe. Glint again. The barrel of a telephoto lens rested on the flattened surface of a rock, protruding from a thick, spiky bush that leaned out towards the road. The barrel-image made his heart pump for an instant, until its photographic innocuousness was established. He grinned again. Same car— same men?

Where was the mike?

He lowered the glasses and looked towards the terrace. Wei and Aubrey patrolled it almost self-consciously. He looked at his watch. Three minutes gone. These men would wait on after Wei and Aubrey retreated into the house, but they would be more alert, less focused in their attention, more available to the information of moving earth, disturbed vegetation. He stood in a low crouch and moved to his left, treading warily but still disturbing little showers of rock, little puffs of dust. He remained above and behind the watchers until he found a shallow dry gully. He dropped into it and began to wind down with it, sliding his body like a dancer through its narrow course. He raised his head twice, the second time finding himself slightly below the position of the two men, and twenty yards or more behind them.

Bright shirts, cropped heads, thick necks, concentration in their hunched shoulders.

Camera and binoculars. A slow voice speaking quietly into a microphone. Small recorder lying on the flat earth behind the lip-reader. Hyde craned his head, listening. A murmur, with hesitations and pauses. Large silences. Click, wind-on, click; the whirring of the camera as a succession of pictures was taken.

Hyde ducked his head and continued down the gully. When he was only a few yards above the level of the road, he climbed out of the gully into the shelter of a small, stunted, drunkenly leaning bush. One of its thorns scratched him. He studied the miniature contours of the lower slope. The cameraman and the lip-reader above him were invisible to him, he to them. He moved rapidly now, after glancing at his watch and discovering that another three minutes had passed. If the long-range mike was here at all, it would be on the other side of the house.

Dust and pebbles skittered away, his breathing became more rapid and uneven, his back ached as he continued to move in his adopted crouch. If he was seen, he was seen. But it was unlikely while Aubrey and Wei held the stage of the terrace.

He paused and looked up. Rain gullies, scattered bushes, dry yellow earth, rocks. A head moved within the camouflage of a low bush, bobbing up and down. Hyde began to climb again, hurrying. When he was no more than fifteen yards from the bush, he slid behind a rock and waited until his breathing calmed. Then he rose on his haunches and looked over the rock.

Glint of the lens from the other side of the house. Nearer, the back of a man's head, a white shirt stretched over broad shoulders, a darkened patch between the shoulderblades. A sunhat pulled forward to shade the eyes. The cigar shape of the microphone protruded ahead of the man like a grey loaf of French bread. Voices, tinny and unsubstantial that might have been coming from the microphone, reached Hyde. Evidently, Aubrey and Wei had reached this side of the terrace in their patrol. The grey submarine of the mike rose from the bush, titillated by the voices, seduced to attention. At that range, with no mush except the dim whispering of the city below, every word would be clearly recorded.

Hyde looked at his watch. Ten and a half minutes gone. The voices vanished, merged with the city. The microphone withdrew. The man's head appeared above the bush, watched the terrace for a moment, then dropped down again. Then the KGB man's voice crackled out in Russian, and there was a furry, treble reply. Walkie-talkies. *Da, da . . .*

Hyde retreated, guessing the next move. He used the shadow of the rock until he reached another rain gully, and began to hurry down it towards Peak Road, skipping almost as surely as he might have done down the steps from the house. The gully bent towards the tarmac drive from the road to the garage at the rear of the house, and he climbed out of it and dropped down onto the hot, sticky tarmac. A grey, dented VW Beetle nestled in the drive. Godwin had borrowed it from an acquaintance at Government House, a Foreign Office official with respectability. As far as Godwin could ascertain, the KGB office would not suspect it.

Hyde got in. The air in the car stifled him, despite the fact that the windows were open. He slid down in the driving seat, and waited. Three minutes later, the microphone operator passed across the entrance to the drive, glanced once at the apparently empty VW, and walked out of sight, whistling softly with a self-congratulatory descant. Hyde sat up, grinning. His hand touched the ignition key. He listened.

He had seen, when he first climbed the hillside behind the house, that a second car was parked further up the slope of Peak Road, as if it belonged to visitors to another house. He had not expected any of the watchers to return to the KGB office the moment Aubrey and Wei disappeared. The business was evidently urgent; the Rezident was evidently concerned. Outside the timeless, indolent scenario of Aubrey's interrogation of Wei, other people and other plots were moving more quickly. Aubrey had underestimated, ignored, was in error. These people were like flies around a jam jar.

The engine of one of the two cars fired, roared, and then the tyres protested as the car was turned round on Peak Road. Hyde turned on the Beetle's ignition, then edged the car out of the drive.

The dusty black saloon was already moving away up Peak Road, ascending into a haze, its exhaust shimmering behind it, seeming to melt the car, allow the tar of the road to absorb it. Hyde accelerated after the black car. Victoria Peak and the tramway loomed to his left as the road twisted and began to descend towards the central district. The two cars, Hyde keeping a hundred yards behind and allowing two other vehicles to slip between them, slid into the thronging cars and bicycles and motor scooters and rickshaws of the central district. The Botani-

cal Gardens promised coolly to Hyde's right, and then he
plunged the car into the congealed traffic of Caine Road.

He was hot, edgy, and tired of negotiating the traffic by the
time the black car pulled up onto the pavement of Tung Street in
the Sheung Wan district. The KGB office, behind its facade as
an antique shop, looked unprepossessing. The KGB man got out
of the car, locked it, and went in. Hyde drove on down the
narrow street, but found nowhere to park. Irritatedly, he circled
the block and entered Tung Street once more. On his fourth
circuit, he edged the Beetle, with a hideous scraping noise,
between two other cars only twenty yards or so from the antique
shop. A Chinese, presumably the nominal owner, stood in the
doorway, demonstrating the decoration on a vase to two evidently American tourists.

Hyde picked up his camera from the passenger seat, and
settled down to wait. He looked at his watch. Ten-forty. In the
narrow, shadowy street the rich odours of food tugged at his
stomach, and the temperature became like heavy, hot clothing
around his body. Sunlight spilled between blind buildings in
molten slabs of light emerging from a furnace.

Customers. He photographed even those who created no sense
of suspicion; the ones with slung cameras, straw hats, striped
shirts, shorts, mini-skirts, denims. Older than possible, younger
than likely. He reloaded the camera, considering there were only
two possibles in thirty-six frames. The ubiquitous and titular
owner of the antique shop appeared in perhaps half the shots.
Eleven-fifteen.

Another possible. He adjusted the focus with more care as the
man weaved between the rickshaws and bicycles. A pause, as if
to be photographed with clarity, then he entered the shop. He did
not re-emerge. Then another, then the little man Vassily at the
airport. The suspicion grew that Godwin would not know all the
faces, that these men were new arrivals, drafted in. The scenario
that enclosed them was accelerating, had moved into another
gear. It did not matter what Aubrey wished, planned or performed.
The initiative was swinging towards the KGB. They had the fish
on the slab, and the gutting knife was poised. Another one,
click, wind-on, click again as he ducked his head into the narrow
dark doorway. Eleven-thirty.

And then, stepping out of a taxi, with a small suitcase and one
piece of cabin baggage, his face pale and unexposed to the Hong
Kong sun—Petrunin. The shock of recognition caused a sharp,
coronary pain in Hyde's chest. His breathing was difficult. The

man had tried to have him killed, less than two years ago. Eighteen months ago, on Cannock Chase. Petrunin.

His hands were shaking, the shots would be out of focus, but Petrunin had already paid off the taxi and had turned to the building. A smile of amusement—click—a moment of hesitation, his eyes drawn by a slim, small, elegant Chinese girl—click, the girl out of focus, Petrunin grinning ruefully—then he walked into the shop, body disappearing—click . . .

Hyde put the camera thankfully on the seat beside him. Tamas Petrunin, formerly Rezident at the Russian embassy in London, forced to get out when an operation blew up in his face. Tamas Petrunin, who had been promoted to a new job in one of the geographic departments of the KGB's First Chief Directorate—was it China, or the rest of Asia? Hyde could not remember.

Wei was a target. In that moment, at eleven thirty-six in the morning, Petrunin's arrival in the Hong Kong KGB office made Wei a target. The scenario was now in top gear, and Aubrey no longer had any control over it.

Petrunin.

He saw, immediately, a station cleaner who brushed diligently and whose head moved continuously like that of a feeding, nervous bird; the last sigh of steam from the locomotive was like a sound that might have escaped from Liu's tight chest, an expression of his tension. A railway policeman—perhaps, but he was not certain, the bulge of an unfamiliar gun beneath his uniform jacket—strolled with care and deliberation past the carriage window, turned on his heel and came back down the platform as the train finally stopped. Liu avoided looking at the man, and tried to smile the smile of an arriving passenger at journey's end towards Captain Feng, as the policeman passed the grimy window again. Across Liu's mind flitted images of factory chimneys belching smoke, of green parks with small, robotic figures engaged in martial exercises, of temples and hotels and modern concrete towers; as if the last minutes of the train's journey had been left imprinted on the coloured slide of the window. He tried to push the images from his thoughts, but it was as if his mind was trying to retreat back down the line to Canton, out of the crowded, sprawling city.

Shanghai, and they were waiting for him. He was expected. End of the line. A clipped, laconic defeat possessed him. When Feng stood up, merely to reach up to the luggage-rack for his suitcases, Liu's body jumped.

"End of the line," Feng said, grinning. He looked tired, and wary.

"What?"

"End of the line—thankfully."

Their two remaining travelling companions, an old man and his plain daughter, squeezed past Feng out of the compartment. The old man had been silent for most of the journey, sleeping as uprightly as he sat, except when querulously demanding food. The woman, who might have been twenty or forty, had read assiduously hour after hour. To Liu it had seemed as if they were aware of the conspiracy against him, and had chosen deliberately to ignore him.

Liu stood up, pulled down his one small case from the rack, and turned back to Feng. The man's black, raisin-like eyes studied him. They were red with tiredness and drink. He swayed slightly, but more like an attacker than a drunk. Liu's own head was clear, but unable to grasp and hold. Images of anticipated arrest flitted through his mind and fell across his concentration like cobwebs might have fallen across his eyes. He could not think. He was jumpy, aware, unnerved.

"After you," he said.

"After you."

Liu led Feng along the corridor to the carriage door, already realizing that he should have debouched as soon as the train stopped and worked himself into the first rush of passengers to the barrier. The old man was climbing with painful slowness down onto the platform. The platform sweeper's face was beyond the old man and his daughter. *Come on, come on . . .*

Liu felt a rush of adrenaline overwhelm him, and fought to control it, dampen it until he might need it. His body prickled with tension, jumped and twitched with the need to act. The old man tottered away on the woman's arm, and Liu stepped down. Feng's hot breath on the back of his neck as they had waited revolted him. The platform sweeper became more assiduous. The railway policeman was further down the platform now, talking to a second policeman. Feng hurried at Liu's side, both suitcases held in one hand, his left. The fact and the implication registered. They passed the two policemen. Liu sensed them fall in behind himself and the captain. Perhaps—no doubt—the man with the broom was there, too. Liu accelerated slightly, and he and Feng drifted slowly into the last of the crowd. Liu worked himself through, burrowing with arms and elbows. Feng remained at his side.

Four more handsome Chinese, mounted on a flying horse, raced towards the year 2000 on a poster they passed. Overhead, smoky steel carved and perhaps once gilded flung itself in a series of narrow bridges on which pigeons perched. The crowd flowed towards the barrier. The adrenaline accumulated, waiting to be employed.

The platform sloped slightly upwards to the ticket barrier. Beyond it, over the heads of waiting relatives and friends, Liu glimpsed the ornate station concourse, its green plants and fountain, its carving and statues, as a park-like apparition. It seemed a freedom he would not reach; rather, be hustled through to the waiting police van. He could not see the girl who was supposed to meet him, and he could make no move until he did. She had to see him, see what he did, where he went. And she had to be professional when he did move; watch and wait, be ready. If she lost sight of him, or lacked the expertise, if she panicked, then he was lost. He would be alone and running in a city more than two thousand square miles in area, amid eleven million people. The girl had to see him, and understand . . .

Feng's right hand was sharp, end-of-finger-like in the hollow of his back. A gun. More handsome Chinese on a poster, racing forward under the wise leadership of Deng, banner-bearing, grinning with gleaming eyes at him; mocking him now. As if the gun had been a signal, Liu saw two, three railway policemen move down from the barrier towards him. The figures on the poster now stared into a far perspective unlike his own immediate future; they ignored him. He and Feng had paused, the gun nudging his spine. He envisaged the damage and pain possible from the officer's Type-59 nine-millimetre pistol with startling, unnerving clarity. The crowd straggled away from him, reaching the policemen. Feng was too close, it would be easy . . .

The girl, the girl . . .

The foremost policeman was a matter of thirty yards from him now, arms at his chest, buffeting like a swimmer through the turbulence of the crowd. The railway policeman and the platform sweeper might be closing, or merely blocking his retreat. His eyes frantically searched for the face of the girl. There was no way in which she could have been wearing something distinctive, all they could instruct her to do would be to . . .

Wave the *People's Daily* like a flag, and there she was, her stick-like arm aloft. *No, no*, another woman, older, similarly waving, then embracing someone. His confidence ebbed. Twenty yards now.

"Don't do anything stupid!" Feng instructed, his breath hot on Liu's cheek as he leaned forward, the alcohol tangible. The man was in the perfect too-close, off-balance position—*where was the girl*? She was afraid to wave, because of the police. She'd given him up already . . .

Feng moved back—now he might step too far away. The nearest policeman was ten yards away with a second drawing level with him. Then the thin arm, the newspaper, waving twice, quickly and covertly; a small, dangerous, ashamed gesture. Confusion and near panic on her face. *Imperialist lickspittle spy.* The words closed on his mind, images of the hysterical accusations of the televised trial of the Gang of Four flickering in the sudden hopeless dark that confronted his reason. Feng was still slightly too close, slightly off balance . . .

Liu turned quickly, his hand reaching behind him, grabbing the barrel of the gun, twisting it upwards; he felt the shudder of the first shot and a scorching sensation in his hand. The explosion was loud and deafening; Feng's now confronted face showed a surprise which turned to rage almost at once, the alcohol wiped aside like sleepiness. Liu brought his knee up hard into Feng's groin, tugged the pistol free by the barrel and thrust Feng aside with his foot.

A hand grazed his clothes, he heard yells and demands. The platform sweeper raised his broom like a tufted lance, the two policemen near him began to move as if their boots were weighted. He shouldered aside a light frame then jumped down onto the tracks of the empty platform opposite the train from Canton. Liu stumbled slightly, hopped to save his ankle from twisting, aware of the fragility of his limbs and torso and of the metal of railway tracks and bullets, then began running.

Whistles and cries. The scorched sensation in his right hand diminished, and he thrust the pistol into his belt. The small suitcase banged against his knee and thigh. He threw it onto another empty platform, and hoisted himself up from the tracks with the ease of a gymnast, the adrenaline making his whole body fluid, graceful. He grabbed up the suitcase. Porters stared at him, and retreated. A distant railway policeman began to run. The first pursuers were on the tracks behind him. Feng was still lying where he had pushed him.

The heartbeat of another train, drowning the cries and whistles. He crossed the platform and jumped again. The locomotive was in front of him, and he could see the driver's startled face in the porthole of the cab. The brakes squealed louder. He heaved himself onto the opposite platform, knelt, then rose into the flurry of steam that was the locomotive's protest at his intrusion. Then the slowing carriages masked him.

A standing train, empty. He opened the door of a compartment, passed through to the corridor, then opened the door down onto the tracks. He was suddenly aware again of the fragility of the bones and muscles and sinew and cartilage in his ankles, so that he lowered himself awkwardly from the carriage, wrenching his arm as he did so. His shoulder burned; heat spread across the back of his neck.

Another platform, this time with a few passengers waiting for some local train. No police. He climbed as purposefully as he could onto the platform, crossed it at a walk, business-like, then climbed into another standing carriage. The train was filling up. He opened the carriage door on the other side, reached out and twisted the door handle of a newly arrived carriage which was still shedding passengers, and stepped across into its corridor. A man turned his head in surprise, but Liu ignored him.

He hurried out behind the man into the crowd heading for the barrier.

No police at the barrier—no, one policeman, hands clasping his uniform belt in complacent self-importance, head turned to gaze down the line of ticket barriers, ears alerted by the whistles. Liu passed through the barrier, his one piece of luck the fact that, as with his own train, the tickets from these passengers had been collected before arrival.

And then the girl was hurrying towards him, pushing through the crowd, small, pretty, alert. Professional. She studied the faces that passed her avidly, as if she might have been searching for a lost child. She collided with him; surprise and relief contradicted each other on her features. Liu felt weak, and embraced her with relief rather than in pretence of recognition.

"Quickly," she whispered in his ear as she returned his embrace.

Light spilled down through the glass roof of the huge station concourse, onto the ornamental fountain. Dragons and gilding. Green bushes and ferns. Liu thankfully walked into the illusory garden towards the exit and the bus stop, the girl's small hand on his forearm as if she were guiding a blind man. The last traces of adrenaline evaporated, and Liu felt desperately tired. Fear, too, began to come back insidiously. His hand shook as he pushed open the exit door, and stepped out into the midday sunlight.

           *   *   *

Hong Kong's noonday gun. Aubrey was too distant to see the small, ceremonial puff of smoke, but the gun's report ascended to Peak Road like a whispered shout, inserting itself into a silence between himself and Hyde. A single gun, firing on China across the bay, Aubrey thought with irrelevance, until Liu's features entered his mind and the ceremony of the gun achieved an allusive importance he disliked. Liu, attacking China single-handed.

Hyde's mood was sullen, disturbed. Evidently the Australian disliked being on the terrace of the house, despite the fact that both Aubrey and Godwin had assured him that their watchers had departed, presumably summoned back to their headquarters because of the arrival of Petrunin.

Petrunin . . . The man obviously worried Hyde.

A heavy, damp wind had sprung up. Cloud was filling in the spaces between the hills like a grey dough. Kowloon thrust a dense crowd of white fingers upwards against the heavy, slow-moving cloud. A cyclone on the way, Godwin had said. The sun had vanished like an illusion.

"Hyde, what is the matter?" He had given no reply to Aubrey's last question.

Patrick Hyde was remembering his childhood. Squatting against the sun-leaking, hot wooden planks of the cramped, carless garage behind the house, his breath still audible from his haste, the air stifling. The *Beano* annual open on his grubby, bare knees. He had found it on top of his mother's wardrobe with the rest of his Christmas presents. Auntie Vi had brought it from London with her. He had only ever seen the *Beano* comic once, a tattered copy for which he had swopped a broken penknife. Now, magically, he had a hundred pages of Lord Snooty and Biffo the Bear and Dennis the Menace. And he had not been able to wait until Christmas Day. He had seen the book's title through the thin wrapping paper that contained it, and had been consumed with a possessive impatience until able to retrieve it from the top of the wardrobe.

And then, as Dennis the Menace in his striped jersey and impossible shock of black hair was about to receive yet more just punishment, he had looked up, giggling, and seen the funnel-web spider emerging from its abode beneath the shelf above his head, the shelf where the old paint cans were stored. Knowing that the spider's bite would kill him, he had sat in rigid, mortified terror for thirty minutes before the spider entered its woven funnel once more and he could force himself to move. He had wet his shorts by that time. His mother and Auntie Vi, returning at that moment, saw the shorts and the *Beano* annual. His spanking was a relief, affirming life and health.

"What?" Hyde said, looking up suddenly. Tamas Petrunin was his own particular funnel-web spider. Eighteen months before, the man, then KGB Rezident in London, had almost killed him in England. And now he was here, in Hong Kong, and he would doubtless already know that Hyde was here, too. Hyde suppressed a new shudder.

"What is the matter?" Aubrey asked, not unkindly.

"Nothing."

"Petrunin?"

Hyde's left shoulder ached with the memory of a wound. "No," he lied.

"You know him?" Godwin asked, surprised. He held in his hand the new, still-wet prints of airport shots of Petrunin, taken that morning. He seemed to be offering them to Hyde, who turned away.

"Slightly," he murmured.

"Formerly KGB Rezident in London," Aubrey explained. "He was recalled, and surprisingly promoted. A clever man. He's now believed to be heading the First Chief Directorate's Sixth Department."

"China," Godwin said.

Hyde turned on them.

"It's very bloody important, all of a sudden, isn't it?" His eyes seemed to accuse Aubrey, remind him of his indiscretions.

"It *is* important," Aubrey replied coolly. "Made more important by what the KGB has recently learned." It was almost an apology. On the Boxing Day, all those years ago, Hyde had gone back to the garage with a burning rolled-up newspaper and fired the web and its occupant. The paint tins and bottles of white spirit had also burned. The fire brigade had put out the fire eventually, leaving the garage a ruin.

"OK," Hyde said grudgingly, beginning to accommodate himself to the idea, and the threat, of Petrunin. "OK."

"It means that Wei is no longer safe here," Aubrey observed. Godwin appeared crestfallen, as if he had failed some stern examination. "Suggestions?"

"Extra men," Hyde replied, his hands in his pockets, the heavy wind distressing his hair. The dampness in the air was as tangible as a facecloth.

"We can borrow them from Government House—police?"

"Yes, Mr. Aubrey."

"Mm."

"Why not move him down to police headquarters or even Victoria Prison?" Godwin suggested. "Then he'd be safe."

"It might very well affect the progress of my interrogation, young man." Aubrey rubbed his cheeks, as if laving them with the damp air. The wind ruffled his last remaining hair, making the grey wings stand out from his temples like horns. "Hyde?"

Hyde scuffed at a stone, kicking it along the terrace. Then he looked up challengingly at Aubrey.

"It's bloody important. They know who Wei is, and what he's offering for sale." The skin of Aubrey's cheeks darkened momentarily and he frowned, but Hyde ignored the signals. "If they're suddenly so interested in Wei, then perhaps they're moving to protect Zimmermann?"

Aubrey appeared dubious, but he said: "Go on."

"If you want further proof, then discover how much they want to get their hands on Wei."

"How?"

"Easy as picking up the phone. Tell police headquarters you want provision for a special prisoner, to be delivered tonight. The KGB have drafted in more men—Godwin's snaps tell you that, Petrunin didn't come by himself—and it might just be the opportunity they'd like."

"A trap, you mean?"

"A both-ways trap. Smuggle Wei to prison, but appear to take him down tonight, in technicolor. A decoy. Find out how much they want to shut Wei up. It might tell you something about your German mate."

"Telephone?"

"Don't tell me they won't have tapped this place by now."

"Agreed." Again, Godwin looked as if he had been accused of failure. "Decoy, mm? You?"

Hyde nodded. "Me."

"You'd take on the—task?"

"It's what I'm paid for."

"Very well." The wind was scouring across the terrace now. "Weather?" Aubrey asked Godwin.

"This cyclone is well out to sea. It will do."

"Let's go inside. There are details to clarify."

Hyde walked away from Aubrey, and leaned out over the terrace, his shirt flapping loosely on his back in the wind. To Aubrey, the Australian appeared vulnerable, small, unmuscular. It was a new and unusual glimpse of the man.

Hyde came back towards them. "The car's back."

"What about—?"

Hyde shook his head. "They're still inside it. Just arrived. Interested, aren't they?"

The girl was silent during their trolley-bus ride from the station through the centre of Shanghai towards the Bund. They crossed Suzhou Creek near the Shanghai Mansions, a thirties-style skyscraper hotel that would not have been out of place in some part of San Francisco or downtown Manhattan. The very familiarity of its red-brown appearance sent a shudder of isolation through Liu. The girl merely tapped him sharply on the arm when they reached their destination. The trolley-bus stopped on Zhongsha Number One Road East, opposite the small Huangpu Park. One old woman descended from the bus with them. Liu breathed deeply, as if for the first time since leaving the station.

The girl guided him across the busy road, weaving them between buses, motorized trishaws, cars. As they entered the park, even though it was crowded with lunchtime pedestrians and the benches were fully occupied, there was a sense to Liu of fugitive peace. The city's incessant noise was veiled, the city's unrelieved crowds thinned, weeded. Movement was slower, the trees bent over slow-motion figures engaged in the shadow-play of *tai ji chuan*, the gentle martial art: an aid to digestion. Hands moving like those of actors in a mime: mimed violence. The harmless images of attack, grasping, damage amused David Liu. There were Westerners, too, engaged in the exercise: businessmen, diplomats, tourists.

"He is there," the girl informed him, touching his arm and leaning to him.

Against the perspective of the river and the modern blocks of offices and flats, its crinkled-sailed junks and sampans and ocean freighters and derricks and cranes, a tall man who could only have been American—grey suit, blue shirt, wide tie, a sleek, groomed presence—was engaged in the shadow-boxing. He stood head and shoulders above the shapeless-capped Chinese men around him. The butterfly wing of a junk's sail moved behind him, a backcloth to his profile. Frederickson, the CIA case officer assigned to him in Shanghai.

Liu looked from the man to the girl at his side. "Thank you," he said.

"Can you practise *tai ji chuan*?" she asked.

"Yes."

"Then join him."

Liu sensed himself as a manipulated puppet, a delivered

parcel. And superfluous to requirements. He had nothing to say to the girl; she resisted intimacy of any kind, confirmed in her role as a courier.

"Very well." Liu crossed a strip of grass towards the river, gleaming like steel in the sunlight. He put down his suitcase as casually as he could, and edged towards Frederickson, who gave no sign of having seen him. Liu raised his hands, palms outwards in front of his chest, lunged slowly forward, swayed to one side, bent his knees, slid and insinuated his hands through the air. No one remarked his arrival.

"Welcome," Frederickson said. "Glad you made it. Any trouble?" The American was glancing towards the girl, who had taken a seat on one of the benches, next to an old woman in a light blue jacket and black trousers. The girl was reading her newspaper.

"Some."

"Yes?"

"An army captain on the train became suspicious." Liu did not mention his arrest after crossing the border. It seemed too distant, and unrelated to Shanghai. "He called ahead, to the railway police here..." Frederickson's reactions as he boxed with the hot, humming air of the park seemed to have increased in intensity. He jabbed and cut and stabbed with his hands as if he faced an opponent.

"What happened?" he snapped.

"I got away—the girl got me away. There wasn't any pursuit, if that's what worries you."

"OK, OK. They don't have your papers?"

"The army captain knows my cover."

"OK, go to your secondary papers. I'll get you a new back-up identity and cover story prepared. Meanwhile"—Frederickson looked carefully around him; the vigour of his shadow-boxing had subsided—"we'll get right to it—your briefing."

"Yes?" Liu traced patterns in the air with his hands. A butterfly seemed concerned to evade his grasp. The horn of a river barge boomed from the far bank of the Huangpu. "I begin to wonder why you need me." He had not, he remarked to himself, meant to make that observation. It did, however, seem true.

Frederickson grinned. Lines around his pale blue eyes appeared as he did so. The grin was twisted, but handsome.

"They're professional, our people here, yes. But they're not trained agents, not trained to look after themselves. They're just agents in place—ministries, factories, communes. They're monitors, that's all. And *I* can't make a suspicious move—I kind of stand out, you know.'' Again the twisted, charming grin, disarming Liu. ''They have no freedom of movement, I have less. That's your job.''

''OK, what have you got for me?''

''A medical orderly, they think.''

''Think?''

''One of my people thinks one of the orderlies at the East China Hospital, right floor, right duties to know about our German pal, might be open to a bribe. They haven't done anything. That's your job.''

''Might, might, might . . .'' Liu observed.

''Right. It's all hazy. Everything's been rushed. Langley and Buckholz want too much too soon. So, I've gotten you one orderly who was working when Zimmermann was in the East China Hospital. And now it's up to you. I can't go near him. He won't talk to a Westerner—at least, not one of my colour.'' Frederickson looked down, as if disapprovingly, at Liu's short figure and his complexion. Liu felt himself weighed. ''You'll make it,'' Frederickson said.

''When?''

''Tonight. You eat at the Clean and Delicate Restaurant, near Fu xing Park, at nine. The table's booked under your second cover. The girl will pick you up there when you've eaten.''

''Where am I staying?''

''Shanghai Mansions. You're booked in under the same cover.''

''OK.''

Frederickson ceased shadow-boxing, and turned briefly and directly towards Liu.

''This is urgent. Do what you have to, but get the information Buckholz wants. Clinch it here in Shanghai if you can—it's going to get more difficult if you have to go upriver to Wu Han. Contacts and back-up are thin on the ground. Understand?''

''Yes. And if I get something tonight . . . ?''

''You'll be in luck.'' Again, Frederickson grinned. His hands wafted in the air now, like parts of a machine running down. ''The girl will know how to reach me.''

Frederickson straightened his knees, adjusted his jacket, and walked away. He waved to a jogger in bright shorts and a University of Minnesota sweatshirt who weaved through the crowd engaged in shadow-boxing. Frederickson's back-up, Liu presumed. Liu picked up his suitcase. The girl had already disappeared from the bench.

Liu could taste, even after the glass of *pi jui* beer and the green tea which followed his meal, the spices and pimento that had been used abundantly in the Si chuan regional cooking of the Clean and Delicate Restaurant. He felt tense, but in control of his circumstances. His papers and reservation at the Shanghai Mansions had been accepted without demur. He had become a railway inspector, by implication rather than statement an inspector of railway security. It elicited a tangible, though understated, deference, and a larger room than he might have anticipated. He had dozed with ease. In the restaurant, too, a corner table at which he ate alone had been the result of the appearance of his identity papers.

As if the wiping of his lips on his napkin had been a cue, the girl entered the restaurant. Her hair had been done in a fuller, softer Western style, and her jacket was a bright red, above black silk trousers. She caused some heads to turn, and the waiter's glance indicated that such a companion was only to be expected for a Party official involved in matters of policing. Liu went through a mime of asking the girl to sit, but she indicated, pleasantly, that there were other matters at hand, and Liu settled the bill and they left.

"Where are we going?" he asked as he stood on the pavement, his arm crooked to hold the girl's hand. The Fu xing Park's dense, heavy trees loomed against the warm stars. There was a distant chatter of monkeys from the small zoo in the park. Motorized trishaws puttered along the street. Warm streetlamps, the occasional car, bicycles. The city had a feeling of well-being. Liu felt strangely at home, anonymous, safe.

"It is in the Old Town—a shanty."

"Transport?"

"Bicycle, of course." The girl smiled. She indicated two bicycles standing together in the rack outside the restaurant. "A friend brought yours," she explained. "Are you ready?" She seemed to be gently mocking him.

"What do I call you?"

"Liang will do."

"Very well. Lead on."

Liu mounted and followed the girl, with a more unsure and wobbling action of the bicycle, to the junction with Fu xing Road. More lights here, the noise of the city conducted along the street as if it were an air duct, hundreds of bicycles and dozens of motorized trishaws. An old-fashioned city, bustling, crowded, noisy; yet humming rather than yelling with life and vitality. Eventually they crossed the circular Zhonghua Road, the perimeter of the Old Town. Then Liang led him into the rabbit-warren of blind, narrow, softly lit streets, beneath overhanging upper storeys of richly carved wooden houses, past rows of whitewashed, thatched shanties, winding and twisting all the time so that within minutes he knew he would never find his way out of the area without the girl's help. The district was no longer a festering slum; it was bright, almost aseptically clean, thronged, even light-hearted.

Near the Yu Gardens, the girl slowed to a halt outside a still open shop selling carvings, lanterns, even birds that still sang in the artificial day of the streetlamps. Fish drifted through weed and fern and bubbles in great tanks, mouths opening and closing with a philosophical slowness. Liang pointed ahead, to a low white shanty with a new thatched roof.

"There," she said. "He will be at home now."

"You'll come in?"

"If you wish."

They approached the door of the tiny, one-storey shanty. The girl knocked. Almost immediately, as if he had been waiting behind the door for their signal, a young man with quick, wary eyes opened the door and beckoned them inside. They pushed their bicycles into the narrow corridor. The house was scented with a mild, sweet incense. The place had a familiarity for Liu: friends' places, relatives' homes when he was a child. The whole of the crowded, cramped, vivid Old Town seemed familiar, as if transplanted from America. Any Chinatown, anywhere.

"Please come in, please come in." There was a quick, guessing, acquisitive intelligence behind the bland courtesies. "Welcome to my home."

The young man waved them through a door which he opened. The scent of something more than incense. The young man was bribable. Opium. The scent of Shanghai's past, the city's former wealth, power and corruption. The incense was intended to mask the smell of the opium. Old men in his childhood had smoked it, the smell had been everywhere. The young Chinese used a needle in America; here, old traditions remained alive. The smell explained the quick bright eyes, the searching glances. The man had a habit that was expensive, and difficult. The Party disliked opium addiction; it demanded addiction to itself, its propaganda-fixes. He had been left above the high water mark by politics and history, without Tongs and Triads and connections to feed his habit easily. The hospital would be a useful source, but he was probably greedy.

He might lie, then ...

The young man indicated cushions on the polished wooden floor. A woman brought in tea, bowed and left. Liang seemed to dislike the old-fashioned, subservient courtesy the woman expressed. Liu drank the proffered tea before he spoke.

"I am led to understand," he said easily, "that you could be of help to me."

"Perhaps. My name is Xu Bin, by the way."

"My name is not important," Liu replied. "You work as an orderly at the East China Hospital? Is that so?"

Bin nodded. "Yes."

"Well, Bin, you had a visitor—a patient—at the hospital some time ago, one you might not have expected. Is that not so?"

"We have many." Liang sat cross-legged and silent. Both men ignored her. Liu felt a small pulse of excitement begin in his temple. The bright eyes caught the light of the single lantern above them; preternaturally bright, opium-bright. Clever and greedy, too.

"Ah, yes, but this one was not Chinese."

"We have many Westerners, also."

"Germans?"

Bin sighed. "Ah. Not important Germans, perhaps." He shook his head. His hands clasped his shins as he sat. They quivered slightly. "You wish to know about this man." It was not an enquiry.

"I do."

"You are prepared ... ?"

"Why would you not talk to the American? I am American, though not white. What difference is there?"

"I do not want ..." The young man made a sweeping gesture with his hand. "You smell something?"

"Yes."

"That would be only the beginning, yes?" He smiled. "I am not ready." He looked darkly towards Liang. "This is something I may do, for money. But I do not wish to become an *employee*, you understand. They might offer me—something in kind, something to smoke, and I would take it, and then they would control the supply, and the habit. This way, with you and with money, they do not have control."

"The habit must be hard, here?"

"I inherited it. It is, perhaps, genetic. My family have been addicts for generations. Once, I thought myself cured. But that was untrue. I—manage. A little more money would be welcome, however."

Liang's face was creased into lines of contempt, but she said nothing.

"Of course. How much?"

"One hundred dollars."

"Impossible."

"Ask, then. I shall provide some information, as a sign of worthiness."

"This German—his name?"

"Zimmermann." Liu recognized the name, despite the difficulties of Chinese pronunciation.

"Describe him, please." Bin did so. "Good. Then, you saw him?"

"Many times."

"What illness was there?"

"Food poisoning."

"What visitors did he have?"

"What have I earned so far?"

"Five dollars."

"Ten at least."

"Seven."

"Very well. Visitors—there were many."

"All Chinese, all Western?"

"Both."

"What shift were you working?"

"Night shifts."

"He had visitors at night?"

"Many. How much have I earned?"

"Twenty dollars."

Bin nodded. Liu noticed that the opium scent had been swallowed by the incense. Bin seemed to perceive, and regret, its departure. "That is good."

"Visitors at night?" Liu prompted. "Who were these visitors?"

"Police."

Liu controlled his sense of excitement, keeping it from his face and eyes. "Police? Chinese police? What nonsense."

"It is not nonsense," Bin protested, now firmly determined to accelerate the accumulation of dollars. "Chinese police. I know them, their type, their manner. And doctors—"

"In a hospital, of course—"

"Not from the hospital—brought in especially."

"Why?"

"To administer drugs."

"What kind of drugs?"

"To make him answer their questions, I suppose. There are such drugs."

"You *know* this?"

"How much have I earned?"

"Fifty dollars," Liu snapped impatiently.

"Good. I know this—I have seen. Every night, all of the night. Our doctors and nurses not allowed into the room, and not willing to speak about it. Questions, all night."

"I see—"

"Have I earned my hundred dollars?"

"Perhaps seventy. You can, however, earn the other thirty, and one hundred more, tomorrow."

Bin appeared cheated, then suspicious, then avaricious. He said in a small voice: "What do you want?"

"The files. I want to see the files—*all* the files—kept on Zimmermann by the hospital. Temperature charts, diet, all the medical records, including X-rays if there are any."

"I can't—"

Liu stood up, confident, dismissive. "That is up to you. A total of two hundred dollars." He reached into his wallet, and counted out the equivalent in yuans of seventy dollars. Bin's face twisted in rage. "I know that U.S. dollars buy more. Tomorrow I will give you, in exchange for these notes, real U.S. dollars. Two hundred of them—if you have what I want."

"I can't—"

"That is your concern. My gratitude for your hospitality. Good night."

Liang followed him to the door. Bin made no protest or attempt to prevent them leaving. Liu assumed that he was already engaged in computing the risks against the reward. If it was possible, he would bring the files out of the East China Hospital.

"Will he do it?" Liang said with evident distaste when they had wheeled their bicycles out into the street and the silent woman had closed the door behind them.

Liu rubbed his eyes, suddenly weary. The lantern-soft illumi-

nation of the narrow street seemed sharp, hard. Noise from a
restaurant, singing; the mutter of crowds funnelled towards them.

"I think so." He smiled. "We shall see."

"You're tired."

"And satisfied. Will you guide me back to the hotel?"

"Of course."

They cycled slowly through the twisting, crowded streets until
they emerged onto the Renmin Road, another part of the perimeter of the Old Town, of the ring of roads that enclosed it. Liang
pointed northwards along the well-lit Henan Road.

"When you reach the Suzhou Creek, turn right. Shanghai
Mansions is ahead of you then."

Liu nodded. "You're going home?"

"Yes."

"You'll report to Frederickson?" The girl nodded. "Tell him I
shall want to meet him the day after tomorrow—with good news,
I hope."

"Good night."

Liang pedalled off, and was soon lost in the throng of
bicycles. Liu began cycling up the Henan Road, past the Muse-
um of Art and History, a dark and lowering building, his growing
impression one of being in the middle of a pack of riders in some
road race. He was eminently satisfied. Most of all, he no longer
felt alienated and alone. He was anonymous, and confident in his
anonymity, here in Shanghai. The interview with Bin had been
fruitful, more than he had hoped.

The flash of sparks from an overhead cable as a trolley-bus
passed on the opposite side of the road startled him. He wobbled
his bicycle back under control, and shook his head to clear the
mood of satisfied reverie. He could smell the river on the warm
night air, even before he reached the creek and turned right. The
lights of shipping lay ahead of him then, anchored in the river. A
string of lights revealed the presence of a bridge, and he saw the
random pattern of room lights from the Shanghai Mansions.

He slowed outside the hotel, and left the cycle in the hotel
park. He turned to look back at the creek and its bridges, at the
train of barges hooting and sidling beneath it, at the crowds and
their dense, inexorable sense of movement.

The man had evidently not expected him to turn back at the
hotel entrance. He was standing beneath the globe of a streetlamp,
a camera hanging on his chest. He was leaning against a car. He
made no attempt to use the camera, and turned unsuspiciously

away from Liu, bending his head to speak to the car's driver. Two men, then.

Car, camera, two men...

Liu felt chilled as he hurried into the Shanghai Mansions. Evidently he was being followed. He was under surveillance.

FOUR

In Harm's Way

Chancellor Dietrich Vogel handed the laboratory coat and white safety helmet he had worn during his swift tour of the chemical factory to one of his aides. Zimmermann smiled at the practised ease, the sense of confident relaxation that the man exuded. Always, he was able to suggest he was among friends, creating warmth and respect. Here, in an industrial suburb of Frankfurt, engaged in a handshaking tour of one of the I.G. Farben factories, he encountered management, unions and workforce with the same unshakeable good humour.

A second aide handed Vogel his check cap and raincoat, which the Chancellor draped loosely over his shoulders.

"Can I smoke now?" he asked, smiling.

"Not until we leave the building, Herr Chancellor," he was informed with a note of genuine regret by the managing director who had conducted him on his tour of the factory. "I am so sorry."

"I am sorry I haven't given up the habit," Vogel replied, clapping the man on the shoulder and laughing. The businessman allowed himself a moment of amusement, moved to it by Vogel's manner.

"You have time for coffee, I hope?"

Vogel glanced swiftly at Zimmermann, who nodded.

"Naturally—a pleasure," Vogel replied, almost thrusting the managing director in front of him towards the doors of the building and towards the executive offices. "But if I sit down, I may not want to get up again!" The managing director did not seem any longer self-conscious about his laughter. His staff, and that of Vogel, chorused their approval in smiles and guffaws. Vogel turned to wave at overalled and white-coated workers as he reached the doors. Many applauded; among them, Zimmermann imagined, many who would not vote for him. Vogel only occasionally encountered hecklers; always, he dealt with them brilliantly and without offence or humiliation, but much of the time he disarmed criticism by his presence, his behaviour.

The late afternoon sunlight was breezy, grass and concrete patched by clouds pushed across the sun. It had rained that morning. The neat lawns and banks that surrounded the factory and its office block still retained a freshened scent. Sprinklers were already at work, reinforcing nature. Vogel waved to faces at office windows, to lorry drivers, security guards, trailing his entourage and the management of the factory behind him like gulls in the wake of a fishing vessel.

Zimmermann watched what might have been a royal progress from the factory doors to the office block. Vogel fascinated him, even after all these years. So little of it was pretence, too. Most surprising of all.

Zimmermann disliked Frankfurt. The past stirred too easily to life whenever he visited it. Capture, weeks of interrogation by the Americans, the vision from the back of an army truck of a city that had virtually disappeared. He had been, while enduring that long journey to a detention camp, forced to a discovery of the horrors to which Germany had brought herself, allied to a lunatic, himself the leader of a gang of thugs and sadists. The journey, which had seemed to last for weeks rather than days and to have been an endless succession of encounters with the displaced, the bereaved, the homeless, the fleeing, had begun in Frankfurt, and for that he could never forgive the city. Its energy, brightness, urgency now expressed as well as any German city—perhaps better than most—the new order, the recovery, the miracle. Zimmermann never regarded Frankfurt in that light. To him, it was always the first image of his own vision of damnation. He, in uniform, had been a part of the order that had truly destroyed Germany; not the Allies and their bombs and tanks and men, but the Führer, the Wehrmacht that had sworn an oath of loyalty to him, the Abwehr that had been ingested in 1944 by the secret police. By the time he reached his place of detention, he was sickened by his wartime silence, his acquiescence; and he was ashamed of his uniform.

Frankfurt. Gleaming, bustling, handsome Frankfurt. The beginning of that journey which had really never ended.

Wolfgang Zimmermann saw the correspondent from *Pravda* make as if to approach him. The entourage had been whisked into the office block by Vogel as if it were his factory, they his guests, and Zimmermann in his mild reverie had lagged behind. A couple of correspondents stood on the steps up to the glass doors with him, perhaps expecting a sidelight upon the Berlin Treaty. Zimmermann recognized them both, one from *Bild Zeitung,* the other from *Frankfurter Allgemeine.* The newspapers' senior correspondents were still in tow behind Vogel, these two were bright, quick, younger men. He smiled at them almost absently as he ascended the steps lightly, but his eyes were still on the *Pravda* correspondent.

Vogel had encouraged the Soviet and East European press corps in the Federal Republic to involve themselves in his election campaign, lifting travel and access restrictions to aid them. Thus the man from *Pravda,* usually based in Bonn, had travelled with the rest of the pressmen accompanying Vogel. The man at his side, festooned with camera equipment, Zimmermann did not recognize. He recognized the gesture, however; the restraining hand placed upon the *Pravda* correspondent's arm. He recognized, too, the urgency of the man's instructions, just as he understood the seniority of the second man over the correspondent. He saw the hand-waving gestures in his own direction which the man either could not, or did not bother to, disguise. He realized, instinctively and completely, that the man was no mere photographer, because he recognized the type. God, he should be able to. Police. And not German police, either. The two German reporters seemed to hesitate in their approach, perhaps recognizing his distraction. Zimmermann, for no reason he could name, felt chilled in the warm, breezy sunshine.

The *Pravda* correspondent nudged his companion. The policeman looked up, towards Zimmermann. Even at a distance of perhaps thirty yards, Zimmermann could clearly see the urgency on the man's face; and an expression of baffled anger and suspicion. Only then did he seem to remember his cover. He raised a camera to his eye, pointing its telephoto lens at Zimmermann. Zimmermann turned away, rejecting the pretence.

Why now? he asked himself. Why now, of all times, was the KGB watching him? What did they want with him?

The lamplit room was hot, despite the stirring of the sluggish air by the fan above Aubrey's chair. The windows were closed and shuttered. The cyclone, venting its full power on the South China Sea, roared around Hong Kong's hills. When he had shuttered the windows in the lounge, with Godwin's help, the wind had seemed like a solid force outside, pushing at the house. Aubrey had found the impression unnerving.

He laid the file aside and rubbed his eyes, then looked at his watch. Twelve-forty. He had arranged over the telephone that Wei would be transferred to Victoria Prison at one that morning. A car would arrive to collect him. Meanwhile, the senior police officer who had arrived at the house that afternoon had received instructions that Wei, under McIntosh's supervision, would be in reality collected by another car thirty minutes after the departure of the decoy saloon containing himself, Hyde, and Godwin, and escorted by a second police car. If the telephone had been tapped and the instructions overheard, then that car and its escort could expect to be intercepted. Thus ran Hyde's gloomy reasoning, and Aubrey did not have the confidence to refute the argument.

Aubrey was pricked by the realization that it was he who had created the situation which now endangered Hyde. It was for that reason that he insisted on travelling in the car with Hyde and Godwin; insisted on putting himself in harm's way. Atonement; apology.

The wind howled and thrust at the house. A shutter, loosened somewhere, banged distantly. The noise of the wind swamped the cassette-recorder on which Hyde had left some jazz piano music playing quietly when he went upstairs to begin the process of turning himself into a replica of Wei by dyeing his skin. Superstitiously Aubrey left the music playing, despite his dislike of jazz.

He was impatient for events to unfold and impatient for the arrival of the Zimmermann files from London. Buckholz's interrogation he had read and re-read; the files he had brought with him from London on the German's post-war career, which were now on his lap, had become familiar and dull and unrevealing. Both sets of documents, separated by nearly forty years, revealed a man he did not know. Aubrey, whether from instinct, superstition or vanity, believed that revelation would come from his own interrogation of the young Abwehr officer in 1940. He needed to re-understand *that* man. The seeds of his later life would have been there.

Aubrey clenched his hands into fists in frustration and ignorance. If he recalled every word, relived every moment, he would know Zimmermann. Then Wei and the 1945 file and the general files and Liu's journey and the Berlin Treaty would all exist in a clear, revealing light.

He waved his hand in a dismissive gesture. The fond illusion
of an old man, he told himself. He stood up, stretching, hearing
the old muscles and sinews protest, the old bones and joints
creak and crack. He regretted his determination to accompany
Hyde and Godwin in the car, but knew he could not now
withdraw. He looked across at the stairs leading out of the
lounge. Wei. Twelve forty-five. Perhaps . . .

He climbed the stairs and passed along the landing to Wei's
room. As he went, images of Zimmermann's career flickered
through his mind like the quick life on the surface of a pond; but
in shadow, meaninglessly, to no purpose. Business success, local
political office, family, widowhood, appearance in certain Nazi
trials in the Federal Republic during the sixties, some journalism
of a portentous and semi-philosophical kind, without humour;
wealth from the sale of his business interests, his attachment to
Vogel when the Chancellor was no more than a junior minister;
Ostpolitik, television and radio interviews which were no more
than declamations under Erhard and Brandt and Schmidt of his
support for a united Germany; opposition to NATO, his roving
commission as a publicist for *Ostpolitik* and for Vogel; visits to
the Soviet Union, Eastern Europe, America, China . . .

And the younger man, the brilliant schoolboy, the army
intelligence officer attached to the Condor Legion during the
Spanish Civil War, his capture by the Republicans, his wartime
career in the Abwehr, his high estimation in the opinion of
Gehlen, his chief . . .

A man Aubrey did not know. A web of nerves and shadows
and clues. Aubrey could not decipher the symptoms presented to
him. He pushed open the door of Wei's room, pushed Zimmermann's files from his mind.

He received an immediate impression of the sardonic smile on
Wei's face. Then a mirror-image, dispelled in an instant but
nonetheless disconcerting, as a head turned to him: Hyde, face
dyed to Wei's colour, wearing the same bright shirt that the
Chinese colonel had exhibited on the terrace that morning, the
same colour slacks. Godwin grinned at Aubrey's momentary
discomfiture, while the young duty officer simply watched Wei
from his chair against the wall.

"Well?" Hyde asked. "You likee?"

"What does this pretence signify?" Wei asked languidly.
Aubrey recognized an effort to appear casual, unconcerned. It
suggested the possibility of nerves, the beginning of fear. As if
on cue, Hyde removed, checked and replaced the eighteen-round

magazine of the Heckler & Koch VP 70 pistol with which McIntosh had issued him. Wei's eyes were immediately attracted and held by the gesture and the weapon. Hyde thrust the pistol into his waistband at the small of his back. "What is this?" Wei repeated.

Aubrey did not look at Hyde. "Yes, indeed, Colonel Wei, this man is intended to pass for yourself—in the dark, of course, and in a car."

"I forgot to tell you that there might be certain—um, impediments?" Wei nodded. "Ah, forgive me. This charade is merely a precaution."

"Against what and who?"

"Certain interested parties, shall we say."

"The ministry?"

"No. Revisionist elements would be nearer the mark."

"KGB?"

It was Aubrey's turn to nod. Hyde watched Wei's face twist in surprise, then grow livid with an undisguised fear. The man's eyes assessed the room in quick, darting glances, as if the walls had suddenly grown transparent, glass-like. He evidently felt unprotected. The sensation devoured his confidence, his reticence.

Aubrey smiled. Excitement was like an appetite about to be sated on a fine meal. "Yes, I'm afraid so. They've become very interested in your arrival."

"How? Why?"

Aubrey shrugged. "I couldn't say, old chap. Don't worry, though. I doubt any harm will come to you."

"This is some kind of—"

"Danger? It is not a bluff—at least, not one for your benefit." He transferred his glance to Hyde. "Yes, Patrick, I think you'll do."

"All Chinamen look alike," Hyde observed. "Especially to a Russian."

"This is preposterous!" Wei protested, swinging his legs off the bed. Sensitive to Aubrey's intentions, Hyde drew the pistol and motioned the colonel back onto the counterpane. Wei retreated, drawing up his legs, sitting upright against the headboard of the bed. "Preposterous. I demand to be handed over to the Americans immediately."

"Please, Colonel, do not interrupt me. Matters are—time is running out. Excuse me. Hyde, come with me . . ." Aubrey turned to leave the room.

"Schiller!" Wei called at his back.

"Not one of my favourite German poets," Aubrey replied. "However, I'm surprised you're familiar with his work, Colonel. Do you read Rilke?"

"Schiller is the man's name," Wei hissed, his face creased and small and venomous.

"I'm sorry?" Aubrey appeared bemused, and irritated at the delay. "Whose name? What man?"

Wei's voice rose to an exasperated shout. "There was an officer captured with Zimmermann in Spain! *His* name was *Schiller*! Now do you understand?"

Aubrey crossed swiftly to the bed. His face appeared angry.

"How much do you really know, Colonel? How much could you really tell us if you tried?" A car horn tooted dimly from the drive outside. A swift frown of anger crossed Aubrey's features. He had established the circumstances and now had to abandon them. In Victoria Prison, Wei would have time to rebuild his defences before their next meeting. "Of what importance is Schiller, pray?" he asked icily, contemptuous of Wei's information. He could see Wei already beginning to reconsider, as if the car horn had been a warning to him to remain silent. He did not answer. "Very well, I leave you to consider matters..." He turned his back on Wei once more. Hyde and Godwin had now joined him at the door. The car horn tooted for them again. Aubrey cursed it under his breath.

"They were in the hands of the NKVD in Spain!" Wei snapped out, abandoning whatever comfort he had derived from the noise of the car. Aubrey turned on him. The man looked as if he were being deserted.

"NKVD?"

"Zimmermann was in the hands of the NKVD—a Colonel Aladko, one of those NKVD people with a passport that belonged to a dead volunteer in one of the International Brigades, I forget which one. Zimmermann and Schiller were both under the close supervision of this revisionist Aladko..." The words had emerged in a flurry; the desperate display of identity documents.

The car horn tooted, impatiently.

"Where is Schiller?" Aubrey asked greedily. "Is he alive?"

Wei shook his head. "I do not know. Hans-Dieter Schiller. That is all I heard..." Wei subsided into his fears. Aubrey clenched his fists, then said: "You will be taken care of, Colonel. You have nothing to fear." Wei seemed not to hear, but to be engaged in some renewed, and fiercer, inward debate.

Aubrey left the room. McIntosh was waiting impatiently in the lounge, like a host anxious to see the last of his troublesome guests.

"The car's waiting . . ." he began unnecessarily.

"Take the greatest care of Wei," Aubrey replied. "He's far from played out."

"Of course."

The cassette tape on the recorder increased in volume. Aubrey turned his head. Hyde was standing by the recorder, listening. The piano floated a pretty, high melody into the room, delicate, ethereal, syncopated. The pianist provided a grunting, breathy, unintended accompaniment. Hyde's eyes were closed. Then, savagely, he ejected the tape with a loud click like the magnified cocking of a pistol.

"For luck," he said. "OK." He breathed deeply, shrugged his shoulders, and followed Aubrey through the hall and kitchen of the house to the rear entrance.

Two cars. Two peaked-capped policemen in wind-flapped shorts standing by the empty car. They seemed relieved to see Aubrey.

"Get in the car—and you, Godwin," Aubrey fussily instructed. Then he turned to McIntosh. "In case I have an accident," he said above the wind's noise, "get a signal off to Shelley at once. A full check, pre-war, wartime, post-war, on a Condor Legion officer named Hans-Dieter Schiller—presumably Abwehr like Zimmermann—captured with our German friend. I want to know whether he's alive, and where he is. Soonest."

"Very well. I'll do that right away."

Aubrey felt reluctance grip him like a great weariness, then he merely nodded, and crossed to the car. Godwin was seated next to the driver, Hyde in the rear. Aubrey slid in next to him. A police officer bent his head to Aubrey's window.

"Everything's arranged, Mr. Aubrey. You'll be the second car. We won't be far ahead, and we'll keep our eyes and ears open. Your driver will call us on the radio as soon as there's any sign of trouble." He paused, then added: "You're sure you're being sensible, sir?"

"No, I'm not. Nevertheless, I'm here."

"Very good, sir. You think there will be trouble?"

"I don't know. We shall see."

The inspector hurried off to the escort car and climbed in. Aubrey wound up the window, and the booming, howling wind above which the inspector had had to shout lessened its protest. Its rage seemed conveyed to the chassis of the car, as if the

police saloon was being buffeted by some large animal. Aubrey
brushed his remaining hair flat, irritated at his dishevelment.
Hyde had the Heckler & Koch across his lap. Aubrey heard the
click as Godwin cocked his Walther, before the noise of the car
engine increased as they turned in the drive to follow the escort
car. Hyde seemed audibly engaged in breathing exercises. Aubrey
felt the hot water of a potential field engagement with a meta-
phorical elbow; aware, unusually, of his seniority, of his significance within SIS, of his age, of all the mouldering and mint-new
secrets in his old head—aware, perhaps most evidently, of the
unfinished business to which this escapade was no more than a
sideshow. Uncomic relief. He disliked the manner in which the
chessboard always seemed, finally, to resolve itself into the
killing-floor, the arena, the bullring. Papers, microfilm, micro-
fiche, codes, signals, instructions, operations, missions, objectives; all in the end becoming a matter of living, killing, dying,
wounds and pain. He had no business here. He had the wrong
adrenaline—he had an old man's covetous, remembered, dry
adrenaline—for this kind of business . . .

The stars seemed to be moved by the wind, motes of bright
dust. Mount Kellett loomed to Aubrey's left as the road began to
drop away towards the scattered, strung-together lights of Hong
Kong. Across the dark strip of the bay, beyond Hyde's dyed
profile, it seemed that the lights of Kowloon were dimmer,
failing. The wind was opaque, light-absorbing. Aubrey was
surprised at his increased, almost hallucinatory awareness.

Victoria Peak to Aubrey's left, another humped, shoulder-
turned mass protecting itself against the cyclone. The lights of
the car escorting them disappeared as it rounded a bend. Their
driver accelerated slightly to catch up.

The black, lightless car rammed into the side of their vehicle,
emerging suddenly from the white-walled drive of a house on the
bend, a house without lights, like the car. Aubrey's driver
wrestled with the wheel as their car was slewed across Peak
Road towards the steep slope below the road. The black saloon
drove on like a bull-dozer, a heavy American sedan with a big
engine. Aubrey's driver managed to slow their car, halt it with
its nose jutting into darkness over the stones at the verge of the
road; the force of the other car expended itself in rending the
metal of the wing and door. Aubrey felt the plastic of the door
lining bulge against his knee. He could see the face of the driver
of the American sedan as the car's nose slid along the side of

their own vehicle. The wind howled against Aubrey as Hyde pushed open his door.

"Down!" Hyde yelled, dragging at Aubrey's elbow. "Radio!" he yelled to the driver, who was clasping his shaking hands together to still them. Then Hyde was gone, rolling out of the door of the car.

Hyde rolled away from the car and rose to a sitting position, the pistol held stiffly out in front of him. The driver, almost lost in the howling wind, was radioing the escort car. Then there were two distant shots, and then only the crackling voice from the radio, creaking through the ether and the storm. The wind jolted him in the back. He knew Godwin would be unable to get out of the car with the American sedan jammed up against the door. He was, effectively, alone.

The battered radiator of the sedan jutted out behind the police car. He waited. Beyond it, the whitewashed wall of the house was like a backcloth, a sheet against which might be played some improvised children's drama, full of high voices and shouting and stiff, unreal poses. He remembered them from his infants' school days, his own attempts at characterization much like the stiff-armed pose he now adopted, holding the pistol.

We have followed the star to Bethlehem, to bring gifts of gold and frank—frank—frankissence . . . In a nervous, heavily accented, piping voice, his mother in agonies, unable to prompt him, in the front row.

A shadow against the whitewashed wall, moving out from behind the American sedan. Hyde fired twice, and the shadow— *myrrh*—flicked aside, leaving the wall whole and clean once more. Hyde rolled again, then got to his knees. The lights of the city behind him would outline him, so would the wall across the road. He got to his feet, swaying like a drunk in the wind, the rough wine of adrenaline coursing through him. Bent almost double, he began running.

Shouts, whipped away by the wind. Shots, a high whine near his head, then he had reached the steps that climbed up to the house with the white wall. He turned back in the darkness and saw two, then three figures detach themselves from the massed lump of the cars. Someone was trying to climb through the sunroof of the police car—Godwin's light suit. Two stabs of flame, almost no noise, and one of the figures stumbled and fell.

A second car roared round the bend and screeched to a halt. They must have passed it without seeing it, back up Peak Road. Men debouched from it immediately, two of them firing in the direction of the crash. Godwin's light suit slipped back into the interior of the car, and Hyde could not tell whether the man had been hit or was merely taking cover. He felt chilled to the bone and turned, racing up the steps, then thrust himself into and through the bushes that flanked them. He emerged into the open space of an ornamental garden. He felt water on his face, the wind flicking the spray of the fountain across the garden. The moonlight was faint and low, and he crouched in the lee of the fountain.

Voices, shapes that might have been illusion or only shadows; no noise of a car arriving. The pretend-urine from the penis of the boy's stone statue on top of the fountain was funnelled up and away from him in a fine spray. A dark shape was altered by the flaring of a blown overcoat. Hyde fired. The figure dropped to the grass. His fire was returned from others. Chips flew from the stone boy, grazing his cheek. He fired again, and the figures scattered. He wondered, with an excitement that threatened to topple into dread even as he experienced it, whether Petrunin was one of those illusory shapes. He doubted it.

How safe was he? Alive, or dead? Did it matter?

Then the shadows seemed all around him, perhaps five—no, six?—becoming visible and solid as the rising moon peered above the peaks; a slender nail-paring, but enough to cast shadows.

"Give up." He did not know which shadow spoke. "Chinaman," it added. The shadows moved closer, flapping, bulging, changing in outline at the wind's demand. "You understand? Night-sights, you understand? Night-glasses? We can see you. By the fountain."

Hyde listened for the noise of a car. If they had taken out the escort car? Twenty seconds or more was enough time. Where was it?

They'd kill him when they discovered the dye, the lack of slanted, almond eyes. In rage and frustration, they'd kill . . . Car engine? No lights in the house. Siren?

The shadows moved closer.

"Stay away!" he yelled. "Stay back!" The shadows paused. Engine, siren? Voices? Running boots, lights? "Stay away from me!" he yelled against the wind, a high, panicky protest.

Siren running down, running footsteps, cold running water on his hand from the fountain. The shadows dispersed. Stabs of flame in the night, sparks from a policeman's boots as he skidded into stillness on the steps, yells, more shots . . .

Then only the wind. Hyde rose to his feet, the policeman's hand supporting his forearm and his weight.

"Thanks, mate. How's—?"

"Hyde? Hyde, are you all right, man?" The querulous voice of an old man whose occupation or leisure had been disturbed. A bent black figure on the steps up to the house, the police inspector standing beside him. "Hyde?"

"I'm all right."

"Thank goodness."

Hyde walked unsteadily, not because of the wind's buffeting, across the garden to join Aubrey. Relief became aggression the moment he reached the steps.

"You won't want any more bloody proof, will you?" he snapped. Aubrey stared at him in surprise. The inspector seemed personally affronted. "They'd have killed a bloody dozen to get hold of Colonel bloody Wei, wouldn't they? Because you told them about him—because you're here in person to talk to him!"

"Hyde—"

"You want more bloody proof? You've had a copper killed, and one of your own people—"

"Godwin was merely grazed," Aubrey remarked icily. "He'll be all right."

"Wei's telling the bloody truth, though, isn't he?"

"They wanted you alive, did they not?"

"Y—yes . . . Why?"

"If they *knew* already everything there was to know, perhaps they would simply have killed you? Perhaps they know as little as we do?"

"Balls! They're panicking because Wei's told us about their precious sleeper!"

"Perhaps they're panicking because of the Berlin Treaty? Perhaps that is important enough to justify the interference of Petrunin, the capture of Wei?" Aubrey was shouting now, both of them battling each other and the wind. The police inspector had walked away from them and was engaged in inspecting the dead constable further up the moonlit steps. "I'm sorry, but we know only a little more than we did this afternoon, Hyde."

"Then I got shot at for nothing?"

"To protect Wei, I'm afraid."

"Christ! You're wrong, you know. Wei's genuine, and the Russians think they're up shit creek."

"I am *not* convinced—"

"I bloody am, mate! Zimmermann's as guilty as hell! He's a bloody KGB agent!"

"No," Liu said, shaking his head reluctantly. "It's not enough. These files have been washed, I'm afraid."

"My money? I have done as you asked. I have earned my money."

"You'll get your money," Liu assured him, handing back the files, letting them slip out of the pool of white lamplight under which they had lain as he studied them. They became shadowy in the room's lantern light—the electricity supply for the block of workers' apartments had failed an hour earlier, and they had had to climb fourteen flights of stairs to this flat—and their shadow-nature seemed highlighted to Liu. He had learned nothing from them.

Except that, on the assumption they had been washed, there must have been a serious reason to tamper with hospital files. Unless the tale was untrue, all of it. Wei's story in Hong Kong, the orderly Bin's story here in Shanghai . . . The suspicion had insinuated itself, sneaking up on his awareness, like the attribution of an unworthy motive to a friend.

There were four of them in the room, apart from Bin. Himself, the girl Liang, and the young couple who occupied the flat and who were part of the loose federation of individuals that the CIA described as its cell in Shanghai. For security reasons, Frederickson had instructed Liang not to take Liu to Bin's house in the old city again. Instead, he had been brought here to a newish concrete block in a northern suburb of the city, and the young man's wife had brought Bin.

David Liu stood up, stretched casually, then crossed to the window of the small living room. He tugged back the thin curtains. The afternoon was heavy with cloud. A trolley-bus passed along the tree-lined avenue fourteen floors below him. Beyond the road, the suburb came to an abrupt, neat end. Tiny figures were watering the year's winter wheat crop on the flat green expanse of a commune, a sulky, hesitant wind whipping the hosed jets into tendrils of spray like peacocks' tails. Beyond the green were the pylons and wires and transformers of a power station. Specks in white shirts moved on bicycles along a distant road near the power station.

Liu felt himself in control of his situation, even though frustration at Bin's purloined files thrust itself into his awareness, made his skin prickle with a desire for action, for results. He urned back to study the occupants of the room. A look passed etween Liang and Bin which he could not identify, but which eemed to possess a familiarity, even an intimacy, their supposedly light acquaintance would not have engendered. The residents of he flat, the young man and his wife, also seemed enclosed within the circle of the glance and smile, both of which winked ut like lamps as he turned to face them. Liu suddenly felt solated, alone—confronted?

It was an almost feline sensation, something to distrust, not ased on fact. Mood, insight, feeling? Mistrust of his compan-ons asserted itself, and he did not resist it; surprised, neverthe-ess, at its appearance. He endeavoured to control his features.

"My money?" Bin requested sullenly, holding out his hand, gripping the files on his lap with his other hand. Liu withdrew his wallet and carefully counted out ten notes, each of twenty dollars. Bin fished the yuans out of his pocket, and offered them n exchange. Liu watched his face carefully.

"Keep those," he said. "You did your best. Here." Bin's nthusiasm hesitated beneath his skin for a moment, then bloomed n his features.

"Thank you, thank you." It sounded rehearsed. Liu felt himself adrift in a mass of contrary emotional, physical, and ubconscious information. He had to leave them, get away omewhere and consider, reflect, analyse.

"There's nothing more you can tell me?" Liu's inclined head ndicated the files.

"No. None of it is here, is it?"

"No, it's not. Pity."

"You believe me? I was telling the truth."

"Yes, I believe you," Liu replied levelly. He turned back to he window, his eyes seeking out the distant power station, then he road and the white-spot cyclists, then the green wheat fields being watered with peacock's-tail sprays, then the tree-lined avenue and . . .

A car. Parked on the opposite side of the avenue from the block of flats. He could not tell whether or not it was occupied. With a sure and chilling instinct he knew it was a surveillance car.

That morning he had been certain he was being followed. The car had been parked outside the Shanghai Mansions all night—he had checked on it periodically. Foot-surveillance all morning by someone who followed him even into the restaurant where he had lunched. Then, perhaps half an hour before he was to meet

Liang, nothing. Surveillance withdrawn—or only dreamed in the first place, figments of stretched, raw nerves. Now, another car. He would note whether it returned to the city centre in the wake of the bus he would have to catch.

What did they want? They had to be PSB or MPT—the department did not matter. He was the object of their attention perhaps the girl, and now himself as a contact? Perhaps, too, the people in this flat, perhaps even Bin?

He turned back into the room. No, it would have to be Frederickson who answered his questions, not any of these people. These he did not know, could not trust.

"We must go," Liang informed him, as if deliberately breaking a tension of which she was subtly aware.

"Yes, of course." He had to get away from the girl now. The car in the street, and the medical orderly. His mind focused on those three objectives. How? How could he wait around, without the girl? "Thank you," he said once more to Bin. "And thank you." He had not been introduced by name to either of the flat's residents. They stood and bowed formally. Liu returned the gesture. Bin appeared in no haste to depart. "We'll leave first," he said, for Bin's benefit—for the benefit of all of them.

"Yes, yes." Bin now seemed eager to see him gone. He had folded and pocketed the two hundred dollars. The yuans, however, lay carelessly on the floor by his chair, as did the files, theatrical props that had served their purpose, Liu could not help reflecting.

Why had the young man drawn the curtains? The flat was not overlooked. Had it been a signal? It had seemed natural at the time, covert, properly secretive. But there had been no need. Had the room been bugged?

They descended the stairs. Suspicion gripped Liu, fear assailed him like waves of nausea. He imagined or guessed no motive for his suspicions, simply entertained the doubt itself, the subtle, corrupt aroma of the set-up, the mantrap. The meat being used as bait was beginning to smell. The girl, descending flight after flight in front of him, seemed unaware of his tense and altered mood. Her slight back and narrow shoulders became objects of revulsion to him. He wanted to beat the truth from her.

Outside, the wind flapped and billowed the girl's thin cotton trousers. It searched his drab suit. He forced himself not to look across the avenue at the parked car beneath the trees as they walked the few hundred yards to the bus stop. An old man and two children waited for the trolley-bus. Liu held himself under

control with an increasing effort, answering the girl's few innoc-
uous comments as casually as he could. The car was occupied,
he observed. Two men. They were too distant to betray whether
they were watching the bus stop.

He did not know what he could do, even at the moment when
the trolley-bus arrived and its door sighed open. He helped the
old man onto the bus, indicating to Liang that she should board
first, with the two children. The old man's wisp of beard bobbed
his feeble gratitude. His lips worked as if he were chewing the
reassurances Liu supplied thoughtlessly, his mind racing, the
beginnings of action occurring to him as a sketchy, grainy film of
physical activity.

Bus stop, pneumatic doors, shelter, flats, car, trees, Bin...

"OK," he called to the driver further up the bus. The doors
immediately began to sigh shut. Liu stepped nimbly backwards,
onto the pavement again. Liang's face moved through surprise,
then shock, then a narrow and enraged suspicion. As the doors
closed, masking her features momentarily until she moved her
head to keep him in sight, Liu admitted that he must surrender to
his suspicions. The realization chilled him. The trolley-bus
moved away down the almost deserted avenue, beneath the trees.

The parked car did not move. Liu watched it from the shelter
of a tree, craning his head furtively round the bole to keep it in
view. He felt foolish and inadequate; he fought to keep his sense
of isolation under control. It was too raw and potent to be
ignored. He did not have much time. Liang would get off the bus
at the next stop, come running back...

He studied the block of flats, counting the floors up to the
fourteenth, but he could not satisfactorily locate the window of
the room which contained Bin and the married couple. Would
Bin come out, and soon?

The medical orderly emerged from the flats. Liu immediately
glanced behind him and saw that the distant blue speck of the
bus had stopped. His heart pounded. Bin glanced towards the
bus stop, then immediately crossed the avenue to the parked car.
Even though it was the evidence he desired, Liu could not
believe what he saw. His mind, for its own peace, attempted to
reject the information. Bin leaned into the car, handing the files
to the passenger.

Liu turned his head and looked down the perspective of the
avenue. A single distant figure. He sensed it was running in his
direction. Liang. Perhaps no more than a minute away. Bin and

the police. Doctored files. The girl was part of it, too. The whole of Frederickson's Shanghai cell? How many others were there?

Bin climbed into the back of the car. Carefully, assessing that the trees masked him from the car and from the flats, Liu began to walk towards the running figure approaching him. It was the girl, and she was running. He strolled, composing his features and his lies. He had to talk to Frederickson.

The girl slowed as she saw him coming towards her. He grinned, and held his arms out in a gesture of helplessness, apologetically. The girl's face was bland, out-of-breath, her eyes searched his face, then looked beyond him towards the car.

"What were you doing?" she asked in a tone of reprimand.

"Sorry. I was fazed." She appeared puzzled. He tapped his forehead. "Not thinking. Helped the old man on, forgot I wanted the bus myself." He broadened his grin. "Sorry. Mind on other things."

"Oh." She evidently did not believe him. Her eyes kept straying between his face and the car. She seemed, however, to decide to accept the transparent fiction of his excuse; no doubt, Liu concluded, that would last only until she received orders. "I thought you might have forgotten something."

"No. There's nothing more to be learned here," he said lightly.

"No, I suppose not," she agreed.

"What time's the next bus?"

"What? Oh, another ten minutes."

"Let's walk on to the next stop, then."

"Yes," she agreed eagerly.

Liu took her arm, and they began walking. Somewhere behind him, he heard the noise of a car engine starting, then the retreating sound of its engine as it drove off.

Frederickson, he thought. I have to talk to him.

Strangely, he did not feel endangered, not in any immediate sense. For some reason, they were letting him run. These people were . . . misleading him, yes, that was it, for a purpose. He could not imagine why. Misinformation. Presumably they were covering up the Zimmermann business. They were the smoke-screen around the subject. They contradicted Wei.

He kept a tremor of excitement under control as he held the girl's arm. Wei could be right, then. *Was* right? There *was* something to hide. They were trying to lead him by the nose.

Frederickson. He would have to talk to the CIA man himself, but not via the girl.

"You have heard, of course, of the unfortunate events of this afternoon?"

"Right. Your people messed up."

"I do not think that your accusations are justified. Perhaps your man is not as naïve as you suggested."

"He's suspicious now."

"In what way, precisely?"

"I don't know. He hasn't called."

"He will. I suggest a smokescreen, a diversion."

"Like . . ."

"The arrest of the whole cell, everyone he has met. To take place when he is present. A convincing arrest, perhaps with one or two wounded, even dead. That is not important."

"Wait a minute—"

"Conviction is of the essence, my friend. Liu must be persuaded of the truth as Wei has told it."

"Give him the truth, then."

"Not yet. He must work for it. Then he will believe it. In Wu Han, perhaps."

"OK."

"You must make arrangements for Liu to reach Wu Han. Please inform me of his report, when he makes it. Then I shall make the necessary arrangements for our smokescreen."

"If he's too suspicious, if I can't persuade him—"

"Then he, too, will become the responsibility of the ministry. But please try to avoid that."

"I'll work on it."

"Please do so."

In the darkness, Frederickson was no more than a shadow, a reassuring yet mysterious bulk. Couples, hand in hand or with their arms around each other, strolled past the bench on which Liu and Frederickson sat in Huangpu Park. A breeze moved the smell of the river and its noises towards them. The boom of a barge's horn, the creak of wood, the slapping of water against concrete and vessels. Navigation lights sidled past them like low constellations. The lovers, hundreds of them, were like a formal, erotic garden, or another elaborate mime. Vertically, they imitated coition, suggested an organised, ritualised privacy tolerated by the State. The murmuring hubbub of their conversations imitated the dialogue between himself and the American, suggesting a community of secrets. Somewhere, a transistor radio played approved music.

"What does it all amount to, Liu?" Frederickson asked bluntly, his profile just discernible against the warm stars. "What exactly do you suspect?"

Liu had telephoned the consulate and cryptically arranged the meeting without identifying himself. Now, hours after the bus doors had shut and he had seen Liang's face, hours after Bin had leaned into the car, he was uncertain, hesitant, inclined to disbelieve his own senses.

"I—am not sure."

"You think this guy Bin was bait?" Frederickson listened to the silence from Liu, realizing that he might have voiced a point of view that had not occurred to him.

"Bait? How do you mean?"

"It's not impossible they know who you are, why you're here. Bin was a risk—he's not one of our people. You think he was planted on you?"

"But he confirmed Wei's story, at first."

"To gain your confidence, maybe?"

"But the girl . . ."

"She never trusted Bin."

"I don't mean that. I mean, on the bus—she panicked when I got off."

"She told me. She was worried, about you. You're her responsibility, man."

"I see . . ." Liu sounded hopefully thoughtful to Frederickson. The American was glad of the darkness. Murmuring lovers strolled past against the lights of a small freighter. "Then Bin is hiding the truth?"

"Wouldn't the Chinese like you to go home and disprove everything Wei's telling them in Hong Kong?"

"Of course, but—"

"Then maybe that's the name of the game? You were there, Liu. Do you trust Bin?"

"He's an addict. If they have him by that rope, he's theirs all the way down the line . . ."

Frederickson hesitated before he spoke. Liu's quiet voice sounded as if he were on the point of convincing himself; taking the hook.

"Well?"

"Perhaps."

"OK. We'll wrap things up here. Get you to Wu Han tomorrow, or the day after."

"Won't they be expecting me?"

"I'll get you a new cover. Things are too tight in Shanghai. Maybe up-country they've been more slack, or people may be readier to talk." Frederickson stood up. "I'll be in touch. And Liu—"

"Yes?"

"Watch your back, uh?"

"Yes."

"South Australia? You're certain?" Aubrey glared at Hyde, who had guffawed with surprised laughter. "Near Adelaide?"

"I never liked Adelaide," Hyde murmured into his beer.

"Shut up, Hyde," Aubrey snapped. Godwin smothered a companionable grin, an expression which turned to one of discomfort as the plaster on his temple tugged at entrapped hairs.

"You can't drink the water," Hyde added.

Aubrey looked up from the signal pad that McIntosh had brought with him from the cellar of the house where the communications equipment was housed. McIntosh seemed to hold himself responsible for the information from London. He appeared guilty and evasive.

"That's what it said, Mr. Aubrey. That's Shelley's signal."

"And the 1940 files?"

"I've sent through another request. He doesn't mention them."

"I see that. I *must* have those files." Aubrey looked at Hyde, slumped on the sofa, the headphones he had been using to listen to the stereo system lying like a dark crab on his lap. "Hyde?"

"Sir."

"Does all this sound likely to you? I know absolutely nothing about Australian wines, but I find it difficult to imagine a former Abwehr officer inheriting a vineyard in South Australia. Do you?"

Hyde shook his head. "You've missed a lot that's worth drinking," he said.

"Forget the salesmanship, Hyde."

"Adelaide's surrounded by vineyards—it's the capital of the Australian wine business. Where is this vineyard—Barossa Valley?"

"Yes. How did you know?"

"It used to be a German settlement, in the old days. They brought the vines. There's still plenty of Krauts speaking pure 'trine up there." Hyde grinned. "A relative died, Schiller—

fancied a change, packs his bags and goes off to grow grapes. Why not?''

"This wine is of good quality?" Aubrey asked ingenuously.

"The best is really good." Then Hyde's eyes narrowed. "You'll get the chance to taste some, won't you?"

"I—haven't decided."

"You want to talk to Schiller?" McIntosh asked in surprise. "In person? But, sir, what about Wei?"

Aubrey passed a hand over his eyes. He had spent most of the day at Victoria Prison. He was weary of Wei, prepared to flee the man's intractable company. "I cannot break him," he admitted. "He has retreated again, just as I foresaw, now that he believes himself safe. Perhaps Buckholz..." He looked at the signal again. "A fresh approach, for two or three days." He cleared his throat. It appeared to be Hyde that he wished to convince, unless the Australian was no more than a mirror in which Aubrey was carefully arranging his features. "Everything we have learned goes back to Spain, and to 1938. It was there, if anywhere, that Zimmermann was recruited by the NKVD. This man Schiller was with him. I think it's worth the journey—worth the distraction."

"I agree, sir," Godwin intruded.

"Yes," Hyde added.

"Very well. McIntosh, I shall want two tickets for Adelaide, for tomorrow. Understand this, however. Mr. Buckholz is to have full access to Wei, but he is not—I repeat, he is *not*—to remove Wei from Victoria Prison."

"Don't worry. The Yanks will have to wait."

"If he interrogates Wei, it is to be with one of you two present, and everything is to be recorded."

"How much do you think Wei knows, sir?" McIntosh asked.

Aubrey shrugged. "Everything? Nothing? I don't know. To him, information is wealth, and he has become miserly—until he sees we are doing something for his future. No, at the moment, I am more interested in what Hans-Dieter Schiller, late of the Abwehr and now of the Barossa Valley, has to offer in the way of information."

"Will he talk?"

"If he doesn't, I think he will encounter all sorts of problems with the Australian authorities."

"Sir?" Godwin asked.

"Yes?"

"What about Petrunin and his friends?"

"As long as they do not find out, then they're not a worry."

The dead Russians had, improbably, all been carrying Irish passports bearing the proper stamps and visas. Aubrey had ordered that close surveillance be kept on the antique shop, and then had chosen to ignore the KGB in Hong Kong. Wei was safe, and that was the end of the matter.

"I see, sir," Godwin murmured dubiously.

"Make sure they don't find out. Whatever measures are required, Hyde and myself must leave Hong Kong secretly."

"Yes, sir."

FIVE

Trapdoor

"I am afraid there can be no quibbling with regard to your people."

"Look, when we agreed to make them known to you, for the purposes of this operation, you guaranteed their safety."

"That is true. It is the safety of the operation, however, which is paramount. Would you not agree?"

"Of course I have to agree—"

"Then Liu must be convinced. If your people have to die, then that is regrettable, but necessary."

"I can't see it that way—"

"As agents, they became inoperative as soon as we were told their names. You cannot use them again."

"That's not the point—"

"Isn't it, my friend? Well, in deference to your Western ideas of the value of human life, I will see what can be done. But if it is necessary, then you will have to mourn them. Their families, no doubt, will be taken care of. Very well, instruct the girl to contact Liu."

Liu had slept badly, a twisting, perspiring repository of anxieties, fears and expectations. His clarity of thought had been gradually eroded by his sense of isolation and dependence. Frederickson's explanations and answers had not been satisfactory, but he had no solutions of his own upon which he could depend, and the CIA station head in Shanghai was the only person he inclined towards trusting; his senior officer, his case officer. David Liu could not rid himself of the sense of being entirely alone. He was an American with a yellow face in the middle of China's most populous city; the police were tailing him and his confederates seemed engaged in betraying him.

He eventually got up, shaved and washed, and took up a

stance at the window, gathering strength to go down to the hotel restaurant for breakfast. From his window, he could not see the police car he knew must be watching the hotel. What he did see, however, was the girl walking on the road below him, beside the Suzhou Creek. Red tunic, black trousers. As he watched her, his body masked by the curtain and the window frame, she periodically glanced up as if searching for his window. Her walk, her pause, her upward looks, all conspired to enrage him. What did the girl want? What could she possibly have to say? How would she explain . . .

Buttoning his jacket, he left his room and took the lift to the ground floor. He strode through the hotel foyer, oblivious of any police surveillance, and swiftly jostled his way across the crowded pavement, then whisked alertly like a matador between the rush of cycles, until the girl was no more than a few yards from him. At that moment, she saw him approaching.

"What do you want?" he asked coldly. The hesitant smile slipped back inside her mouth.

"Frederickson sent me," she said hurriedly. "I have your papers—your new cover." She seemed to wish to lead him out of the throng. Liu followed her. Papers, cover? Frederickson still trusted her, then.

They walked down concrete steps to a narrow towpath beside the creek. Here the bustle diminished and the age of the pedestrians increased dramatically. Old people engaged in *tai ji chuan,* shadow-boxing, moving slowly and aquatically in deference to ageing sinews and muscles, or sitting calmly on the benches, watching the river traffic. A train-like convoy of barges sidled towards the bridge and the Huangpu River beyond it.

"My papers?" he demanded, his hand held out to her. Their pace was slow, imitative of the other inhabitants of the towpath.

Liang reached into her red tunic and removed a small package wrapped in clear polythene, secured with elastic bands.

"Here," she said.

"What are Frederickson's instructions?" He slipped into the habit of trust. The papers were like securities, bankers' drafts on her loyalty to the CIA.

"Why do you not trust me?" she asked. "Bin was a mistake. Bin was not my fault—everything was so hurried . . ." She appeared hurt rather than angry. Her crumpled, expressive features were appealing. "It was a risk. He must have told the police."

"Perhaps," Liu replied, not unmoved. He scanned the towpath for surveillance. Unless it was one of the grandparents here, there was none. A barge horn sounded a dragon-like bellow, startling them both. Liu grinned.

"I ran back to you," she said, "because Frederickson made you my responsibility . . ." she explained lamely. Her very hesitancy implied amateurishness rather than deceit, and Liu accepted it as such.

"OK," he said. "Bin's scrubbed out. Are the police still watching the hotel?"

"When I arrived, yes. Then the car left."

"I wonder why?"

"Perhaps a change of shift?"

"Maybe. OK—Frederickson's instructions?"

"You leave for Wu Han tomorrow on the morning train. Your tickets are with your papers. Your cover is as a minor Party official being transferred to Wu Han from Shanghai—promotion." She smiled. "Frederickson himself will be there—there is a U.S. delegation of businessmen travelling to Wu Han by air tomorrow from Peking. Frederickson, as Trade Attaché, will accompany them during their visit." Liu felt absurdly, overwhelmingly comforted by the knowledge that Frederickson would be on hand. "You will be met at Wu Han station. You must, however, ensure that you are not observed boarding the train." Liu nodded. With the pale blue sky behind them, the figures walking across the bridge over the creek looked like mechanically swimming ducks in a shooting gallery. It was an unnerving, unbidden image.

"Anything else?"

"There will be a suitcase at the station—here is the locker key." She handed it to him, and he pocketed it as swiftly as if it had been stolen.

"A gun?" he asked involuntarily.

"No."

Liu recovered. "Of course not."

"Do not book out of the hotel here."

"Naturally. Anything else?"

"Tonight . . ."

"What about tonight?"

"We have someone for you, to make up for Bin."

"Who?"

"A policeman."

Liu appeared stunned by the information. "What?"

"No!" the girl cried as if he had struck her. "One of our

people, one of *Frederickson*'s people. He is a police clerk, no more than that. He is not often used, he has little access..."

Liu recovered himself, and prompted her when she faltered. "Go on. A police clerk?"

"Frederickson put him to work as soon as Bin became suspect. He may have something by tonight..."

"Is he known to be one of your cell?" The girl shrugged. "It's important. Through Bin, you're known, so are the couple in the flat. Who else?"

"I cannot tell. No one has been near him since—since the error with Bin."

"What information?"

"Who visited the German, how many times, perhaps what records were kept, I do not know. It will be dangerous for him, but he will try. Will you meet him?"

Liu hesitated, then he said: "Why can't this clerk feed his information through you or one of the others?"

Liang appeared shamed. Looking at her feet, she said: "Frederickson does not trust us—we are not trained agents. Who knows if this man is secure? He wants you to judge, not us."

Liu nodded. "Very well. Tonight. Where?"

"The Yu Garden, in the Old Town. Directions are with your other papers."

"What time?"

"He will finish his shift at ten. Ten-thirty will give him time to reach the meeting place."

"OK. Now, leave. I don't want to be seen with you again, not today. You, keep off the streets, keep away from your flat. Understand?"

"Frederickson, too, has given me the same instructions."

"And me—I'll try not to get arrested." The girl looked fearful, but Liu grinned. "Don't worry, somehow I don't think they're ready to pull me in yet. They don't know enough. After all, if they keep close to me, I could lead them to every agent Frederickson's got in southern China, couldn't I?"

Aubrey, like a child with a new comic delivered with his father's morning paper, could not resist glancing through the record of his interrogation of Zimmermann in 1940 as he ate his late breakfast. The files had arrived in the Bag on the day's first flight from London. Pineapple, boiled egg, toast and marmalade, fruit juice, coffee. He bit and swallowed each mouthful of his meal without noticing what he ate. His eyes, alert and gleaming though they appeared, were not focused on the breakfast table, even on the dining room. Hyde, with the previous day's *Daily Telegraph* propped against the condiment set, was enjoying his fried meal and the complete county cricket averages on one of the sports pages. He had already, wistfully, read the racing page.

"What time are you expecting Buckholz?"

"What? Oh!" Aubrey's damp blue eyes cleared and narrowed their focus. "Americans seem to have invented an atrocity called the working breakfast. He should have been here by now. I postponed the meal-time as much as I could." Aubrey's look of ironic amusement vanished, and weariness possessed his face. Hyde wondered whether the journey ahead daunted the old man, or if Wei dragged at his optimism. He was locked as tightly as a cuckolded, worshipping lover into the unsatisfactory relationship with the Chinese defector. Whatever Aubrey learned in the Barossa Valley, it was to Hong Kong he would have to return, and it was that relationship he would have to take up once again.

He attended to the buff folder and its closely typed, grimy-edged sheets of paper. There was a musty smell of age and blind alleys vying with the smoked bacon in front of Hyde.

"Schiller may have the answer, you know," Hyde suggested, slicing his fried bread then neatly apportioning a slice of bacon and egg to it before opening his mouth. "He could say, yes it happened, or no, it wasn't like that."

"Do you think I could believe him if he said no?" Aubrey asked in irritation.

"Then why ask him?"

"As you remarked, he might say yes. Or I might be able to tell he's lying if he says no." Aubrey sighed. "I *have* to ask him." Aubrey looked up. Buckholz entered the room, ushered in by Godwin. Aubrey, almost furtive with haste, closed the folder on the table and slipped it beneath his copy of the previous day's *Times*. "My dear Charles!" he exclaimed, with a bonhomie that was transparently false to Hyde, as he stood up to welcome the American.

"Kenneth." The two men shook hands. Aubrey indicated a chair. Buckholz acknowledged Hyde's presence with a slight, though not dismissive, nod.

"What would you like?"

"Just coffee." Buckholz appeared on edge, undecided whether affability or bullying would serve his purpose. Hyde ate attentively, the *Telegraph*'s close print blurring as he pretended to study it. "Kenneth—"

"Yes, Charles?" Aubrey poured coffee for Buckholz and himself. "What can I do for you?"

"It's about Wei—"

"Yes?" Aubrey was at his most ingenuous. "What about Wei?"

"I think it's time we got our hands on him."

"But you have. It's your interrogation, from today."

Buckholz watched Aubrey, his grey eyes alert, his cropped, whitening hair and broad shoulders implicitly threatening the small old man. "You know what I mean, Kenneth. Wei is, in all but name, our responsibility already. He wants asylum in the States, it's us he really came to. China's our sphere of influence. So is Germany, for that matter. I want him, Kenneth. Transfer him to my custody."

Aubrey's eyes narrowed. His cheeks seemed more lank. His brow was furrowed, as if he was inwardly debating the administrative difficulties involved. Hyde knew he was gathering defiance.

"I'm sorry, Charles, it just isn't possible." Buckholz's face coloured slightly. "You have complete freedom of access to him—"

"In company with one of your people! What's the matter, Kenneth? You don't trust me?"

Aubrey's lips pursed in displeasure. "It is not a matter of trust, not at all. Wei was fished out of the harbour by members of the Hong Kong police force. He is, therefore, my country's responsibility. Quite definitely, and quite properly. Until my investigations are completed, he remains in Victoria Prison where, incidentally, he is most secure, under the closest supervision."

"And that's your last word?"

"It is."

"You're making a mistake."

"I hope not."

Buckholz shrugged, and grinned slowly and reluctantly. When he spoke again, his voice had lost its cutting edge. "This guy in Australia, Zimmermann's old team-mate. You think you'll get results?"

"I really don't know." Aubrey was mollified by the American's change of tone. "I hope for clues, at least. If Wei is lying, then we will have to establish *why* he is lying."

"Simple anti-Soviet smear campaign."

"Quite likely. If he is telling the truth, and this man Schiller helps in any way to confirm the story, then Zimmermann will have to be exposed."

"Which would bring down Chancellor Vogel's government, and stop ratification of the treaty. Vogel's opponents wouldn't sign it."

"I realize that. That is the decision of politicians, not intelligence services. They must make up their minds in London and Washington on the basis of the facts—the *full* facts."

"And, hell, you're going to supply those facts," Buckholz said with a grin.

Aubrey smiled deprecatingly. "I hope to do so."

Buckholz stood up. "OK, Kenneth. I'll read the files you sent over on Wei's story so far, then I'll meet with him. It should be very interesting."

"As soon as I have anything—*if* I have anything—I'll be in touch with you, Charles." Aubrey stood up, and the two men shook hands once more. Buckholz left the room with an easy step that in no way lessened his bulk.

Hyde looked at Aubrey enquiringly. "What was that all about?"

"Probably irritation at sitting on the sidelines, nothing more."

Aubrey poured himself more coffee. McIntosh entered the room.

"Mr. Aubrey, it's all arranged." Aubrey indicated that he should join them at the table. "You and Hyde will board the aircraft thirty minutes before the other passengers. To all intents and purposes, you'll still be at the prison interviewing Wei when you're on your way to Australia." McIntosh seemed genuinely delighted with his arrangements.

"Good. You're certain no details of our journey will have reached our friends in the KGB?"

"Not unless they've got taps and ears in places we don't know about." McIntosh shook his head. "No, I think you can be assured they know nothing about your little jaunt to the colonies."

"Why is, Aubrey booked to fly to Australia this afternoon?" Tamas Petrunin demanded. Vassily, perched respectfully on the edge of a hard chair on the wrong side of what was normally his own desk, looked crestfallen. "Sydney, and then Adelaide? Why on earth should he leave Colonel Wei to take such a holiday?"

"I do not know, Comrade General," Vassily murmured with abject respectfulness. Petrunin, as Vassily glanced at his face from beneath drooping eyelids, did not seem flattered by the use of his rank. "We have been unable to ascertain from our sources—*any* of our sources—what connection this might have with the Englishman's investigations."

"Australia?" Petrunin muttered, as if to himself. "This matter concerns the Chinese, the Germans, the British, the Americans. It does *not* concern the Australians! You've signalled Moscow Centre?"

"Yes, Comrade General. Requesting priority time on the central computer. That was three hours ago."

Petrunin looked at his watch. "Aubrey will be leaving in two hours. You have the reservations held for Singapore?"

"Yes, and through to Perth, then Adelaide."

"Disposition of forces?"

"Sydney embassy will be organizing support in Adelaide for you—" He paused, as if he had blurted some embarrassing secret. Petrunin smiled.

"You guessed?"

"Your personal interest, Comrade General, your very great interest . . ."

"Yes, yes. I shall go, if the game seems worth the entrance fee. The man Hyde—he, of course, I know of old. A very good operative. Aubrey would not chase off to Australia on a wild-goose chase, oh, no . . ."

The telephone rang. Vassily's hand reached out automatically, then he hastily withdrew it, as if he had been burned. Hand and figure seemed to Petrunin, as he picked up the receiver, to retreat into the shadows of the hot, airless office above the restaurant. Petrunin had retreated from the antique shop which was now under close police surveillance. He expected no more provocative action from Aubrey. The smells of cooking from below were omnipresent. The fan whirred and grunted and sighed over their heads, making no inroads on the room's midday temperature.

"Comrade General?"

"Yes, yes."

"A reply to your signal, from Moscow Centre."

"Yes?"

"They've come up with a name—Schiller, that's S-c-h-i . . ."

"Never mind the spelling! Who is this man?"

"Another Abwehr officer, one who served in Spain with the repressive forces of Fascist capitalist imperialism . . ."

"The Condor Legion?" Petrunin asked with affected boredom. "Skip the ideology and get to the point. With Zimmermann?"

"Same unit—and captured in 1938 with him."

"Remarkable. And . . ."

"Schiller is now an Australian citizen. He lives in South Australia—"

"Near Adelaide?"

"Yes, Comrade General."

"You have a precise address?"

"Not yet."

"Signal Sydney—get them to find him at once. And send up the full text of the signal. Thank you." Petrunin put down the receiver. "So," he murmured, "Aubrey thinks this Schiller is worth the journey. I wonder, precisely, what Herr Schiller's importance is in the scheme of things. Don't you, Vassily?"

"Of course, Comrade General."

"Hm. Very well, hotel reservations in Adelaide. Sydney must arrange support. I want Schiller before Aubrey finds him."

"Why, Comrade General?"

"Why? How should I know? Schiller, perhaps, will tell me." Petrunin leaned forward across the desk. His eyes were bleak. "Zimmermann *is* the Berlin Treaty. Moscow feels—and I agree with Moscow—that whatever is going on, it threatens Zimmermann's position. Therefore, it threatens the Berlin Treaty. And therefore it threatens *us*. The Soviet Union. The Chinese certainly don't like the Berlin Treaty—perhaps they want to ruin matters by ruining Zimmermann? But what tale they could spin about him, I have no idea. Schiller might." He leaned back in his chair, then added: "Well, get on with it! There isn't much time if we're to be first past the post."

The clouds below the aircraft were lit by the full moon. There was no real downward perspective, and they floated like sandy islands on the glimmering sea thirty-five thousand feet below. Aubrey dozed, replete with champagne and a lobster dinner on the 747. The film being shown in the first-class section seemed demented and banal without its sound track, and created no desire to use the uncomfortable headphones. The sea below possessed more attraction, moonlit like pale lace, especially around the coastlines of the Philippines and then the Moluccas.

The record of his interrogations of Zimmermann in 1940 was locked once more in his briefcase. Zimmermann's face and voice, however, still occupied his half-sleep. Once again, Aubrey returned, in a strict chronology of recollection, to the farmhouse near Flize and the remainder of the first night of the German's capture.

He had persisted in questioning Zimmermann, even though the

man refused to admit the Abwehr connection on which Aubrey was now convinced. Zimmermann had an armour composed of quick-wittedness, humour, and courage. Aubrey, reluctantly and amid his growing frustration and self-criticism, was forced to grant the man a grudging admiration. Some impersonal part of himself, which in reality was the kernel of his future talent as an interrogator, recognized the professionalism of his prisoner.

"You are not an infantry officer, you are an officer in the Abwehr, German military intelligence," he persisted once again. On the humming aircraft, his lips moved in union with the inwardly-heard statement, and his facial muscles reproduced their twist of dislike which was his reaction to Zimmermann's easy, relaxed, patronizing smile and the shake of his blond head.

"Nineteenth Panzers," he replied.

Aubrey the old, dozing man shook his head vigorously. The laughter of some other first-class passenger at an episode of the film almost roused him. Then he slipped back to the smell of dung and hay and the oil-lamp. Rembrandt again, the little group of himself, the German and the two French brothers—both of them asleep—like a secular Nativity, lit by a warm light, with shadows gathering around them. The stamping of a cow made the two horses shuffle in their stalls. The half-dreaming Aubrey thrust himself back into the past.

"You persist with your story?"

"Of course. It is the truth." Zimmermann waggled his identity tags at Aubrey again.

"I've seen those before." Aubrey, acting by instinct, had stood up at that point and moved to the edge of the pool of light from the lamp. "Frankly, I think they're fake—but fake or not, you're here and we have the guns. I can't say I think much of your experience, your cleverness, your superiority, you know." The young Aubrey drawled and postured, imitating a debating society contempt for an opponent's argument. Some instinct guided him, indicated he should irritate the German, unsettle him. "You're my prisoner, whether you talk or not." He turned and smiled. "I'm quite pleased with myself, really, you know. First time out, and all that. A *real* German officer!" Then he had laughed softly.

"I seem to be captured quite often," Zimmermann replied, seemingly unmoved. "I must tell you that I'm used to it. I've been interrogated before, by experts."

"Captured before? Dear me, how clumsy of you. How inexpert," Aubrey mocked.

"It may be foolishness, of foolhardiness, or bravery, I do not know. I should warn you, however, that I do usually manage to get back to Berlin in time to collect my medal." Zimmermann was smiling easily. "Still," he added, "you are beginning to learn the game." Aubrey walked back into the lamplight, his face expressionless. On the face of the old man in the aircraft, there was an amused smile.

"What game?"

"The interrogation game. You are very young."

"You'll be here long enough to teach me, I'm sure."

"I doubt it. Yes, but you are learning. It is a craft at which we must work hard." He grinned. "Ignore the plural, I am only an infantry officer," he added easily. "I remember," he went on quickly, before Aubrey could interrupt, "being held in Spain, in Aragon, when I was a young officer with the Condor Legion..." It seemed to Aubrey that the far-sighted look that entered Zimmermann's eyes at that point was not assumed but real. He was looking back to some better, cleaner time, his mouth suggested as it pouted with regret. "Yes, I was interrogated by a Russian then..."

The old man, his head leaning near the window, his face gilded by the moonlight so that he was the colour of the pale clouds, the silvered sea, sensed the excitement he had experienced earlier. Not forty years or more before; then he had felt only a kind of envious curiosity towards the German's story. No, it had been just before dinner was served, when he had been reading through the files as if they had been a novel, beginning at the beginning, immersing himself in that first night of his acquaintance with Zimmermann. He had felt his heart pound, his breath become short. A steward had enquired after his health. He had requested champagne with a quite conscious sense of celebration. He had *known* Zimmermann had spoken of his capture and of his Russian interrogator, but he had needed the proof that lay in the record of that night and the subsequent days and nights.

"Go on," the young Aubrey had prompted when Zimmermann had paused at that point. Zimmermann had nodded, seeming to agree with some other part of himself that the tale had no military or intelligence significance...

The dozing Aubrey admitted that his recollection had been interrupted by dinner. His stomach had betrayed him, the gastronomic part of his imagination had greedily flooded his mind with images of lobster, a kind of imaginative mouth-watering. He should have pursued the moment, brought it back, *seen* it . . .

Zimmermann's face now, how was it? What was its exact expression? The old man's face was puckered and contracted in the gleam of moonlight from the window. Zimmermann had paused. "Go on," Aubrey had said, hardly noticing the pause or understanding it simply as a moment used to weigh the pitfalls and traps of telling it. Then the German had said:

"Yes, I remember the Russian. Aladko, he called himself. I presume he was a Soviet intelligence officer." Zimmermann shrugged. *There, there,* the old man told himself in his dream. *The very name that Wei supplied.* Zimmermann had passed over the name, mentioning it only once. He had gone on to talk of the man's beard, his smell, his bad German, his brutality, his cunning as dark and narrow and enclosed as his small black eyes by his inflated cheeks.

His face, his hesitation? the old man asked, rousing himself to an upright position in his seat. He concentrated his newly awake mind upon that moment of hesitation and attempted to see the German's expression. He had continued because there was no cause for retraction, for hesitation or caution. The story had emerged naturally, and seemingly in full. Zimmermann's eyes had been full of recollection, not calculation.

Aubrey looked out of the cabin window at his side, down at the bulk of an island slipping through the sea like an unlighted vessel. Then there was only the gleaming flat sea again, and pale islands of cloud. He was no further ahead. In fact, he was more confused. It had happened then, according to Wei's story. Zimmermann and Schiller and a small unit, on a reconnaissance, had been captured by Republican forces. During the few days before they made good their escape, Zimmermann had, apparently, become a Soviet agent.

Yet he had recounted the incident without hesitation, without secrecy?

The narrative had been interrupted by the arrival of a major from an intelligence unit of the British Expeditionary Force. He had been like the turning out of a bright white light. He instructed Aubrey that he and his prisoner should move north, at first light, to the BEF's intelligence headquarters at Louvain.

The recollection of the major fully awakened the old man. He shook himself like a hound, sat up and rubbed his eyes. The vivid memories faded and paled, became sepia prints of dead grandparents on a lounge wall. Aubrey yawned. A nagging curiosity had begun to develop like hunger in his stomach. He knew that he had to talk to Schiller in Australia. He suspected that Schiller held the key to Zimmermann.

Spain. The Condor Legion, 1938, Aladko of the NKVD . . . Schiller held the key, of that Aubrey was certain.

In the warm, gathering dusk David Liu walked into an old and vanished China. The Yu Yuan, the Garden of Leisurely Happiness, was like the recreation of something from a dinner plate. The last of the light rendered the garden in the blue-black and cream of the willow pattern on bone china. However, his knowledge that it was the basis of the pattern's design did not reduce the sense of surprise, even wonder, that he experienced. Pleasure subdued tension. For a few minutes he was alert only to the shapes of buildings, the last sunlight held in calm water, the whisper of man-made waterfalls, the hum of late insects.

He crossed the zigzag Bridge of Nine Turnings, past the ornate teahouse whose lights glowed in the dusk, and observed the heads of customers at the windows. The gardens were still crowded, but emptying with a regularity that was disciplined and somehow depressing.

He was an hour early for his meeting with the police clerk. He had returned to his hotel room to inspect his papers after leaving the girl, then he had gone out, not to return. There was a new surveillance car, but he lost his tail by plunging into the crowded, rabbit-warren streets of the old city, using the morning to inspect the Yu Garden, memorize its lakes and halls and towers and trees. It was an intricate trap, and there were a hundred trapdoors. He was satisfied.

For the remainder of the day, he had walked the streets or spent the time in restaurants and teahouses.

He had no idea whether a trap had been set. The exact meeting-place was the Hall that Looks Up at the Hills, at the northern end of the garden. He walked towards it beneath trees hung with lanterns. If it was staked out by the police, then he would know it. As yet, they would not be fully alert, fully concealed.

He spent fifteen minutes inspecting the surroundings of the hall, and its shadowy, warm-lit interior. Banners, lanterns, heavily-carved furniture in the rooms, ornate beamed ceilings. It was alien, and familiar; alien to his experience, familiar to a wistful, deracinated part of himself. Beneath the upcurved, elaborate tiled eaves of the hall, he wished, for one fleeting moment, that he was not an American.

No one. It was not a trap, then. He found a bench which gave him a clear view of the hall and the small lake and Rockery Hill beyond them, and seated himself to wait for the arrival of Liang and the clerk.

The garden was almost empty by ten-twenty. The flow of people out of the Yu Yuan had become no more than a trickle, individuals loitering like raindrops sliding down a window. There had been no remotely suspicious activity in or near the Hall that Looks Up at the Hills. Then he saw Liang, following the main path. He would be shielded by bushes from her view when she passed him. He enjoyed the moment of secrecy and concealment. Then he saw the couple from the flat, and picked out in the next minutes two more people he did not recognize but whose patterns of movement were familiar. All four of them were engaged in surveillance.

Back-up. Frederickson was looking after him. Perhaps all the Shanghai cell was here, protecting him. He watched them post themselves around the building, and continued to wait. Liang went into the hall, and a few moments later appeared on the carved railing of the first-floor balcony, standing beneath the glow of a lantern, alone.

Still he waited, his breathing light and quick, his senses alert for noise, his eyes, accustomed to the darkness, picking out each moving shadow. By ten twenty-eight, there appeared to be no one in the garden other than Liang and those who formed the security screen around the hall.

Then a man joined Liang on the balcony. They greeted one another. Liang immediately began studying the paths around the hall, presumably for him. He stood up and stretched the tense cramp from his limbs, then began walking slowly towards the hall. In a pool of lantern light, the young woman from the flat nodded to him reassuringly. He smiled. He entered the building and climbed the stairs to the first floor.

"There you are." Liang greeted him like a friend rather than a co-conspirator as he appeared on the balcony. Directly below them, the lake gleamed with reflected light, as if luminous paint had been flung into the water. Further from them, the water was dark, pinpricked by the reflections of the lanterns adorning Rockery Hill. The hill, surmounted by a tiny pagoda, loomed black against the stars like a child attempting to imitate a giant. "This is Huang."

The police clerk nodded politely. His nervousness was evident to Liu, as was his sense of the importance of the occasion.

"Huang," Liu acknowledged. "Thank you for coming. Have you any information for me?" Liu's senses and mind were alert, tuned.

"Let us look at the lake," suggested Liang, with an insight Liu admired. Movement, slow, deliberate movement, might calm the clerk, loosen his tongue. They began to stroll around the balcony, out of sight of the path leading to the hall.

"It was difficult . . ." Huang began almost immediately.

"I understand that," Liu replied soothingly, encouraging conversation.

"Some things I have discovered—"

"Yes?"

The lake seemed larger at night. Rockery Hill was decked with lanterns, its pagodas at summit and base like huge paper lanterns themselves.

"The records were, you understand, not available. I had to use subterfuge, purloining the keys . . . I did not have much time to examine them . . ."

"I suppose not," Liu murmured.

"It was my good fortune to have the small camera that Mr. Frederickson supplied on my person when I obtained the keys."

The path below the hall was empty, except for the woman from the flat who was keeping watch.

"You have photographs?"

"Yes. I left my duties early, claiming that I had contracted a cold." Huang sniffed in amusement. "I have developed some of the film. Mr. Frederickson taught me to do this."

"Yes, yes."

"You will understand that I had time to take very few of these photographs, but I selected the documents I imagined would be of most interest—"

"Show me," Liu demanded like a greedy child being offered sweets.

Huang bowed slightly, and reached into his jacket. He brought out three stiff, folded sheets. Liu carried them to the light of a lantern while Liang and Huang stood in silence a few yards away.

He unfolded the three stiff enlargements and inspected them, turning them in the light in order to read the Chinese character and figures they presented. Dosages of drugs, were they—? It seemed like. Pentathol, he translated, excitement plucking at hi heart. He examined the second photograph. The sheet had been laid out under a bright lamp. The writing was almost bleached away by the glare. Assignments: a requisition for men with medical and psychiatric qualifications. The names meant nothing to him. The third photograph was of a letter, written by MPT General Chiang to a senior member of the Politburo in Peking. A progress report on the rehabilitation of the German's raked-over, scrambled, drugged mind; pasting over the cracks so well that he would not recall, even in dreams, the interrogations he had undergone. The Harmony of Thought unit's repair work after they had finished with Zimmermann.

He pocketed the photographs and turned to Huang, who appeared relieved, even happy. Liang opened her mouth as if to speak to him, but the first whistle from the other side of the hall drowned even her intention of speaking. Other whistles answered, there was a shout and a single shot from close by. It had been a woman's voice, raised in warning. The girl from the flat . . .

Liang appeared stunned, betrayed. Huang could not move. Panic had locked his muscles—no, he appeared almost relaxed. More shots. When Huang fell forward against the carved railing of the balcony, his face exhibited a vast and final surprise. Liu, even as he concentrated on survival and escape, registered Huang's final living posture, his last strange expression, and the sprawl of his body across the balcony rail.

"No, no, no . . ." the girl was murmuring over and over again as she stared at Huang's body. "No . . ." She had been damaged by shock, unable to move, unable to act. Liu moved towards her, his hand outstretched, before self-preservation motivated muscle and sinew and brain and he backed away.

Whistles, shots, commands uttered in a magnified voice. "Keep still! Do not move! Police! You are all under arrest!" The stutter of an automatic weapon, the slither of something heavy on gravel.

Liu looked over the balcony. Feet pounded on the wooden stairs to the first floor of the building. The lanterns illuminated the water. The silvery glide of a carp's body distracted him momentarily, and then he climbed onto the railing and jumped, praying that the lake was deep enough.

He hit the water, it cushioned his fall, and then his feet and ankles jarred against the slippery bottom of the lake. He struck out underwater, disorientated and blind, the lantern light above him shimmering and diminishing, the blood pounding in his ears, his lungs straining for relief. He grazed a rock, his hands slipping on weed. He clung to the rock and climbed it to the surface.

He drew in lungfuls of air and looked back, flicking his wet hair from his eyes. Racing figures were surrounding the hall, the girl Liang's bright red tunic was visible among them as she was herded away; two policemen were carrying Huang's corpse between them, head and arms lolling.

Torches flickered over the water, seeking him. A few hopeful shots plucked at the calm dark water. Liu submerged again, swimming towards Rockery Hill and the boundary wall of the Yu Garden. When he came up for air again, he was on his knees on a ledge of rock.

The pagoda's lanterns cast deep shadows along the base of Rockery Hill and the white boundary wall curved away behind it, the recumbent form of a sleeping dragon lying along its top like a guardian. Liu crawled up the slippery rocks towards the base of the wall. He reached it, and touched the surface of the wall with gentle, enquiring fingers. Rough, pock-marked, chipped. It would have to do.

He let his breathing slow. The white wall was a screen against which he would perform his small, desperate mime of escape. Eight or nine feet above the base of the wall, another six or seven feet below the sleeping dragon, were upcurved carved scrolls and boughs together with regular, tusk-like protrusions. He stood upright, and jumped.

His hand rubbed against one tusk, but failed to grip it. Immediately, as if he had touched some electronic alarm, whistles and shots could be heard across the lake. Brick and white-wash dust spat from the wall. He jumped again, held on with one hand, wrenching his arm in its socket, then flung his other arm upwards, grabbing the upcurving tusk. His feet scrabbled violently, then he found purchase and heaved himself level with the tusk. The dragon slumbered above him. He felt the bullets striking the wall, heard them whining away. He rolled his body sideways and over the tusk, sweating profusely, driven by panic. Then, pressing himself against the wall—he could hear orders and running footsteps now—he stretched his body like a cat until he stood upright on the tusk of stone. His hands, reaching blindly above his head, encountered the folds of the dragon's stone scales. He tested his grip and heaved, drawing himself up until his eyes were level with the empty basilisk stare of the carved dragon. Gratefully, he slumped over the dragon's neck.

The poorly lit street outside the garden was almost empty. He swung his body weakly over the wall, straddling it, then lowered himself. On that side, it was no more than ten feet to the pavement. He let his body lengthen against the wall, then dropped.

He stumbled, staggered with exhaustion, but then the whistles prompted him. He began running away from the Yu Garden, the three incriminating photographs water-damaged, sodden, still inside his jacket, their information now safe in his head.

Gradually the whistles faded behind him.

1940: 13–15 May

13 May 1940

At first, the noises were part of Aubrey's fitful sleep. After the effort of making precise and detailed notes of his long conversation with Zimmermann, the reverberations and duller, heavier detonations seemed only to serve to underline the diconnected words and phrases that belonged to the German and his own unanswered guesses and questions.

He awoke. The voices faded, the noises were amplified. Artillery fire. Bombs. Eastwards, towards the Marfée Heights and the river Meuse. He rolled onto his side and found Zimmermann, handcuffed and guarded by a soldier, watching him wake. The German smiled. The major from military intelligence had supervised the making secure of the prisoner. Aubrey seemed to remember his heavy eyelids falling to the accompanying click of the bracelets on Zimmermann's wrists.

The barn door was open. Sunlight spilled across the straw, and cool, sweet air seemed to follow it. Aubrey smelt coffee brewing. He patted his jacket pocket, touching his notebook. Zimmermann's smile broadened.

The major entered, purposeful, long-striding. He was almost as tall as Zimmermann, and powerfully built. Aubrey wondered whether his dislike of the man related to his physical impressiveness or to the hardly concealed contempt that the officer had displayed towards him, his methods of interrogation, even his civilian clothes and status.

"What's happening?"

The major paused in front of Aubrey, who proceeded to brush straw from his jacket and trousers. "I was just about to ask Fritz here the same question." His stick tapped lightly against his creased trousers. The soldier appeared immensely efficient, thoroughly competent. And experienced. Aubrey realized the major had become an object of envy on his part.

"Yes," he replied, nodding. The soldier turned away from him.

"Well, Fritz?" the major asked, standing in front of Zimmermann. Aubrey was unable to see the German's face. "What *is* going on?"

Aubrey saw Zimmermann's shoulders heft in a shrug. "I do not know."

"Don't give me that. Our friend here"—he indicated Aubrey with a small, dismissive motion of his stick—"may believe that rubbish about your infantry status, but I don't. You're Abwehr all right, and you *do* know what's going on. Eh?" The stick tapped his thigh, predicting the future. Aubrey found the display distasteful, but enviable. Authority, as expressed by the major from intelligence HQ at Louvain, cast an unflattering light on the inexperience and youth of Kenneth Aubrey. "Come on, Fritz, what's up? What's the game across the river?"

"I cannot answer your question. What is happening out there? I have not seen it. You have."

"Corporal, get him outside. We'll give him a look at what's going on. Quickly!"

The corporal thrust the butt of his rifle into Zimmermann's back, jolting him off the bale of straw onto his knees. Aubrey saw pain distorting the German's face, then Zimmermann rose lightly to his feet and faced the major. They appeared well-matched opponents. Zimmermann was shoved towards the door of the barn. Aubrey, still brushing his coat, followed the three soldiers. As soon as he reached the door, he saw in the distance smears of smoke against the sunlight and the pale blue sky. Above the smoke wheeled what might have been birds, black and quick. Henri and Philippe were standing with two soldiers, watching the aerial display. There was an ominous freedom about the swooping black specks. Stukas protected by Messerschmitt 109s.

"I see," Zimmermann murmured, turning to the major. "It appears the French are being attacked on the Marfée Heights."

"You arrogant bastard. Is Guderian going to attempt a river crossing?" The corporal thrust his rifle butt into Zimmermann's side. The German gasped with pain. "Is he?" Thrust. Zimmermann's knees buckled, but he did not fall. "Where else are they going to cross?" Thrust again, a quick, heavy jab. "How many crossing points?" Zimmermann staggered from another jab in the back. "What is the timetable? How soon? What units? Come on, you German bastard! How soon? How many? *Where?*" The corporal jabbed downwards at the prostrate Zimmermann, who groaned at the force of the blow, but said nothing. Aubrey brushed at his clothing with a furious desire to ignore and escape. Wisps of straw dropped from him like innocence. "Very well, corporal, that'll do for now." The corporal appeared relieved to step away from Zimmermann. The major turned to Aubrey, his face livid with frustrated anger and something that might have been self-contempt. "We'd better get this hero back to Louvain at once," he remarked in a tight, choked voice.

Aubrey nodded slowly like a halfwit. "Yes, yes," was all he managed to say.

"Breakfast first. Keep an eye on him, corporal." The major strode back into the barn. The black birdlike shapes wheeled and swooped like vultures against the painted blue of the sky.

It was well after eight by the time they were ready to leave. Aubrey was placed in the rear of the second of the two open cars in which the major and his unit had arrived at the farm. Zimmermann, lowering himself gently into the seat and being careful to keep his arms away from his ribs, was next to him. Aubrey, in compliance with the major's instructions, ostentatiously displayed his pistol on his lap. Henri, on Zimmermann's other side, was similarly posed. Philippe sat next to the driver. The corporal and the three remaining members of the major's unit were crowded into the leading car with their officer. Aubrey was grateful for not having to travel with the major.

They followed the farm track down to the main road. In the market town of Flize there were anxious faces, some cheering at the sight of British uniforms, an abiding impression of attention and concern and even fear directed towards the oily-clouded east. Smoke hung like a thickening curtain less than twenty kilometres ahead of them. The major had decided to view the situation at the Meuse before heading north along the river towards Louvain, east of Brussels, where the British Expeditionary Force under the command of Lord Gort had its GHQ.

The hamlet of Dom-le-Mesnil seemed full of people talking, moving slowly, forming groups, waiting. Zimmermann studied the faces of the French they passed. The sight seemed to gratify him, to lessen or make worthwhile the pain he had suffered. The breeze of their passage blew his fair hair off his forehead. Aubrey decided there was something irresistible about the man; he represented a superior, overwhelming force. The essence of what he knew could be discerned on his features. Victory. The impression chilled Aubrey. He felt himself a child playing at hide-and-seek, who had dug into a heap of autumn leaves or pulled back the branches of a bush only to discover some hideously mutilated corpse or some act of obscene violence in progress. In Zimmermann's face, the war expanded, enlarged, lengthened through years ahead.

Two slow, lumbering, underpowered Morane-Saulnier 406s in French air force colours droned overhead, heading towards the circling black specks. Zimmermann, looking up, watched them with a fascination Aubrey could only imitate. The aircraft moved ahead of them, losing feature and colour. Three or four black specks seemed to detach themselves from their attentions to the rising ground ahead and move towards the French intruders. It was a matter of seconds before they encountered the two Moranes, and then only seconds more before each of the newcomers was spiralling towards the hummock of the Marfée Heights, trailing thick black smoke. The German specks returned to their flock.

"Useless bloody Frogs," the driver murmured, oblivious of the presence of Henri and Philippe or perhaps ignoring them through some process of adoption, "just the same as the last lot. We only 'ad any time for 'is mob," he added, tossing his head to indicate Zimmermann.

Aubrey looked at Zimmermann. The German shrugged, then pain squeezed his face into narrow contour lines. The shrug indicated superior planning, equipment, men. Irresistible.

The cars began climbing through wooded countryside, up towards the heights. The narrow road twisted and turned, climbed and dropped. For a moment or two, until the whine of the Stukas and the drone of Messerschmitt engines insisted their presence, Aubrey could imagine they were engaged in some pleasant social outing. He lost sight of the aircraft.

Aubrey let his awareness smear the distinct sounds of the attack ahead into a general loud insect-like buzzing, hearing the explosions much as he had done in the moments before he woke. He felt drowsy as if with heat. Strangely, as the car climbed again and he was pressed further back in the cracked leather seat, the drone of engines became louder, as if he were lying in tall grass and bees were buzzing very near his head. The insect-noises grew louder and louder, became like the ceaseless ripping of cloth. It began to hurt the ears...

Then he realised that Zimmermann had moved. His handcuffed hands were over the driver's head. Aubrey snapped awake, only to realise that Henri and Philippe, instead of struggling with Zimmermann, were staring behind the car, faces mirroring the same growing expression of fear. Zimmermann was yelling.

"For God's sake, get the car off the road!" The driver was struggling to retain control of the steering wheel as Zimmermann wrenched at it. Aubrey fumbled with his pistol, opened his mouth to warn Zimmermann to sit down . . .

The Messerschmitt behind them opened fire, its four smaller machine guns and one 20mm cannon tearing at the engine noise, ripping and stuttering like cloth torn in a fury. The sound deafened Aubrey as he turned to watch his own death leaping upon him.

Leaves flickered and dissolved, the road coughed dust and chippings. The three-second burst pursued them, leapt after them. The mottled camouflage of the Me 109, its black propellor hub, white belly and painted shark's teeth grinning, filled Aubrey's vision. The car swerved wildly out of control and lurched at the edge of the road, dropped its bonnet, began to roll down a shallow slope. White belly after shark's grin, tailplane; the flash of flame, a distinctly heard scream from the other car—then Aubrey's world was shaken and flung upside down as the car overturned. He dropped his pistol, grabbing the yielding substance of Zimmermann's body and uniform to him like an eager lover.

They spilled from the car together. Aubrey, winded, watched the car right itself with a shuddering bump, and stop. The driver lolled ominously over the door, his head at an impossible angle. Philippe lay prone and groaning a few yards behind them. Henri was on his knees, near the road, clutching his reddening shirt at one shoulder, his head hanging like someone vomiting. Aubrey held Zimmermann, his hand gripping the chain between the two bracelets of the handcuffs as he levered himself to his knees. He had fallen on top of Zimmermann, who seemed unconscious.

"Philippe, Philippe! Quickly!"

The younger Frenchman sat upright with a quick, jerky motion. His gun was still in his hand. He looked around at Henri, and appeared about to move in his direction.

"Henri—"

"Philippe, I'll look to Henri. *You* watch the prisoner." Zimmermann opened one eye. He smiled, presumably at his continued existence. Aubrey staggered, regained his balance, and began running towards Henri. A pall of smoke belched up into the branches of the trees that overhung the road, to be masked by the greenery before emerging like a signal into the sky. "Henri, how is it?"

"It hurts, M'sieur. It hurts a lot." Henri groaned. Aubrey studied the wound. The bullet had passed directly through the shoulder.

"Hang on, I won't be a moment," Aubrey murmured, climbing the last few steps onto the pockmarked road.

The leading car had stopped burning. A few flames flickered from the upholstery and from some dark and foreboding lump heaped in the rear seat. The thin trail of smoke was moved by the slight breeze into twisted, anguished contortions. Aubrey approached the car slowly, reluctantly.

They were all dead. The smell of scorched and burned flesh was hideous, making his stomach heave. There were bullet holes in charred flesh and uniforms. The major, the corporal, the driver and the remainder of the unit: all dead. His nerveless hand touched the sill of the driver's door. He withdrew it, yelping with pain, sucking it furiously as if to absorb himself in a lesser, physical distress. He felt his stomach revolt once more, and hurried back down the road towards Henri. He helped the Frenchman to his feet, cradling his larger frame as he assisted him to their car. Philippe had ordered Zimmermann, hand-cuffed though he was, to remove the driver's corpse. It lay reposefully on the grass beside the car.

Aubrey searched the car for its first-aid kit. Zimmermann, ignoring the protests of the two brothers, examined Henri's wound.

"He's losing a lot of blood," he commented. Henri's face was pale and drawn. "Give me that," he added, as Aubrey held up the tin box bearing a squat red cross. "And unlock these." He held up the bracelets on his wrists. Aubrey freed Zimmermann's hands without hesitation. Then quickly and expertly, Zimmermann bound up the red-lipped wound that gushed on Henri's shoulder.

"Thank you," Aubrey murmured when he had finished. "For—" He shrugged expressively.

Zimmermann shook his head. "Self-preservation. The pilot couldn't see my uniform. I regret the driver. Perhaps not the major or his corporal quite so much . . ."

"Can he travel?"

"Yes, but he must receive attention soon."

"Very well. I'll leave him at the nearest field hospital." Aubrey turned and explained the situation to the two brothers. Strangely he felt more intimately bound to Zimmermann; perhaps the man's coolness and his expertise was something to cling to. Aubrey was confused by his feelings.

"Where are we going?"

"To Louvain, I suppose," Aubrey replied. "GHQ." The cryptonym had a comforting ring to it. Solidity. The immovable

bject confronting the irresistible force represented by Zimmermann
nd the Me 109. That swooping, shark's-grin death . . . charred,
vithered flesh . . .

His stomach revolted again and he fought to control it, feeling
iis body shake, change temperature as if each part were some
eparate climatic region. Zimmermann placed a steadying firm
and on his arm.

"I remember the first dead body I ever saw," he said quietly,
"in Spain, three years ago. A peaceful appearance, like someone
leeping. A child. When I got closer, it was like a broken
ggshell. One side of the head had gone . . ." He gripped
Aubrey's arm, and shook it almost fiercely. "Welcome to the
var, Englishman." There was sufficient scorn and mockery in
he tone of his voice to diminish Aubrey's horror. He shook off
Zimmermann's hand.

"Get in the car!" he snapped.

"It will start, by the way," Zimmermann drawled. "It is no
nore than dented and shaken—like us."

"Philippe, Henri, in the car." Aubrey was almost officiously
recise and clipped in his tone. He bustled in imitation of
fficiency, expertness. "We'll continue. Do the major's job for
im. Philippe, keep an eye on the prisoner."

Aubrey started the car. Mud churned from beneath the wheels,
hen they moved, climbing the bank slowly until they reached the
oad. Aubrey steered with exaggerated, narrow-focused care
round the burned-out car and its bodies, then accelerated as
oon as they were beyond it. The smoke from the wreckage was
ow the thinnest of grey streamers, without the spirals that
uggested a human frame in anguish.

Within an hour, they had reached a point only half a mile from
he place where they had captured Zimmermann the previous
ight. Their progress had been slow, threading their way through
nits of the French 55th and 71st divisions of the 10th Corps of
General Grandsard which occupied the Marfée Heights and the
lefensive positions on the left bank of the Meuse. Zimmermann
ad been alert and absorbed. He studied faces more than disposi-
ions, the atmosphere more than the defences. And his confi-
lence of mien steadily increased. He appeared sunny, uncon-
erned, almost amused. The divisions were composed almost
ntirely of elderly reservists with limited training. To Aubrey,
hey now appeared an illusory counterthreat to Guderian's Pan-
ers across the river. It was as if daylight had turned a powerful
lream into a pale ghost of itself. Guderian, Aubrey now be-

lieved, would cross the river that day, at his own choosing and almost on his own terms.

Ammunition in short supply, Aubrey heard. Untrained, unskilled units. Fat and flabby troops. The front, twenty-five miles long, was too thinly defended at any and every point. Many of the pillboxes along the river were unfinished, unarmed. The concrete wouldn't withstand the Stukas' bombs. Troops slaughtered in their trenches . . .

The bombardment had already lasted for three hours. It was unceasing, terrifying. And the German artillery hadn't even opened up yet . . .

Aubrey wanted to flee the Marfée Heights, as from the scene of a disaster that had already occurred. Instead, he remained in the immediate area for perhaps an hour, making furious, continuous scribbled notes. The major's persona occupied him, pushed away the recollection of the man himself, and his charred body. Zimmermann, with amusement, pointed often across the river whenever a gap in the trees allowed them a view of the field-grey tide waiting on the right bank, the concentrations of armour, the silent artillery, the numbers of troops.

Aubrey became charged with a sense of mission. It was like some swift religious conversion. He wished the truth to reach Louvain, not the reassurances he knew would be passed by telephone and coded signal. The front at Sedan was about to erupt, bulge back, be broken. He must get that news to the BEF . . .

Zimmermann seemed reluctant to leave; a spectator for whom the main actors were yet to come on stage. Aubrey drove the car as recklessly as he could away from the ramparts of the Marfée Heights, away from the smoke above the town of Sedan.

They drove north, following the river towards Charleville-Mezieres. The town was filled with people, its approaches beginning to clog with the Belgian refugees driven before the German advance through the Ardennes. Carts piled with possessions, upturned chairs and mangles, small pianos and waif-like empty-faced children who already predicted the future in unequivocal terms. Dust, the smell of petrol on the air that had gone sour with fear and uncertainty. Zimmermann, seated in the rear of the car, an army raincoat draped over his betraying grey uniform, passed through the scenes with a lordly, comprehending satisfied indifference—or so it seemed to Aubrey. The Englishman discovered himself hurled into an adult, irrecoverable world. His espionage career had been little more than a game by comparison ith what he now witnessed. He felt diminished and inadequate; hamed of himself. Pipesmoke, scarves wreathed beneath unshaven ins or wrapped over women's heads. Countless, endless grey ces. These people were prophets, forerunners. They had already witnessed France's future.

By lunchtime, they reached Montherme, where the French 2nd division had prevented the Germans from crossing the ver. Aubrey was delighted.

"No aircraft," Zimmermann observed laconically.

Above them, through the trees and over the fields to the west, ench aircraft circled and droned and waited. The Luftwaffe had t arrived. Artillery crumped and wailed, but no Stukas howled d terrified.

"It isn't going to be as easy as you thought," Aubrey marked with an irritated bravado, munching on some sausage d bread that Philippe had managed to obtain in Charleville. enri was being fed by his younger brother in the car. Aubrey d Zimmermann had carried their food and wine some yards wn the slope towards the river. A picnic above the battle. nits of the French division were dug in on the slopes around em: casual, confident, relaxed. Below them, on their side of e river, German units were pinned down, protected only by the ns of the tanks drawn up beneath the trees on the opposite nk. Cigarette-smoke ascended into the trees in company with e smoke of rifle fire as the French enjoyed their advantage. mmermann, frowning as he studied the dispositions, seemed vertheless undeterred.

"Perhaps not," he said. There was a note of pity in his voice.

"I shall leave Henri with the medical unit of this division," ubrey announced. "That shoulder needs treatment."

"I agree."

"You claim you are not a Nazi," Aubrey said suddenly, vallowing a lump of bread and sausage. Rifle fire crackled ound them, followed by cheering. The cannons of the tanks awn up on the other side of the river were evidently conserving nmunition. The sky above them was silent except for the casional French fighter.

"I am not."

"This is a Nazi war—you are a German, brought up under the azis for the last seven years. A veteran of Spain and the ondor Legion, fighting with the Falangists and Franco. Those e impressive credentials for a non-Nazi, wouldn't you say?"

Zimmermann studied Aubrey carefully, then he nodded. "My

father was an army officer. I am an army officer. It is a famil
tradition. That is all.''

"Where were you born and brought up?''

"Wittenberg.''

Aubrey smiled. "Is that propitious, Martin Luther's city?''

"I doubt it. I went into the army when I was seventeen. I am
now twenty-three. It seems a long time between. I fought in
Spain because soldiers are trained to fight. That is why I am here
now. The Wehrmacht is full of non-Nazis. It is why France and
England have no need to worry. Gestapo and SS—you have
heard of them?'' Aubrey nodded. "They are not everywhere or
all-powerful, you know.''

"Organizations like them have a way of becoming so—at
least, history seems to indicate as much. You were captured in
Spain, you said?''

"Yes. By one of the International Brigades, in Aragon. The
15th, I remember—Yugoslavs, French, British, Americans.''
Zimmermann smiled. "And Russians, of course. Certain Russian
officers operating on American passports, attaching themselves
like limpets to idealists and materialists alike. If you wish to
make pronouncements, perhaps you would like to apply them to
the NKVD. That is the sort of organization that even the
Wehrmacht could not control.''

"Mm. You're talking about an ally of Germany.''

"The honeymoon will be short—as soon as Stalin is ready
he'll change sides.''

"Interesting. Where in Aragon?''

"I was on patrol—reconnaissance. In March. East of Saragossa
behind the Republican lines. Much as now.'' He spread his hand
and grinned. "Even though they were in retreat, they still
managed to take and keep us for a few days.''

"And you met this Russian officer?''

"Russian secret policeman. Aladko. He was quite open about
his real name and identity.''

Zimmermann had begun massaging his ribs.

"Sore?''

"Memory makes the bruises worse. Aladko liked inflicting
pain. Not like your major this morning, working himself into the
right sort of rage before he could give the order.''

"Beatings?''

"He had plenty of cooperation. Russians, one or two Amer

ns, even local Communists enlisted in one or other of the
agonese units. Especially the local Communists . . .''

"And?"

"I kept my mouth shut. Others didn't."

"After that?"

"Courage or cowardice made no difference—the Republic was
eady beaten and they knew it."

Cannon shells whistled overhead, burying themselves beyond
e lip of the hillside; presumably to discourage reserve units
m moving up. It was strangely unreal as a war. The refugees
Charleville had been more real than this. This was a kind of
r-game. The ground shuddered for a moment beneath their
t. The trees at their backs remained unmoved.

"Go on," Aubrey prompted, swigging at the wine before
ssing the bottle to Zimmermann.

"Oh. Then came the softer approach. The idealism. I made no
cret of my dislike of Nazis—officers in the Legion, visiting
nerals and policemen and politicians. Boot-stamping, salutes,
llshit. Grubby little men without education, without back-
ound. And some soldiers who should have known better than
have been taken in by it. Aladko tried to recruit me, would
u believe?"

"Did he?"

Zimmermann shook his head. "Of course not. I am not a
ommunist."

More shells whistled across the river, smashing into the
ench positions below them. It was as if events had suddenly
en orchestrated to impress Aubrey. Screams, smoke, flying
rth and stone. It was not a game, just a period of waiting
fore the full fury of the storm broke. Men groaning; the lower
pes obscured by flame and smoke. Ammunition exploding.

"Come," Aubrey said, remembering the pistol as he got to
feet. "We'll get Henri to the field hospital."

It was another hour or so before they returned to the road that
ralleled the Meuse. Philippe was now driving, apparently
ieved at leaving his brother. They headed north once more,
wards Dinant, forty miles away. As the afternoon advanced and
eir progress, though slow, remained unimpeded, it became
ore and more evident to Aubrey that the Germans now overlooked
e Meuse from Sedan to Dinant. A great flood behind a dyke
ll. One crack, and the Panzers would pour across the French
ains towards Paris and the coast. It was an enervating, depress-

ing journey. The confidence, the good humour of the Frenc
units they encountered seemed empty, wilfully blind to reality.

South of Dinant, the Meuse's sharp meanders and thick
wooded, high escarpments improved Aubrey's grim mood. Here
at least, the Germans could be held. To the south, well . . . Bi
here, yes. It could be done.

"Colonel Aladko," Aubrey mused. "Not a likeable mar
then?"

"No."

"How important was he? The information may be of futur
use if, as you suggest, we become allies of the Russians."

Zimmermann smiled. "Before then, the war will be over."

"Nevertheless—"

"I would say he was an important officer in the NKVD. No
by his bearing or manner, but by his experience, his shrewdness
If he was not important, then his skills had neither been recog
nized nor used. While he dragged us north with him as the
retreated, I studied him. Learning the craft, as it were."

"The craft of the infantryman, naturally."

"Naturally."

"Aladko had all the correct credentials. He was with Leni
and the Bolsheviks in Petrograd, later he distinguished himself i
the Civil War—*their* civil war, Red and White. The Party relie
on him greatly, giving him a roving commission to check on th
loyalty of unit commanders in the field." Zimmermann's smil
broadened. "He was boasting about the number of people—c
all ranks, even up to Commissar or general—he'd had shot. Th
was an occasion where he was threatening me, rather than tryin
to enlist me."

Philippe turned the car off the road, down a country track. Th
road beyond the turning had been bombed. It was torn an
holed. The car bumped along the rutted lane.

"I see."

"I suspect Aladko was very important, and still is. In Moscov
or wherever he is now, he will have an influential post. Do yo
know what he once said to me? *All power springs from the nap
of the neck.*" Zimmermann made a pistol of his right hand, an
pointed his finger at Philippe's neck. "Pfff. That's all there is.
think he was joking." Aubrey shuddered involuntarily.

Black smoke hung over the river behind them, now that the
were away from the wooded escarpments of the Meuse.
seemed denser, heavier, more pall-like. Artillery fire was omn
present; the black bird-shapes in the distance were Messe

schmitts and Stukas. It was too like Sedan, and broke Aubrey's confidence in topography.

"Philippe, head north as soon as you can," he said.

"M'sieur."

Philippe skidded the car into a narrower lane, jolting his passengers between the tall hedges. The lane twisted through blind corners; the ruts of tractor and wagon wheels flung Aubrey and Zimmermann into constant physical contact. Ahead of them, at the end of their green tunnel, there was smoke hanging over the town of Dinant. The track rose gradually, and the cornfields sloped away from them in bright sunlight towards Charleroi to the north-west. An unsmeared sky. A farm tractor chugging audibly in one moment of artillery silence, a breeze moving the fields in a slow, soporific rhythm. All of France beyond those fields. Aubrey regretted the vision as mere illusion, turning away from it towards the real sky, heavy and oily with smoke.

14 May 1940

Aubrey had awoken in the shabby hotel room in Dinant experiencing an image which remained vivid even after he had opened his eyes. The south coast of England, the previous summer; distant specks that had been German aircraft, patrolling the Channel—practising for war. He had seen so many of those ominous specks the previous day, in earnest. As he dressed, watched by Zimmermann who was handcuffed to the bedpost, the illusions of 1939 left him.

A scrappy breakfast in the almost deserted hotel dining room was followed by an hour which they spent searching for petrol for the car. It was as if events had already overtaken Dinant, that the Germans had already passed through it leaving a bereft, provisionless, dazed town in their wake. Eventually Aubrey was able to fill the tank and the two jerry-cans in the boot, and with Philippe driving they headed north once more along roads that seemed perpetually clogged with Belgian refugees, wagon-trains of people already purposeless and defeated. Yet the allied armies became more evident and unscathed. Discipline, equipment, uniforms were still burnished, pressed, polished.

"Why did you choose that hotel instead of a more secure army unit?" Zimmermann asked soon after they had passed the village of Anhée and the road had become a disciplined, orderly artery down which units of the Belgian army flowed. The sight heartened Aubrey, even impressed Zimmermann.

"I—" Aubrey paused to consider. "I think I was reminding myself I was a civilian."

"There aren't any civilians any longer," Zimmermann observed drily. Aubrey looked down at the pistol held loosely on his lap. His grip upon it tightened involuntarily, a reaction which disturbed and disheartened him.

Aubrey felt he had stepped perhaps two or three days back in time. Troop movements and dispositions, unblooded divisions, a stillness over the country, while further south at Sedan and Monthermé the Germans were poised to cross the river, attacking fiercely, beginning to win. Here, nearing Namur, the front was entirely secure, settled, quiet. He began to wonder whether this quiescence was not somehow to the German advantage. Zimmermann, he suspected, would know the answer.

"We have it wrong, don't we?" he snapped. "It isn't here that the main brunt will be borne, is it?"

Zimmermann's face clouded, then cleared into a look of denial. "I don't quite understand—"

"Yes, you do—and so do I!" Aubrey snapped.

Zimmermann shrugged. "If you say so."

"I do!" Aubrey's knuckles were white where he held the butt of the pistol. His other hand gripped the barrel, as if to prevent him pointing it into the German's side. Zimmermann appeared to be awaiting the outcome of Aubrey's inward conflict. "Oh, yes, it's in your face—at least it was for a moment—you *do* know. You understand the whole strategy, don't you?" Aubrey felt a clarity of mind he had not previously experienced. Obliquely, scenes and impressions had conspired with his curiosity to provoke the sudden question.

Zimmermann looked at his watch. "It's too late," he said. "Everything I have seen, yesterday and today, tells me it is too late."

Philippe slowed the car and pulled onto the road's grass verge. A French unit, armoured cars in the lead, light tanks close behind, approached and passed them. Aubrey saw Zimmermann tug the British army raincoat up over his uniform. The dust choked them, obscured the faces of the tank commanders. The armoured unit was moving south towards Dinant. In a matter of a few minutes, the road was empty again in front of them. An industrial haze hung over Namur to the north as the dust of the tanks' passage settled in the warm air.

"Too late?" Aubrey asked as Philippe drove off.

"That was a reserve unit, being deployed at leisure. This road, *all* roads south, should be choked with military traffic."

"Sedan?"

"Yes. You know the German word *Sichelschnitt*?"

"*Sichel*—sickle?"

"Scythe. The sweep of a scythe." Zimmermann moved his arms, imitating a scything action towards Aubrey. "It has begun, it cannot be countered."

"But we captured most of your *Fall Gelb* invasion plans in January—"

"They were revised. Bock's Army Group B is waving the red flag. He has only twenty-eight divisions. Do you know how many Runstedt has in the south? Forty-four, including seven Panzer divisions." Zimmermann smiled gently. "At least, that is my understanding of the plan."

"So we're wrong?" Aubrey asked wildly, looking behind them back down the road to Dinant.

"I am afraid so."

"My God!"

"If I had told you two days ago, it would not have mattered. The French are inflexible, believing in the Maginot Line, even in trench warfare. If I had told your major yesterday, it would have made no difference. There is nothing that can be done. There is no remedy. What I have told you is valueless now."

Aubrey was silent for a moment, then he snapped: "Philippe, put your foot down. Drive faster! I want to be at GHQ this afternoon. It's fifty miles or more. Hurry!"

Zimmermann's face was almost saintly with the sad patience it expressed.

15 May 1940

Aubrey held out the packet of Gold Flake cigarettes to Zimmermann, dismissing the guard with a curt nod of his head which encompassed the German, the army represented by the guard's uniform, and the preceding twenty-four hours. Zimmermann, who had been lolling on the bed, sat upright, stretched, then took a cigarette. Aubrey lit it, then his own. Blue smoke curled to the damp-stained ceiling. It was a narrow, high, attic room in the three-storey building temporarily commandeered by the intelligence units of the BEF's headquarters in Louvain.

A tank rumbled along the cobbled street outside.

"How are you?" Aubrey asked solicitously.

Zimmermann inhaled, exhaled noisily. "Quite well," he replied frostily. "Very tired, of course." He shrugged. When he continued, his voice was more pleasant, less acrimonious. "Ah, there is no point. Before this war is finished, interrogation methods will have improved dramatically. Then there will be no hope for any of us. Your people—bright lights, a hard chair, no sleep—but no beating."

"You told them everything?"

"Everything that mattered. Precisely what I told you. What one or two reconnaissance aircraft could now tell them. Forty-four divisions can't be kept secret."

"No."

Zimmermann lay back on the bed once more, cradling his head against the wallpaper with one crooked arm. Aubrey sat in a chair whose horsehair stuffing was beginning to thrust like some tough weed through its shabby, worn upholstery. The room was shadowy in the pale light from the single, high, narrow window that sloped above their heads. The bare floorboards were rough and dusty.

"And your day—how has that been?"

Aubrey smiled. There seemed to be an amicable conspiracy between them. "Much the same as yours. Without the bright lights, of course. A hard chair, and ceaseless questions. Going over and over the inevitable."

"Today the order for retreat will be given. Now that the strategy is perceived, and has begun to work, there is no alternative. Your BEF will be ordered to pull back."

"How far?"

"Perhaps the Schelde. I cannot say."

Aubrey rubbed his smooth chin. Zimmermann had evidently not been issued with shaving tackle.

"I—you're transferred back to me, by the way. To SIS, that is. You're my responsibility again."

"Ah. Soon, then, I shall attempt to escape."

"Perhaps. I convinced them that you had information of general interest to SIS, apart from your military knowledge. They did not appear reluctant to let you go."

"I don't know any more. I am not familiar with the tactics, only the general strategy. Apparently, they have become persuaded of that."

Artillery fire made the window above them rattle. A slight dusting of plaster drifted slowly to the floor.

"Yours or ours?" Aubrey asked.

"Ours."

"Army Group B on the move?"

"Perhaps. If so, it means that all three bridgeheads across the Meuse have been secured—as you will have guessed."

"Yes."

The shells landed at some distance from the building, making deep, hollow crumping noises, rattling the window again, making Aubrey flinch.

"I shall take you back with me," Aubrey remarked almost casually.

"Where?" Zimmermann was alert, though apparently he was staring sightlessly at the ash on the tip of the cigarette.

"London."

"London?"

"I'm sure you can tell us a great deal about the workings of the Abwehr—about agents in England, et cetera, et cetera."

"You are learning, Mr. Aubrey. Yes, perhaps so." Zimmermann's frame was rigid with tension. Aubrey opened his jacket to reveal the pistol stuck in his waistband. "I understand," Zimmermann murmured.

"Incidentally—to return to Aragon and your last period of captivity—would you be prepared to talk about this Russian, Aladko, and his interrogation of you? His attempt to enlist your services?"

"Of course. As you said, you may well have such an ally one day. It would be well to be prepared."

"Thank you."

The artillery had become a constant deep rumbling, like rippled hollow drumbeats in a quick pattern, interspersed with the closer explosions of the shells they fired. Lighter, closer noises could also be discerned.

"Ours again," Zimmermann explained before he was asked. "Tanks. Our Panzers. Less than half a mile away."

Aubrey felt frightened, yet detached. An observer in a high room, enclosed and unmindful. It was as if the war had been drained from him during his long night of questioning. Zimmermann, too, appeared to relapse into a state of half-alertness. Aubrey watched him carefully for signs that he was bluffing.

"Did you consider his approach to you to be the only one he made?"

"No. Everyone captured from my unit was put through the same thing. The hopeless cases, the ones who believed in Hitler through thick and thin, they were taken out and shot on Aladko's orders. In the nape of the neck. They could look at the snow on the high Pyrenees, the smoky cold air out of which the forests loomed, as they knelt to receive the benediction of the pistol." Zimmermann's face twisted in contempt. He evidently envisaged himself in the identical situation, but Aubrey had no idea whether the contempt was for Aladko or some future image of himself. "I stayed alive, so did Schiller and the others, by playing Aladko's game. Even then, it didn't save everyone."

"How extensive was Aladko's authority?"

"In the woodsman's hut, in the clearing, amongst the members of the Brigade we saw—absolute. Life and death, as I said." More plaster drifted like snow from the ceiling, coating the backs of Aubrey's hands and Zimmermann's stained and crumpled uniform jacket. Zimmermann watched the last motes of plaster and waited until the rattling of the window had subsided. "Absolute. And his real purpose was recruitment, not execution."

"We're aware of the Communist involvement in Spain."

The drone of aircraft became an increasing whine that in turn became a howl. It seemed to originate directly outside and above their single window.

"Stukas!" Zimmermann's face revealed a genuine, unexpected fear. He rolled off the bed, then beneath it. Aubrey hesitated, then crouched against the wall, the tired, sagging chair in front of him. He could see Zimmermann's pale face beneath the bed, saw his lips moving, but he could hear nothing except the hideous howl of the bombers and his own blood beating in his ears as he clamped his hands over them.

The building shook. Plaster rained down. A vivid snake-like crack whipped its way across the wall above the bed. The window shattered, flinging glass into the room.

The dust settled. Aubrey got up. His shoes crunched as he moved. He picked two pieces of glass from his hand. Zimmermann emerged from beneath the bed. Whether from relief or rage or his own and Aubrey's temporary deafness, he was shouting. Gradually, as a background to his words, the noises of the German artillery returned to the room.

"You don't realise their real purpose—they're looking ahead, always ahead."

"Who?"

"The Russians, the NKVD. To this war, then to after this war. Long-term. Aladko and the others had a chance to encounter so many people from so many countries during that war!" Realizing that his own hearing had returned, Zimmermann lowered his voice. He went on talking as he brushed lumps of plaster and shards of glass from the bed's coverlet. "Americans, British, Spaniards, French—a royal hunting forest of different people. They were recruiting madly. Of that I am certain. I think they knew the war was lost almost from the beginning—once we arrived, perhaps. Their main purpose was—agents. Long-term agents." Zimmermann looked up and smiled. "One day, you may thank me for that information."

Artillery closer now.

"Ours," Aubrey said with a grim smile, brushing plaster dust from his hair. "And you—did he succeed with you?"

After the deafening ripple of the BEF artillery barrage, in the silence before the explosions which only seemed to emphasize Zimmermann's own silence, a ruffled, disturbed bird chirped in protest somewhere in the eaves of the house. The snake-like crack behind the German's head had put down spindly, spider-like legs towards the floor, becoming some giant stick insect instead of a serpent.

Then Zimmermann shook his head with a slow smile. "No," he said, "he did not succeed with me. I was not available for purchase."

The explosions shook the house. The door opened, as if flung wide by the blast, and the guard-corporal put his white-dusted head into the room.

"Everything all right, sir?"

"Yes, thank you, corporal." Self-consciously, Aubrey brushed his jacket and trousers. "We're both fine."

Another violent ripple of artillery fire seemed to buffet the house.

"Monty's giving 'is lot what for," the corporal explained, tossing his head in Zimmermann's direction.

"What's happening, corporal?"

"Jerry launched an attack, sir. Third Division's in the process of booting 'em out again." He grinned, his teeth discoloured by nicotine, his expression satisfying to Aubrey.

"Thank you, corporal." The guard shut the door once more. "Well?" Aubrey asked Zimmermann.

"A temporary setback, I assure you. I suspect you're fighting for a town you will be leaving tomorrow." There was something narrow and calculating about Zimmermann's expression that Aubrey failed to notice.

The plaster dust stirred on the floor and furniture as lighter, more distant shellfire was answered by the closer, heavier British artillery.

"Aladko—did he recruit British agents?"

Zimmermann shrugged. He seemed intent upon brushing his counterpane clean of dust and creases. He moved slowly to the foot of the bed.

"Possibly. I would not know. A lot of English would have been sympathetic to his approach, I suspect?" He glanced at Aubrey assessingly for a moment. Once more his hands brushed the coverlet at the foot of the bed. A lump of plaster crackled beneath his boot, another thudded on the floorboards.

"Perhaps," Aubrey admitted thoughtfully, his mind filled with unexpectedly lurid images of Russian agents within his own organization. Zimmermann might know, Zimmermann could point the way . . .

"Sorry," Zimmermann murmured, and then his clenched fist struck Aubrey on the temple. At the same time, his left hand grabbed the barrel of the pistol, twisting the weapon out of Aubrey's grasp.

Aubrey saw Zimmermann's detached, calm face, saw the gun held up like a prize, saw the stick-insect marching frozenly across the wall, heard the protesting bird in the eaves drowned by artillery fire, then his head was tilted back by a blow to the jaw. His eyes perceived the broken skylight rapidly darken. He felt the floor against his body without the sensation of falling. He dimly heard the door open, the guard's surprised challenge. The noises of a struggle—slipping, grinding boots, grunted breaths, a cry of pain—faded and disappeared. He entered a silent, close, warm darkness.

PART TWO

The Tortoise and the Hare

The tortoise goes round once how slow,
Twelve times as fast the hare will go;
But watch the tortoise, watch the hare,
At twelve o'clock you'll find them where?

—old rhyme on a child's clock

SIX

In Vino Veritas

Liu's clothes had dried quickly in the warm night and because of the heat of tension and relief his frame exuded. In the crowded streets of the old city he lost himself and any pursuit for two slow, endless hours. Eventually he felt able to enter a teahouse and eat something, drink dry white wine and smoke two *tai shan*, miniature cigars. He choked back his coughs and tried to let the aromatic smoke and its taste and inhalation finally calm him.

It was after midnight when he crossed Suzhou Creek, passing Shanghai Mansions, and headed for the railway station. Surprisingly, the hotel did not present itself against the warm, starlit night as a refuge or a burrow into which he wished to run. It was simply an empty room, shed as lightly as his last persona. Now he was a Party official; the papers in his breast pocket, still wrapped in polythene, were a portable safe house. When he shed the crumpled, stained suit he was wearing, he would leave Shanghai and its dangers. It would be a fresh start.

The station was crowded with people waiting for the first trains of the morning. The police seemed more in evidence than on his arrival, but not especially alert. He hurried to the luggage lockers, used the key the girl had given him—pausing for a moment with it in his hand to indulge the new sadness and regret with which he could now regard her—then took the small suitcase of scuffed mock leather to the toilets. He changed quickly, put the crumpled suit and underclothes back into the case, then washed and smartened his appearance. The two small wads in his cheeks fattened his features. The padding beneath his jacket gave him a slight but noticeable paunch as he studied himself in the mirror. He parted his hair on the opposite side. A new man smiled with mild, resigned sadness out at him. He picked up his case and made his way back to the station's main

155

concourse; the illusory gardens were made more artificial, almost plastic, by the hard lighting in the roof.

He sat on a bench near the fountain. Its mild noise made him feel drowsy. His paunch was visible as he slumped more comfortably. It amused him. His companions on the bench also seemed sleepy. Liu settled into rest, his suitcase held in front of him between his feet, hands resting on the unfamiliar paunch. His papers, unwrapped and ready for inspection, served him like a shield and comforter.

Idly, he looked at his watch. A little more than four hours until his train to Wu Han. The girl . . .

What she could tell them, might tell them? The fountain whispered, an out-of-sequence drip making the sound less than perfect, reminding him of the mechanics involved in the swish of water. What could she tell them?

His papers, his new identity?

Not unless she had looked. And the girl was sufficiently professional not to have looked, not to clutter herself with information that would damage, hurt, betray. Liang assumed a new and beatified reality in his thoughts. Her capture hurt him. He repressed the shudder that accompanied images of her interrogation.

No, he was safe. In Wu Han there would be no delays, no time lag. Swiftness, contact, extraction of information, escape. He would keep ahead.

The drip subsided into the distant, general noise of the fountain and the whispers of waiting passengers. Liu slept.

The Ansett Boeing 727 from Sydney via Melbourne floated above its own drifting shadow towards Adelaide. Aubrey, at the window seat, watched that shadow slide across the low, green-stubbled sand dunes of the Coorong and ripple across the wrinkled water trapped between the coast and the Younghusband Peninsula. The bright midday sun glinted off the sea, making it as polished and terrain-like as a dented shield. Then they were crossing the delta at the mouth of the Murray River, and the heights of the Lofty Ranges were hazily before them, looming out of the heat.

The memory of the blows to temple and jaw that had been inflicted on him more than forty years before were as vivid as a current physical sensation to Aubrey. Time had not distorted the physical images. Yet he doubted the recollected days of May 1940. He could recall the sensations, the activities, the locations of that journey from Sedan to Louvain, but he was uncertain as to what Zimmermann had said, the expressions his features had revealed, the implications of his opinions and his narrative.

Sydney Airport had been a confused, half-perceived experience, his awareness fogged with tiredness and memory. Hyde had left him like a parcel while he collected their luggage, and Aubrey had drifted back through the years noting, like a signpost unseen when he first passed it, the prophetic nature of many of Zimmermann's observations concerning the NKVD's recruitment of agents in Spain. He had interrogated some of the people, the "moles," that were the fruit of the International Brigades. It was only from Zimmermann, however, that he had heard the name Aladko.

Doubt, however, had strengthened on the crowded Ansett aircraft from Sydney. What game had Zimmermann been playing with him? Any game at all? Was the man telling him the truth? *I was not available for purchase.* Was that true? Had he even said it? To an awakened Aubrey, taking in the landscape that slipped green and blue and brown and gold beneath the belly of the 727, the words had a suspiciously familiar ring. It was like something he might have said himself. In the files, the account of Aubrey's tussle with Zimmermann and the German's attempted escape made no reference—except in generalities—to the conversation that had immediately preceded the two blows to Aubrey's face.

The Boeing banked, its shadow melting and sliding and becoming as fluid as oil as it rose against the slopes of the Mount Lofty Ranges. Then the land dropped away again, and Aubrey was immediately struck by the sight of vineyards. Their regular green patterns on the lower slopes and spreading towards the coast of the gulf shocked him, and he felt his body itch with a fierce, younger man's anticipation. *Schiller.* Yes, Zimmermann's friend. Zimmermann had referred to Schiller being interrogated and bribed by Aladko, without success. He was, perhaps, the key.

The aircraft turned north. Adelaide lay ahead of the port wing, submitting to an envelope of visible heat. As the Boeing began its descent towards the city's airport, the haze revealed trees and parks, beyond which like a bastion stood the white towers of office buildings. The northern suburbs extended until they vanished in the heat. Aubrey experienced a sense of the illusory, as if he were pursuing the city, never to reach it; never to obtain his answer. The Barossa Valley lay somewhere north of Adelaide, in what appeared to be an impenetrable haze.

The sensation depressed him.

Hyde collected their luggage, then the key of the hire car from the Avis desk, once more depositing Aubrey in the passenger lounge like an elderly, geriatric relative until he had completed his chores. He used the locker key he had been given at Sydney airport, and collected the pistol that had been left for him. Another Heckler & Koch VP 70. Three spare magazines. He slipped it into his suitcase. Ten minutes later, they were threading through Adelaide's noonday traffic towards their hotel.

Aubrey remained silent for several minutes, as if Hyde had been no more than a cab driver, then he said: "I must call Shelley when we reach the hotel." It sounded like an order to a member of some imagined entourage.

"Welcome back to the world," Hyde replied. "I thought you'd gone walkabout."

"No," Aubrey remarked in a pinched, offended little tone that admitted the half-truth of Hyde's observation. "Far from it."

"Anyway, welcome to Adelaide."

White, windowed columns, palm trees lining the street, the strikingly cloudless sky; spring becoming summer almost as Aubrey watched.

"The 15th International Brigade, was that it?" he murmured.

"I was in the Scouts, not the Boys' Brigade."

The hotel was opposite the Cheltenham Racecourse. Hyde turned the car off the road and into its drive.

"Shelley can verify that. I remember that number, the 15th. Locals. Spanish volunteers. The Aragonese units in the area..." the old man muttered with increasing excitement. "There must be survivors, perhaps still living in the area. Madrid station could check..."

"We're here. You just carry on dreaming, I'll register."

"Thank you, Patrick," Aubrey replied icily.

Once ensconced in his room, Aubrey, tie loosened against the open-windowed heat and the humidity, dialled Shelley direct. Absent-mindedly, he emptied his pockets onto the bedside table while Hyde, slumped feet-up in a chair, sipped beer from the room's refrigerator. He stirred the collection of coins with his hand while he waited for Shelley to come on the line. He held up two British one pound coins.

"I told the Secretary to the Treasury, when these were first issued, that it was the experience of the Weimar Republic that a barrowful of notes was easier to push to the bakery than a barrowful of coins," he remarked. "He did not seem to appreciate the advice."

"I never even saw a white fiver," Hyde replied, staring at his can of lager. Aubrey waved him to silence, snapping into a more upright posture, old eyes brightly alert.

"Shelley—can you hear me?" A slight delay, then Shelley's voice was close enough to have come from the adjoining room.

Hyde stood up and walked to the open french windows. He stepped out onto the narrow balcony. Adelaide basked like a mottled animal in the sun. Aubrey's voice murmured behind him. To the north and west of the hotel, the city merged at the edge of shape and contour into the glittering, hazy sea. He breathed deeply, and closed his eyes.

It was some minutes later, when he had ceased to distinguish Aubrey's voice from the general murmur of traffic and insects around the potted plants on the balcony, that he was jolted into wakefulness by Aubrey's impatient voice at his side.

"I think we'll set out at once, don't you, Patrick?"

"You don't want a rest first?"

Aubrey searched Hyde's features for irony, and seemed satisfied. He shook his head. "No. I must talk to Schiller as quickly as possible." He paused, then: "I'm unhappy with the momentum of events so far. Cut off from our Chinese friends—Wei and David Liu—and quite as ignorant and confused as I was whole days ago."

Wittenberg.

"What is it?" Hyde asked, lowering the empty lager can from his lips. "What's the matter?" Aubrey's face had contracted, his eyes become vague. His lips were pursed.

Wittenberg. Zimmermann was born and bred in Wittenberg. He had not imagined that. It was in the current profile dossier Shelley had included.

"Wittenberg," he said.

"What about Wittenberg?"

Aubrey looked out across the landscape of Adelaide, his hands gripping the balcony rail, and saw the city retreating into the heat. Beyond the veil was Schiller. Was he any longer important? Was it 1938, or 1940 or 1945? "Wittenberg is in the German Democratic Republic, Patrick."

"Yes?"

"Zimmermann was born and lived in Wittenberg until he joined the army in 1934. His family, if they survived the war, would have found themselves living in the Russian Zone, and then in East Germany, after the war. Is that the most important fact about our German friend?"

"Christ!"

"He could have fallen into their hands *after* the war. Because of Wittenberg which is now called Lutherstadt. I must talk to Shelley again at once. He must get onto this..." Aubrey retreated into the shadows of the hot room. Hyde closed his eyes again, leaning against the window frame. He heard Aubrey dialling, the telephone purring like a cat as the dial returned after each digit. East Germany? Then Zimmermann could be KGB after all.

Wolfgang Zimmermann watched the rain running in mercury-swift tracks down the window of his hotel room, leaving orange, wriggling traces where the streetlamp shone blearily through. His room was in darkness. He had awoken with the decision to make the telephone call. He had moved to the telephone without thought, and begun dialling. It was one in the morning, but the number he had would enable him to reach Petya Kominski of the Bonn embassy staff in his flat.

Halfway through dialling the number, he paused to consider, and heard his heartbeat amplified in the lightless room, and his ragged breathing. Grinding his teeth, he continued to dial the remaining digits.

He heard the number ringing. He could picture the small, neat flat in Bonn, almost watch Kominski get out of bed, cross his bedroom, enter the hall, reach for the receiver...

"Yes?" Kominski said in German. "Can I help you?"

"Petya—it's me, Wolfgang."

"Wolf—what do you want? You woke me up." The voice sounded almost peevish.

"I'm sorry. I want you to do me an important favour."

"Oh?"

"Yes. You owe me a great many favours, Petya." Zimmermann could not decide whether his mounting irritation was with himself or the mildly truculent young Russian.

"All right. My promotion is largely due to you, I agree. What is it you want?"

"All the years, Petya. All the secret meetings..." Zimmermann reminded Kominski.

"Yes, yes," Kominski replied, sounding bored. "What do you want?"

The young Russian was actually *indifferent*. Zimmermann found it hard to believe. He said: "I want you to find out which of your people are following me around. *That*'s what I want."

"What? You're joking."

"I'm not. Think I can't recognise the type after all these years? There're two who are KGB, and there may be more I haven't spotted, dogging me night and day. Posing as *Pravda* people. Who are they?"

"No one. There's no one—"

"Don't give me that, you young puppy! I've *seen* them!"

"Don't get uptight, Wolf." Kominski's slight American accent, his Moscow Radio newsreader's tones, had always rankled with Zimmermann. Now, expressing amused indifference as they did, they enraged him.

"*I am not uptight.* Don't you realize how dangerous this could be? *Now*, of all times? Within ten days of the Treaty being ratified. If it came out now that the KGB were in close proximity, if *anyone* suspected it, the newspapers on the Right would have a field day. Springer's press would blacken me, and our precious Treaty."

"All right, calm down."

"You don't seem to understand what I'm saying. I've been as good as accused of working for the KGB a hundred times. If those people on my tail were even suspected for a moment, the case would be proved. Get rid of them. Find out who they are and get rid of them!"

At the other end of the line, Kominski chuckled softly into the tense silence. His voice was relaxed, soothing, when he replied.

"You're working too hard, Wolf. You're over-tense. I tell you there's no one. *You?* Why should anyone need to follow you?"

"Tell your masters—"

"No. Sorry, Wolf, but you're imagining it all. There's no one following you, no one investigating you. I can assure you of that. Now, get a good night's sleep."

"Kominski—"

The line crackled with ether for a moment, then clicked and purred. Zimmermann, taking the damp receiver from his cheek, stared at it as if he could not believe that Kominski had put an end to the call. Just like that, without listening, without believing a word. . .

He crashed the receiver onto its rest. The telephone fell onto the carpet. Zimmermann ignored it, striding across the darkened room, ignoring the pain from barking his shin against the metal edge of a coffee table. He squatted on his haunches before the door of the bar. He opened it. His face was twisted and malevolent in the pale light that the interior emitted. His still handsome features became gaunt and hunted in the glow. He removed a miniature whisky, then another, and poured the contents of the two small bottles into a plastic glass. He angrily twisted ice out of a polythene rack into the glass. Then he swallowed almost violently at the drink, making himself cough.

He could not believe it. He simply could not believe the manner of Kominski's reaction, his lack of concern, even interest. Everything depended upon the next ten days, everything. If he became suspect now, if any mud attached itself to him before the Treaty was ratified, then Vogel would lose the election, he would be ditched unceremoniously, and the Berlin Treaty might be abandoned. Couldn't those clowns see that?

He paced the room, sipping at his drink, the ice setting his teeth on edge.

Now, *now,* he kept repeating to himself, increasingly afraid. After all this time, now? Now? Why *now*?

They drove north-east through Salisbury, Elizabeth and Gawler on Highway 20. The suburbs of Adelaide straggled, as if limp and dehydrated by the heat, abashed and daunted by the utterly cloudless sky, towards the foothills of the low Barossa Range. At Gawler, Hyde turned the car onto the Sturt Highway, and they began to climb through a tidy, neat landscape of orchards and small farms before the slopes became neatly, rigidly ornamented with vineyards. Buildings too ornate and large to be farms squatted amid the dark-green trellises of vines; the wineries of the Barossa Valley.

Aubrey sat impatiently next to Hyde like someone forced to divert his course. The refreshment of a shower and change of clothing had already evaporated. The air blowing through the open windows of the car was hot and dusty. His short-sleeved shirt was already beginning to stick to his body.

Hyde turned off the highway at Nuriootpa and headed for Angaston. In his impatience to settle a matter he no longer thought important, Aubrey had not even bothered to telephone the winery. They would arrive like casual visitors, mildly interested. For Hyde, the lack of concern seemed inappropriate. Schiller might still hold the key—at least, one of the keys—to the puzzle. He had known Zimmermann then, after all. The hills rose ahead of them, smokily-blue.

Schiller's Winery was a large, three-storey building surrounded by palm trees and lawns. Sprinklers dazzled as the sun caught their revolving spouts and columns. The winery and vineyards that Hans-Dieter Schiller had inherited had been built and planted and developed in 1851—there was a carved date above the door, in the cool deep shadows thrown by the verandah that ran along the second storey of the building. Aubrey could just make out the date as Hyde brought the car to a halt beneath a palm tree. Attached to the main building was a smaller, two-storey wing of late nineteenth-century design; presumably the house rather than the winery. There was a sense of wealth, quiet but evident, and pride about the two unequal wings. The larger winery indicated the source of the wealth, the house one of its fruits. Huge, merely ornamental, white-painted hogsheads stood beside the door of the winery like a medieval craftsman's guild symbols.

Hyde got out of the car. Aubrey watched a tall, fair-haired young man in rolled-up shirtsleeves and neatly-pressed shorts and white stockings stand for a moment in the doorway of the winery, then come towards them. Aubrey was shocked. The young man reminded him forcibly of his own memories of Zimmermann. Germanic, almost arrogant, at ease and assured.

"G'day, can I help you?" he asked Hyde, merely glancing at Aubrey. His voice and accent were undoubtedly Australian. The image of Zimmermann dissipated.

"Wonder if we could have a word with the owner?"

"Mr. Schiller? You're out of luck, mate. He's gone walk-about. Sorry. What did you want him for?"

"My boss here"—Hyde indicated the car and Aubrey—"wine correspondent for the Diner's Club magazine. Know it?" The young man shook his head.

"Use American Express myself," he remarked.

"He's in Australia on holiday—been drinking a lot of your stuff. Wants to interview the owner. Bloody shame he's away."

"What do you do? Same line?"

"Stringer for a few European magazines—you know the sort of thing. Trying to get the Poms and the rest of 'em to find out where we are."

"Oh."

Aubrey was amused at Hyde's exaggerated, hard-boiled accent and manner. He nodded as the young man inspected him, then crossed to the car and held out his hand. Aubrey shook it.

"Name's Peter," he said. "I'm the office manager. I could help—or Mr. Schiller's daughter?" He leaned closer to the window of the car. "Matter of fact," he confided, "she runs the place these days. The old man's taken up photography. He's on one of his trips right now." Aubrey controlled the disappointment he felt leaking into his expression. "Had a book published last year. Big job, all colour. Cost almost twenty dollars to buy it.''

"I see," Aubrey murmured. "I really had no idea . . ."

"You're a real Pom, all right. Look, you want to talk to Miss Schiller? She's over at the house, going through the accounts for the week. She won't mind being interrupted.''

"Yes, certainly," Aubrey said with forced enthusiasm. He opened the door and climbed out. The sunlight lanced down through the blade-like leaves of the palm tree. "Thank you. If you'd be so good as to introduce us—my name is Kenneth Aubrey.''

Hyde was grinning at Aubrey's affected pomposity.

"Sure. Follow me.''

Peter left them standing in the shade of the first-floor verandah that ran along the house wing of the building. They heard knocking, then voices. A chair creaked, then they heard footsteps. Aubrey negligently held the back of a cane chair that stood to one side of the door, one of four arranged around a white-painted metal table, intricately patterned. Hyde shuffled his feet like a visitor of dubious social standing, hands behind his back.

The woman was about thirty. Her fair hair was scraped back from her forehead, and her eyes were pale blue. Her skin was unsoftened by makeup, except for lipstick, and appeared more tanned than merely suntanned. It seemed incongruous that she should be emerging from indoors. She wore a check blouse and slim blue denims. Aubrey held out his hand. She took it in a cool, firm grip.

"Mr. Aubrey? I'm Clare Schiller. *Signature* magazine?" Aubrey nodded. The woman seemed doubtful rather than flattered. "Peter, bring us some '81 and '82 bottles of riesling. The *qualitats* through to—*auslese*?" she asked, turning to Aubrey again, who nodded once more. "And some of the '77 cabernet.''

"Sure." Peter re-entered the house.

"Make yourselves comfortable," Clare Schiller said, indicating the table and chairs beside the door.

Once they were seated, she seemed to await some utterance from her guests. Her eyes were clear, sharply-focused, and the faint lines around them might have been caused as much by inner amusement as by sunlight. Peter returned, wheeling a wine-cooler and opened it, to display a number of tall bottles. Then he brought the glasses and the bottles of red wine.

The woman poured glasses of pale Schiller's Rhine Riesling

for them. Aubrey sipped in an informed, birdlike manner. Hyde, in persona, swallowed half the glass in a gulp.

"Very pleasant," Aubrey remarked.

"And if you're a wine correspondent, I'm Ned Kelly's sister," the woman commented. She seemed unruffled. Hyde laughed, and wine which went up his nose made him cough. "And your mate's a real connoisseur, I can see that. What do you want with my father?"

"I—um," Aubrey began.

"Look, you're drinking one of our poorest years in the last ten. Can't you tell?"

"Unfamiliar . . ." Aubrey murmured.

Clare Schiller threw the contents of Aubrey's glass towards the sunlight. It glittered, then became a brown wet spot on the drive. She opened a second bottle, and filled his glass.

"Try that."

"Delicious," he said, recognising its superior quality. "The '82, I see."

"Young and beautiful. Now you're drinking the good stuff, tell me what game you're playing."

"Ah." Aubrey reached into his pocket and handed Clare Schiller a folded piece of paper. "You can ring that Canberra number now, if you wish. In turn, to confirm what you might be told, they will put you through to—shall we say the police?"

"Police?"

"Or you can listen to my story now and confirm it later."

She was thoughtfully silent for a few moments, sipping absently at her own wine, then she said: "Tell your story. You—" she added, turning to Hyde.

"Yes?"

"You can go on drinking the '81."

"Right."

Aubrey launched into his explanation. He was frank with the woman, though not entirely. He spoke for perhaps five minutes, sipping from time to time at the wine, the woman filling his glass once while he spoke. Aubrey provided no background concerning the nature of the doubts regarding Zimmermann, merely the necessity of talking to her father about the man's Spanish experiences. Aubrey had decided that a cover story would be inappropriate. It was as if he were already talking to her father.

When he had finished, she remained silent for some minutes.

Her eyes moved over an internal ledger, balancing his account. Then she looked up, and nodded.

"I realise you've told me a lot less than half, but I guess what you've said is something like the truth. My father's on a photography trip. Before I tell you where, I'll ring this number." She stood up and went into the house.

"I'll bet she asks directory enquiries what the number of the British High Commission is," Hyde remarked. "What's wrong with the '81, anyway?"

"I'd be disappointed if she didn't," Aubrey replied. "Well, what do you think?"

"What do you want to do? You want to chase after him?"

Aubrey looked over his shoulder, as if back towards Adelaide and its airport. "I'll be out of touch with Shelley," he fretted. "And yet . . . ? The girl gives me confidence. If she's like her father, he'll have forgotten nothing, he'll be shrewd. He may have a good idea . . ."

"Give Shelley a bloody chance? You only gave him his orders an hour or so ago. You've got—what, a couple of days?"

"I have less than ten before the Treaty's signed . . ."

Clare Schiller emerged from the shadows inside the doorway.

"That extension number you gave me? I spoke to a Mr. Price, a Third Secretary or something at the High Commission. He seems to think you're straight. Quite polite, he was." She nodded mockingly, then sat down. Behind her head, pendulous fuchsias added to the exoticism of a kookaburra's ringing laugh. Hyde's head snapped up, and he grinned. "Welcome home, cobber," the woman drawled with evident irony and amusement.

"Miss Schiller, where is your father?"

She was clutching a large book on her lap. She held it up by way of explanation. *Hidden Australia* was lettered above a photograph of a bird with a small snake in its mouth. The picture was sharp, vivid, keenly alive. The photographer was H-D. Schiller.

"That's what my father does these days. He's quite good, too. Good job I'm as good at running his bloody winery for him, isn't it?" The remark was made with only the slightest tinge of bitterness.

"Where is he now?"

"Cooper's Creek." She looked at Hyde, whose face fell.

"Is that far?"

"North through the Flinders to Lake Eyre, turn right," Hyde said. "Maybe five hundred miles. Trouble is, the Creek's two

hundred miles or more long, just in South Australia." He turned
to Clare Schiller. "Can you be more precise? Can you get in
touch with him?"

Aubrey appeared sunk in some private and disappointed reverie. He paid no attention to Hyde's questions, or the girl's reply.

"He's working the Creek west to east. He calls in every
couple of days."

"When did he leave?"

"Last week."

"Is he going through the Flinders first—taking snaps there?"
The girl nodded. "Where's the last place he called you from?"

She frowned. "Day before yesterday. Um, Wilpena—no, that
was the time before. Nearer Leigh Creek."

"Got a map?"

"Yes."

"Get it. Please."

Clare hurried into the house. Hyde watched the silent, medita-
tive Aubrey and had no idea what decision the old man would
make. The girl was back with the large-scale map of South
Australia within seconds. She unfolded it on the table.

"Here," she said.

"Then he was almost out of the Flinders Range two days ago.
Mm." He looked up at the girl. "When will he ring again?"

"Today, tomorrow . . ." She shrugged. "He'll ring some time.
He always does. Pretends to ask after business." She shook her
head with a smile. "You really do want to talk to him, don't
you?"

Hyde nodded. He studied the map. His finger traced a black
line north. "Birdsville Track. We might be able to head him off,
if we get a bloody move on."

"If you go like a bat out of hell you might," Clare observed.

"Too right. I'll need a Land Rover, supplies, the whole
bloody shooting match."

"What about the wine correspondent?"

"Mr. Aubrey—sir."

The woman's eyes widened in surprise.

"Yes, Patrick?"

"Say the word—do we go or not?"

"I—" He paused, then shrugged. "I must do something!" he
suddenly snapped. "I am at the other end of the world from the
epicentre of this disturbance. Yes—we must go."

"Right, then we'd better head back to town. There's a lot to do, and not enough time to do it in." He looked at Clare Schiller. "Love you and leave you."

"Tell me something new," she remarked with surprising bitterness.

"You asked around?"

"Yes."

"And?"

"The owner of the vineyard, Schiller, is on a photography trip, up north."

"Where, precisely?"

"Cooper's Creek."

"And Hyde and Aubrey must be about to follow him in the Land Rover they have hired. Good, then we must follow—by car and by aircraft, just to be certain. Schiller was a wartime comrade of Zimmermann. Evidently that acquaintance has become vitally important to Aubrey. As it has to ourselves. We'd better find him first."

"Yes, Comrade General."

"Don't call me that! *Mister Jones,* understand?"

"Yes, Mr.—Jones."

SEVEN

Outback

From his vantage point on a wooden bench near the Dingdao Temple, David Liu watched the small, neat man emerge from the door of the hotel which overlooked the East Lake. Behind the hotel, the buildings of the three municipalities of Wu Han reached into a late summer, humid, smoggy sky. Inside, in one of those rooms where the windows were shaded by overhanging, ornamental eaves, Wolfgang Zimmermann had first fallen ill during his visit to the city. And the small, neat man—Liu glanced again at the snapshot in his hand—was the hotel doctor who had first attended him.

The doctor strolled towards the trolley-bus stop near the lakeside. He dabbed lightly and fussily at his forehead with a very white handkerchief, doubtless regretting the absence of the hotel's air conditioning. He walked along the water's edge, seemingly amused by the approach of glossy ducks and the wading intentness of bright water birds.

Liu left his seat, patting his breast pocket to assure himself once more that he carried the details of his cover: his means of questioning the doctor.

Liu's journey from Shanghai to Wu Han the previous day had been uneventful. He had booked into the Sheng Li hotel on the other bank of the Yangtse River, in the Hankou municipality. It was a sufficiently good hotel for a minor government official to use. His room overlooked the river and, beyond it, the dykes and the water country that surrounded the city. Factory chimneys belched smoke, power stations fumed, steel plants—some of which the West Germans had helped to finance and construct, hence one of the motives for Zimmermann's visit—flared and erupted between himself and the green flat plains. The first hills of the distant Tapieh Shan were hidden in humid smog.

He had slept for much of the journey from Shanghai. His

papers had been inspected three times while he was still at
Shanghai station, and another twice on the train; and had held
up. Then they were scrutinized at the barrier of Wu Han station,
then once more at the hotel desk. Each time they had been
greeted by a perceptible deference; at the least, with a recognition of equality. Fleeting, half-seen impressions of the journey
remained with him, particularly the lowering, dark, smog-haloed
monster of an industrial city that seemed to have settled on the
fertile green plain of the Yangtse.

He had rung the East Lake Hotel but had not spoken to the
doctor, merely affirmed his duty shift. He had no idea whether or
not Frederickson had yet arrived in Wu Han, his industrialists in
tow. Strangely, he did not concern himself. Leaving Shanghai, he
had left many things: the girl, Bin, Frederickson, immediate
danger. In Wu Han, he was beginning again, and beginning
effectively, properly. First this doctor, then the specialist who had
treated Zimmermann at Wu Han's Hospital of October 1911. He
would question them both. He possessed an unexpected and
welcome confidence that either or both of them would provide
the answers he sought.

The doctor held his bag in front of him in both hands as he
stood waiting for the trolley-bus. Beyond him, the East Lake and
the low wooded hills of its surrounding parks belied the industri-
alization of the city. It might, except for the temperature, have
been an early morning mist that hazed the air. Liu joined the
small queue for the trolley-bus, three places behind the doctor.

Their journey took them out of the parkland around the lake,
down the wide and tree-lined Wu luo lu Street towards the huge
Changjiang Bridge swooping over the Yangtse. Liu watched the
freighters and barges. The rumble of a train on the lower level of
the bridge was apparent through the soles of his shoes. Cyclists
and pedestrians crossing the bridge lent the city the same sense
of urgency possessed by Shanghai. Hoardings exhorted the
population to continue the semi-sacred work of modernization,
promising them television sets and dreamed-of cars as their
reward for even greater efforts. Liu was stimulated and enervated
at the same time by the messages the hoardings offered.

The trolley-bus trundled beneath the rounded hump of Tortoise
Hill, then crossed the Han River towards the orderly, wide
boulevards of Hankou municipality. Liu watched the doctor as
they neared the residential district off Zhongshan Boulevard.
When the doctor stood up and eased his way through the
standing passengers towards the doors, Liu rose and followed

im. Events were moving his way. The doctor evidently lived
ear the Sheng Li hotel. Keeping fifty yards behind, having
aused to retie a shoelace, Liu followed the doctor towards the
iver. Modern apartment blocks flanked the quiet street. The
eaves were beginning to turn brown and gold on the trees, as if
he humid, hot air was somehow roasting them.

Liu followed him up the steps of an apartment block, now
nly a few yards behind. The doctor, turning his head at the
ound of more urgent footsteps than his own, saw Liu instantly
pproach him, a card in his hand.

"Doctor Tai?" Liu asked, his voice carefully official. The
octor assented with a careful nod of his head which might have
een an embryonic bow; an anticipation of rank. "My name is
iu—Public Security from Shanghai." He flashed the card at
ai, allowing him to recognize the small official photograph and
ead the rank and status of the stranger. Tai nodded his head once
1ore; the bow was more evident. The metamorphosis of the
romoted Party official into a minor policeman had been effected.
iu's authority had increased, required deference.

"Yes?" Tai asked, seemingly untroubled. He, too, was a
arty man, and wore his membership like a protective carapace.
What is it?"

"I wish to ask you some questions."

"Concerning myself?" Worry flickered for a moment in his
ark, tired eyes. Tai was perhaps no more than forty. He felt
imself secure—unless the Party had somehow changed the
arameters of criminality. Deng's uncertain, fearful China stared
ut at Liu for a moment.

"No," Liu assured him, shaking his head. "You may be in
ossession of knowledge we require, that is all. May I come
1?"

"Certainly." For a moment, the seemingly-solid structure of
>octor Tai's life and position had been threatened by a distant
emor. Now that he had established that the epicentre was well
way from himself, assurance leaked back into his features.
Please follow me."

They ascended to the top floor of the apartment block in a
reaking, slow lift. Tai ushered Liu down a narrow, thinly-
arpeted corridor to a dark wooden flush door. He unlocked it,
1owing in his unexpected guest. The plain bare living room
1formed Liu that Tai was a fastidious, unacquisitive bachelor.

"Tea?" Tai asked.

"Perhaps later."

"Sit down, please. Tell me why you have had to travel up from Shanghai to see me." Only some of the assurance was adopted; much of it derived, presumably, from Tai's competence, his secure and unruffled past. Liu felt he might need to shake that confidence. On the other hand, Tai seemed prepared to be helpful.

Liu removed a notebook from his pocket, and a pen. He pretended to consult notes. The room was airless, dry. "My enquiries concern the German diplomat, Zimmermann," he began.

"Yes?" Tai replied, genuinely puzzled. Was that a quick flicker of suspicion, secrecy there? Liu could not be certain. "What of him? That was some months ago. As you know, he was transferred to Shanghai soon after he entered the hospital here. I merely attended—"

"Yes, you attended him when he first fell ill."

"I was on duty at that time. My report is with your superiors in Shanghai, I am certain."

"Yes. I have read it," said Liu slowly, allowing an ambiguity of tone to possess his voice.

"Well, then..."

"I am not necessarily concerned with the medical details, Doctor. My superiors are interested in other matters."

"I see. Am I permitted to know—?"

"Of course," Liu snapped. "Otherwise, you could not help me." Liu leaned confidentially forward. "The illness was most embarrassing, you understand..." Tai nodded cautiously, as if he felt himself being drawn towards the admission of some unspecified guilt. "Anyone responsible for that embarrassment to the People's Republic and to the leadership would be in serious trouble..."

"Responsible? How responsible?"

"I believe you diagnosed food poisoning?" Tai nodded. "Your report does not indicate how many other cases of food poisoning occurred at the same time, in the hotel."

"I—"

Liu felt an inward relief. His briefing by Buckholz had indicated Zimmermann was alone in his induced illness, but the report was based on hearsay, on second and third-hand accounts gathered over more than a month. Yet it had been true.

"There were no others?"

"No."

"Strange. What caused the illness?"

"Snake—I am convinced it was the snake," Tai said hurriedly. "Perhaps the fish, but more likely the snake." Tai essayed a smile intended to charm. "Westerners should not be so adventurous when first coming to China."

"Did any of his party have the snake?"

"I—do not think so. Officer Liu?"

"Yes?"

"What is the purpose of this enquiry? How important is it that the food he ate is known?"

"If it *was* the food that caused the poisoning . . ." Liu said, enunciating carefully. Tai's features paled, then he coughed and again attempted the smile.

"I am certain it was the food—so were the doctors at the hospital here. I was never told what they diagnosed in Shanghai."

"Does food poisoning usually cause delirium?"

"Any fever may, depending on its severity—why?"

"Do you agree, doctor, that there are elements present in our society who wish the failure of the Revolution, who wish to undermine Chairman Deng's glorious Four Modernizations? Who would like to tie China's legs together in the race to the year 2000?"

Tai looked appalled by the jargon and its message of treachery. The ripples he had seen coming in his direction had become a wave buffeting against him, with rougher seas behind it.

"I—suppose so . . ."

"Here, in Wu Han, scene of the first victorious battle of the 1911 Revolution," Liu continued, his voice mounting, his eyes increasingly, deliberately glazed, "home of the National Peasant Movement Institute, scene of key battles with the Guomindang which paved the way for our final victory . . . In *this city*, there have been revisionist plots, trouble fomented among the peasants and workers by filthy lickspittle counter-Revolutionary elements!" Liu had half-risen from his seat. He settled back into it. Tai's face was white, his hands rubbing each other in distress on his lap. His knees were pressed primly together. "You understand me, Doctor? There are elements who would have delighted in the embarrassment to the leadership, to Noble Steersman Deng . . ." Liu flung in the *People's Daily* epithet which always accompanied reference to the Chairman, further establishing his conformist fanaticism to Tai. "Would they not?"

"I—I suppose it is possible . . ." Tai kept looking towards the window as if seeking escape.

"It is very possible. That is my mission, Doctor." Liu leaned confidentially forward in his chair. "Can you say that this Westerner was not poisoned deliberately?"

There was a silence then, long and tense. Liu saw the conflicting emotions on Tai's face with a sense of disappointment. It seemed that Tai perhaps had suspected a deliberate act of poisoning, had suspected there was something unusual, not even logical, about Zimmermann's illness, but he knew nothing. He was certain of nothing, possessed no facts. Liu decided to pursue the line of questioning no further as soon as Tai shook his head.

"To me," the doctor said slowly, his voice diminished and small in the plain, bare room, "there was nothing unusual about the case. You are privy to matters I know nothing about. I am afraid I cannot help you. I know nothing. I merely examined this man, relieved his distress as much as I could, and summoned an ambulance. His symptoms were consistent with food poisoning."

"I see," Liu replied with an evident disappointment which indicated belief in Tai's statement. The doctor appeared relieved. Liu shrugged. "Well, there are no more questions." Tai's relief flourished. "You will, of course, report nothing of this conversation." Tai obediently shook his head and rose unsteadily to his feet. He was taller than Liu, but diminished by his sudden encounter with what he regarded as police authority, police suspicion. Greater authority, confidence and assurance than his own had knocked on his door, demanding entry.

"No, of course not," he said quietly.

Liu was disappointed. Considering Tai, he had believed the line of questioning was right; brutal, sinister, surprising. Yet it had opened no doors for him. Tai knew nothing, was in no way privy to any suspicious circumstances regarding the illness of Zimmermann.

"How did you talk to him? Do you speak his language?" Liu asked.

"An interpreter accompanied me to his suite. Also, one of his staff was there, who spoke Mandarin well."

"I see. Delirious, wasn't he?"

"Not when I treated him, no. Disorientated, in pain—but when conscious, quite lucid."

"I see. Thank you, Doctor Tai. Good day."

"Good day."

As Liu walked towards the lift, it seemed to him that Tai slammed the door with a vast feeling of relief. Or perhaps nerveless fingers could not control the force they applied to closing the door. The echo of its slamming followed Liu down the corridor.

The sky was cloudless, uniformly blue except where it was rendered a brassy colour around the noon sun. Aubrey sat in the shadow of a canopy which was fastened to the side of the Land Rover and supported like a shop awning by two thin metal poles. On his lap Buckholz's transcript of the interrogation of Wolfgang Zimmermann went unregarded for a moment as he attended to Hyde's restlessness.

"What's the matter, Hyde?"

"I—I want to check we're not being followed."

"What?"

"Just to make sure."

"You suspect something?"

"One car—been with us since we left Hawker. Keeping more or less to our speed, well back behind us."

"I see." Hyde was rubbing his bare arms as if, impossibly, he felt cold. "Very well. Where is it now?"

Hyde shook his head. "It passed when we pulled off the road. If it's interested, it won't be far away." Dramatically, and perhaps for self-assurance, Hyde removed the pistol from the small of his back, and checked the magazine. "OK," he said.

"I gather you were looking for bugs under the car just now?"

"I didn't find one. But they don't need one, do they? This isn't London. There aren't too many places to go to on this road." He waved his arm to indicate the country around them.

Hyde had stopped for their midday meal and rest within the boundaries of the Flinders Range National Park. They had already driven more than a hundred miles north of Port Augusta, where they had spent the night in a motel after arriving late from Adelaide.

"Very well. I'll keep alert," Aubrey promised.

"Your gun?" Aubrey patted the briefcase beside him on the blanket on which he was seated. "Right. See you."

Aubrey watched Hyde move away from the shade of the Land Rover, his upper torso bisected by the line of the open bonnet. Almost the moment he was gone, Aubrey felt the heat assail him, making him immediately drowsy. It was as if the heat aided their pursuers, if such pursuit existed. Reluctantly, Aubrey got to his feet and put his straw hat on his head, stepping out of the shade into a fierce heat that might have been emitted from one of the foundries of Whyalla that had flared into the hot night as they drove north towards Port Augusta. All Aubrey recollected of that drive was a fleeting, neon-lit, star-bright landscape and sky which had followed the hiring of the Land Rover and purchase of supplies in Salisbury. Aubrey had telephoned the hotel and the British High Commission in Canberra while Hyde obtained water, food, petrol, emergency equipment.

When Aubrey had climbed into the Land Rover, he had been struck by its air of expedition, the prophecy it suggested of desert and wild place. It had seemed unreal. In a way, even deep into the Flinders Range, it still seemed unreal except for the heat. St. Mary's Peak was steel-grey a little to the south, the river red gums in full dark leaf surrounded the campsite; the hills south of the Brachina Gorge were dark and glossy with vegetation. There was grass as well as dust and stony, flinty creek beds. After the farming country on the edge of the southern extent of the mountain range, this place still did not unnerve or appear alien. Thus far, Aubrey had moved north through seemingly familiar landscapes.

He moved about slowly, watching Hyde as he became a speck of shirt and light slacks climbing the slight incline back towards the road. Then a rock obscured him, the shadow of a group of heavy-boled gums caused him to vanish.

At that moment Aubrey did feel isolated and alone, until he saw Hyde again, climbing slowly up the slope of a shallow, suncrowned cliff. Presumably he was taking some kind of short-cut. He topped the cliff, and disappeared. Unsettled, conscious of the silence which the noise of insects and the laughter of a bird did nothing to lessen, Aubrey returned to the shade of the canopy and to the somehow real companion of their journey: Zimmermann. He remembered lines he thought belonged to Eliot. *Who is the third who walks always beside you?* And again, *There is always another one walking beside you . . .*

He attended to Buckholz's file. Memories of Zimmermann's escape from that attic room in Louvain pricked his consciousness for a moment. Waking with a painful jaw, seeing groggily the chair balanced on the bed, beneath the damaged skylight; the door open where Zimmermann had, for some reason, re-entered the room, to attempt escape via the roof. His own tottering climb onto the shabby chair, its crazy tilting, his effort to heave himself through the skylight and the chair slipping away from under his feet so that he was left hanging above the bed, elbows bent and the perspiration beginning to break out on his forehead and beneath his arms. Then he had heaved his head through the skylight and looked around, his face cooled by a mild breeze.

Zimmermann was crouching at the edge of the sloping, green-tiled roof, Aubrey's pistol still in one hand, his face slowly displaying the familiar smile. Aubrey had scrabbled unathletically onto the roof and inched his way down its slope towards the German. At no time did Zimmermann point the pistol in his direction; it was as if he had forgotten the gun. When Aubrey reached him, the German had shrugged and simply handed it over. They had retreated back up the roof to the skylight to the accompaniment of artillery fire, answered now more hesitantly and distantly, like the shouts of an unsuccessful bully making empty threats, by the German tanks. Zimmermann, pausing at the attic window of another empty room, looked back at Aubrey with no trace of regret or disappointment on his features.

Memory had almost tricked him into sleep. Shaking his head to lighten its sense of numbness, Aubrey conscientiously quartered the scene in front of him, squinting into the hard glare and the shadows thrown by cliffs and gum trees. No one. He attended to the files open on his lap.

It was quite easy now to take up Buckholz's interrogation of Zimmermann like a familiar book. More than a narrative, it had become a drama in Aubrey's imagination. He saw GIs moving armed and unfamiliar and often helmeted, khaki ghosts, through the panelled rooms and flagged and pillared halls of the castle that Buckholz's section of G-2 had commandeered as their headquarters; the stamp and click of boots, the out-of-place accents, the combination of awe and disrespect.

Aubrey read a passage that had intrigued and troubled him earlier. Only Buckholz was present; Lieutenant Waleski was engaged in a separate interrogation, presumably in his inimitable style. There was brandy and cigars, a civilized atmosphere. Notes in Buckholz's familiar handwriting set the scene like a careful dramatist.

Zimmermann had been open, even indiscreet, with the American. There were the phrases—*I would have supported a plot even before the war...Stauffenberg's only error was to fail...Yes, my superior, General Gehlen, has always been loyal—it's where he and I disagree...*

It seemed evident to Aubrey that Buckholz's mind had already turned towards the possibility of recruiting Zimmermann for some post-war intelligence work for the Americans, for the questions proceeded to the Soviet Union in an obvious manner. Zimmermann's answers, too, were clear and pointed. An insect

buzzed near Aubrey's head. He brushed it aside, finding his
temperature rise even from that small effort.

*No, I accept that Stalin made mistakes . . . I don't think you
Americans have much to boast of—what about your Negro
population's freedom? . . .*

Aubrey flicked over the page.

*You must remember that the Revolution attempted, is still
attempting, to drag Russia into the twentieth century—of course
there have been mistakes . . . Yes, there is much to admire . . .*

Aubrey turned another page, then another, as if anxious to
reach the resolution of some dramatic, fictional crisis. He felt his
temperature mounting steadily as he searched the pages.

Socialism—Hitler? Incompatible . . . Aubrey smiled. He could
hear the words on Zimmermann's lips. *Lenin says . . .* Aubrey let
his eyes roam the succeeding pages. *Marx says . . . Lenin says . . .*

He looked up with a jerky movement of his head. The sunlight
beyond the canopy glared at him. The landscape swam into a
haze, reformed. The bald light and inky shadows hurt his eyes.

He closed the transcript after noting that an army stenographer
had been present. It was a faithful account made at the time, not
a later recollection. He sighed with dissatisfaction. Zimmermann?
A Marxist-Leninist mouthpiece, devoid of originality of mind or
expression?

Was Zimmermann playing a game—avoiding any possible
recruitment by the Americans by pretending socialist sympathies?
Was this really Zimmermann, after five years of war and on the
verge of defeat, beaten, captive, weary?

Aubrey patted the transcript, almost smiling. It was as if he
anticipated pleasures to come from an entertaining, enthralling
narrative. Yet he was troubled, also.

Zimmermann was a German, not a Russian. Zimmermann had
encountered the NKVD in the person of Aladko, in Spain. He
had been under no illusions then. He had not swallowed the
conformism of National Socialism—would he have been open to
persuasion now? If he was at pains to impress his lack of
persuasion by Aladko in 1940, why was he so remiss as to
indicate Russian sympathies in 1945? One record contradicted
the other.

Aubrey shook his head. Anticipation, yes. But not of pleasure
or amusement. The file beneath his hand was somehow dangerous—
suspicious and unreal . . .

Unreal?

The word returned, even though he tried to banish it. It was, somehow, unreal. Untrue?

Hyde huddled in the cleft in the rocks overlooking a neat, ordered campsite with its barbecue pit and wooden toilet hut. He might have been no more than twenty miles from the outskirts of Sydney or Melbourne or Adelaide. The shade of a narrow-boled blue gum fell across Hyde's place of concealment. A moment before he had reached it, a pair of rock wallabies had bounced away across the cliffs, causing the men below him to look up. Seeing the moving wallabies, they had laughed and taken no further interest in the rocks above them.

Three steaks on the barbecue grill, sausages enough for three. Only two men, however, in shorts and bright shirts were standing near the van; which meant that there was a third man watching the Land Rover just as he was watching the Volkswagen. He needed to get back to Aubrey.

He studied the two men through his field glasses. He recognised neither of them. Their voices floated up to him, quiet but distinct. Their Australian accent disturbed him as a species of treachery rather than mere danger. He could smell the steaks, see the blue smoke ascending from the grill in a thin, straight line. A kookaburra laughed in the tree above him.

Three men, then. No sign of Petrunin. Even the thought of the man made him chilly. The Russian had achieved the significance of a destiny, a fate that lay ahead even as it pursued him. He did not intentionally enlarge or dignify Petrunin in this way, but his shoulder ached with the old wound whenever he thought of the man. He knew with a fine and chilling clarity, that Petrunin would be happy to see him dead; not even beaten or outboxed, just dead.

He levered himself back among the rocks to the bole of the gum. A bright spider bobbed and wobbled along a thread of its web, spun around a tiny clump of yellow wild flowers. They had been secure, come all the way from Hong Kong to the South Australian outback, and Petrunin was, at least his people were, still no more than a step behind them. Apparently, he was inescapable.

Hyde brushed the spider's web and the tuft of flowers deliberately as he rose. The spider bobbed violently, but clung onto the thread, upside down. The flowers stilled, the thread quieted. The spider continued. Hyde, despite himself, grinned. Then he scuttled his way down the opposite side of the cliff, making his way back to Aubrey and the Land Rover as quickly as he could.

The low wooden bungalow which was the home of the hospital specialist who had examined and treated Zimmermann during his confinement in Wu Han was on the outskirts of the municipality of Wu Chang, part of a privileged development for important professional and Party men near the East Lake. There were other such developments in the conurbation of Wu Han, especially where the banks, offices and palaces of colonial days survived in Hankou.

There was space here, and the trees of the parks around the vast lake masked the industrial city that lay to the west, where the low sun was creating a purpled, smoky gold wash of the sky as its rays struck through the industrial haze. Eastwards, the gold was tinged with pink above the advancing dark blue line of night. Skeletal, fragile pagodas rose above low trees. Delicate willow-pattern bridges arched over narrow inlets where moving swans dragged the water into creases behind them. A few small boats were being poled or oared across the smooth, glass-like water. David Liu breathed deeply. The air was almost fresh after the humid day, with even the merest hint of cold and autumn.

He looked at his watch. Eight-thirty. The specialist had been at home for half-an-hour. He had arrived in a small, fawn car, which was itself another token of esteem and importance, just like the bungalow. There was warm light at the windows, and music from inside. Liu could hear hedge-clippers clicking from an adjoining property, even the whisper of a lawn sprinkler. Wu Han's privileged, its elite, resided beside the East Lake.

He moved swiftly towards the doctor's front door. This, he told himself, was the significant encounter. This man knew the drugs, the visitors, the medical condition. He would have heard the Russian spoken, known the nature of the questions asked under drugs, the quality of the answers given. The man could prove that Zimmermann was a KGB agent.

Or prove the opposite?

Liu dismissed the question and rang the doorbell. It chimed gently inside the house, like a glass bell. He turned swiftly to look once more at the lake as it slipped into darkness, and then the door was opened. A small old man bowed.

"Sir?" he asked. Liu was transported back through time to the China his grandfather remembered. A servant?

"I wish to see Doctor Meng." Liu's voice hinted at authority, purpose. The old man's face crumpled into sharper lines, rivulets of old fears suddenly in spate.

"Yes?" He seemed at a loss. Such people did not come to this house; this refuge.

Liu handed him his policeman's ID. It was the first swift, telling blow in the encounter he had determined should take place between himself and Meng. Inside, the sleek-haired, upright, tall specialist might already be wondering who his visitor was. He had no idea what was coming to him, Liu thought with a certain savage satisfaction.

"Tell Doctor Meng I have some questions for him."

The old man hurried away into the warm shadows of the hall and through a door into a well-lighted room. Soft laughter was silenced for a moment, then there was a murmur of voices, the scrape of a chair, and then a taller figure than that of the old man was coming to the front door.

Meng was wearing a silk dressing-gown in deep golden and brown shades. A dragon appeared at his left shoulder. He was confident, almost amused, slightly puzzled.

"How can I help you?" he asked.

"I—have some confidential enquiries to make, doctor. I believe you can help me."

"They concern me or my family?" Meng asked loftily.

"Not directly, no."

"Then you had better come in, officer—?" He looked at the ID card for a moment, then handed it back. "Officer Liu. Come in. We can talk in my study."

Liu entered the bungalow. Rich and spicy aromas of a meal greeted him, and the smell of incense. There were deep rugs on the floor of the hall.

Yes, he thought. This man is wealthy, intelligent, privileged. He will know. Liu recalled the photographs he had seen the moment before the first shots in the Yu Garden. Drugs, treatment, visitors. This man would *know*. He was almost there . . .

"Herr Professor Zimmermann, are you then prepared to categorically deny the insinuations of this newspaper story?"

The voice of the Press Association correspondent, an Englishman Zimmermann normally respected and to whom he might well have been amicable, seemed a laconic, insulting drawl. The press conference was crowded, of course; not unexpectedly, in view of the story carried by the early editions of the *Dusseldorfer Abendzeitung*. According to the members of Vogel's press staff it was also in most of the principal West German evening newspapers. Foreign pressmen, in particular the British and the Americans, were much in evidence and prepared to shout their questions above the hubbub created by the German press corps covering Vogel's campaign.

"Of course I deny it!" Zimmermann snapped, immediately regretting the evident irritation in his tone. The perspective of the Springer press in Berlin and Hamburg, the popular Sundays, then the weeklies, opened before him, daunting and angering him. A field day, it would be called.

"What, precisely, do you refute?" the Press Association man asked. The conference room of the Dusseldorf Hilton had fallen silent. Eyes watched him carefully from behind a veil of cigarette smoke. Hands were poised over notepads. The two press aides who flanked him were no longer real. He was alone on the dais, behind the long table with its crisp white cloth and water jug and glasses and array of microphones like steel flowers.

Zimmermann leant back in his chair, a conscious gesture of assurance at variance with his feelings. "Everything, naturally. Except the details concerning the Treaty itself—a few of which are correct."

A few droplets of laughter, insufficient to refresh. The room was hot, eager; not hostile—not yet—but the smell of a story, a possible scandal or at the least a *cause célèbre,* was as redolent as blood.

"There are no secret clauses in the Treaty?" the correspondent from *Die Welt* demanded to know.

Zimmermann spread his hands above the white cloth, and shook his head.

"There are not."

"What about the accusations of secret trade agreements—huge trade credits?" *Suddeutsche Zeitung* of Munich. Zimmermann's familiarity with, and knowledge of, the press corps now seemed fatuous and redundant. "The story calls it a massive bribe."

Of course, they were all furious that their papers hadn't carried the story, which had originated with a so-called exclusive in *Bild* that morning. All the paraphernalia—unnamed sources, classified evidence, more to come . . .

The evening papers had gutted it, built on it, speculated and fantasized about it. Now the dailies wanted their hundred marks' worth.

"That is nonsense. The full text of the Treaty has been public knowledge for months."

"But it is asserted, Herr Professor, that there is another and undisclosed document, which exacts the price of the Treaty itself?" *Frankfurter Rundschau*. "Do you deny that?"

"Of course I deny it."

Flashguns flickered and blinded, as if he had said something which betrayed him. The red lights on the portable TV cameras, perched like ugly pets on the shoulders of their cameramen, attracted Zimmermann's glance. Film cameras whirred at the back of the conference room.

"As for yourself, Herr Professor," the correspondent of *Bild* and *Bild am Sonntag* began. Zimmermann steeled himself. Springer's man. Others in the room, too, attended to the tall, bespectacled political muckraker. This was the beginning, Zimmermann told himself. This is the source and this is the rabid animal. My enemy.

"Yes? You should know. It's your story," he essayed. A small trickle of laughter. The correspondent smirked, and bowed.

"Indeed."

"What is your source—the CIA?" Zimmermann suddenly snapped, irrationally irritated, losing his temper plainly and mistakenly.

"The old smear, Herr Professor?" More laughter. Zimmermann cursed himself. "Do you deny any contact or affiliation with foreign agents yourself, Herr Professor?"

Herr Professor . . . After selling his business, there had been that brief, enjoyable period as an academic: economic research at Bremen, funded by the German Research Foundation. Now this odious, cynical man made it appear no more than a shabby pretence, a mask of respectability to be torn aside. Vogel had found him, and enlisted him, at Bremen.

"I deny it, of course. It is ridiculous that I should have to deny it." Zimmermann waited, wary.

"Do you know a man called Kominski at the Soviet embassy in Bonn?"

The silence is going on too long—*answer*! Zimmermann told himself.

He nodded carefully, as if his head was delicately balanced on his shoulders.

"Yes. A member of the embassy staff engaged in preparatory and liaison work . . ."

"Would it surprise you to learn that Kominski is a KGB officer?"

"That is nonsense!"

Then the uproar, the *Bild* correspondent the centre of attention, then Zimmermann. The focus of TV and film cameras swinging like gun barrels between the two men. Unable to prevent himself, Zimmermann nervously brushed his hair with both hands.

He had to leave. He was beginning to perspire. He had to desert the field, or lose in another and perhaps more complete manner. He stood up. The press corps, seeing the movement, bayed at him. A hundred questions, demands. He waved his hands to indicate he had nothing to say. The *Bild* correspondent watched him, smiling; he, not Zimmermann, was the most important man in the room at that moment.

''Kominski—?'' he heard a dozen people about in ragged unison. Petya would, of course, be recalled. Of *course* he was a KGB officer—most of the important people were. Of course they had had to discuss future security with the Soviet secret police and intelligence people. But, how could he explain *that*? He could give no answer.

He walked into the wings of the dais, and mopped his brow. The faces of the two press aides were dark, foreboding. Zimmermann tried to breathe calmly, but he could not; as if his lungs pursued air that was always just out of reach.

''Confirmation, uh?'' Buckholz said with a grin, closing the cell door on Wei.

Godwin shrugged. McIntosh's telephone call had summoned him away from Buckholz and the Chinaman for a few moments, but the news from London and Bonn had been more than sufficient to disobey Aubrey's instructions. Presumably Shelley in London was putting it through in a signal to Canberra, thence to Aubrey himself.

''You think so? *Bild*'s a bit of a rag, isn't it?''

''A popular newspaper, maybe. Doesn't have to be wrong, though.'' Buckholz gestured over his shoulder with an extended thumb. ''That guy in there's been saying the same thing for a week. Now the Germans are raking over their own ashes. And look what they find!''

They began walking along the catwalk of the most secure wing of Victoria Prison; the warder, having locked the door to Wei's cell, was a pace behind them. Through wired, reinforced, barred glass at the end of the catwalk, the blare and flash of

Introducing the first and only complete hardcover collection of Agatha Christie's mysteries

Now you can enjoy the greatest mysteries ever written in a magnificent Home Library Edition

Discover Agatha Christie's world of mystery, adventure and intrigue

Agatha Christie's timeless tales of mystery and suspense offer something for every reader—mystery fan or not—young and old alike. And now, you can build a complete hardcover library of her world-famous mysteries by subscribing to The Agatha Christie Mystery Collection.

This exciting Collection is your passport to a world where mystery reigns supreme. Volume after volume, you and your family will enjoy mystery reading at its very best.

You'll meet Agatha Christie's world-famous detectives like Hercule Poirot, Jane Marple, and the likeable Tommy and Tuppence Beresford.

In your readings, you'll visit Egypt, Paris, England and other exciting destinations where murder is always on the itinerary. And wherever you travel, you'll become deeply involved in some of the most ingenious and diabolical plots ever invented ... "cliff-hangers" that only Dame Agatha could create!

It all adds up to mystery reading that's so good ... it's almost criminal. And it's yours every month with The Agatha Christie Mystery Collection.

Solve the greatest mysteries of all time. The Collection contains all of Agatha Christie's classic works including *Murder on the Orient Express, Death on the Nile, And Then There Were None, The ABC Murders* and her ever-popular whodunit, *The Murder of Roger Ackroyd.*

Each handsome hardcover volume is Smythe sewn and printed on high quality acid-free paper so it can withstand even the most murderous treatment. Bound in Sussex-blue simulated leather with gold titling, The Agatha Christie Mystery Collection will make a tasteful addition to your living room, or den.